She scrambled out o walked toward the cowboy. "What are you doing?"

The cowboy nudged his hat up his forehead and regarded her. His half grin etched a dimple into his cheek. "I'm working."

"Why are the cows crossing the road now?" Paige cringed. But she wasn't making a bad joke. She was serious.

"Simple. More pastures to graze over there."

Paige set her hands on her hips and eyed the long line of cows waiting to cross. "Will this take long?"

"Well, that depends on your definition of *long*." The cowboy settled into his saddle as if he was settling into a long, lazy morning of his own.

"There's more than one definition?" And of course, more than one dimple. His full grin revealed the pair and fully captured Paige's attention. But she was in Texas to figure out how to get her job and life back in Chicago. She wasn't there to get distracted by handsome cowboys and their horses, no matter how beautiful and well-mannered they might be.

Dear Reader,

We have a long list of Christmas traditions in our family, ones passed down through the generations, ones borrowed from friends and even those I wasn't aware were traditions. Until one of my daughters informed me that *yes, Mom, we have to make gingerbread houses that eventually fall over*, or *we have to get toothbrushes and loofahs in our Christmas stockings. It's a tradition*. Simple or grand, there's something about traditions that keeps us connected.

This holiday season, thanks to a Christmas-first list, Evan Bishop and Paige Palmer discover that blending new and old holiday traditions allows them to honor the past and create new memories. Now if the cattle rancher and the veterinarian can open their hearts to more than the joy of the season, they just might learn that love truly can heal. It's Christmas in Three Springs, Texas, where the holiday decorations are plentiful, the December social calendar is full and family is always celebrated. Welcome back.

Grab your family, celebrate a new tradition (or more) and enjoy making those memories together—the ones that will be shared for years to come. Wishing you and your family all the best for the holiday season.

I love to connect with readers. Check out my website to learn more about my upcoming books, sign up for email book announcements or chat with me on Facebook (carilynnwebb) or Twitter @carilynnwebb.

Happy reading!

Cari Lynn Webb

CariLynnWebb.com

HEARTWARMING

*Trusting the Rancher
with Christmas*

———

Cari Lynn Webb

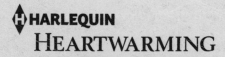

HARLEQUIN
HEARTWARMING

HARLEQUIN®
HEARTWARMING™

Recycling programs for this product may not exist in your area.

ISBN-13: 978-1-335-42649-9

Trusting the Rancher with Christmas

Harlequin Enterprises ULC
22 Adelaide St. West, 40th Floor
Toronto, Ontario M5H 4E3, Canada
www.Harlequin.com

Printed in U.S.A.

Cari Lynn Webb lives in South Carolina with her husband, daughters and assorted four-legged family members. She's been blessed to see the power of true love in her grandparents' seventy-year marriage and her parents' marriage of over fifty years. She knows love isn't always sweet and perfect—it can be challenging, complicated and risky. But she believes happily-ever-afters are worth fighting for. She loves to connect with readers.

Books by Cari Lynn Webb

Harlequin Heartwarming

Three Springs, Texas

The Texas SEAL's Surprise

City by the Bay Stories

The Charm Offensive
The Doctor's Recovery
Ava's Prize
Single Dad to the Rescue
In Love by Christmas
Her Surprise Engagement
Three Makes a Family

Return of the Blackwell Brothers

The Rancher's Rescue

The Blackwell Sisters

Montana Wedding

Visit the Author Profile page at Harlequin.com for more titles.

To Rebecca—everyone should be blessed to have a friend like you. And every conversation should always start with the words *based on a true story*...

Special thanks to my writing gang for sharing their energy pennies, advice and continuous encouragement. Shout-out to the swim team carpool crew: Amelia, Hannah and Macybelle—travel swim meets and deadlines do mix, but let's not do that again. And to my family—I love you more than I can say. Your support means everything to me.

CHAPTER ONE

PAIGE PALMER JERKED her rental car to a stop on the Texas interstate and cut the engine. Her stomach grumbled. She'd skipped breakfast. The line in the Dallas airport coffee kiosk had been too long that morning and she hadn't wanted to miss her connecting flight. As it was, Paige was supposed to have arrived in Three Springs yesterday. But bad weather in Chicago, then mechanical plane trouble in Dallas had delayed her overnight.

Now she faced another delay. And it wasn't airport related.

She scrambled out of her car and strode toward a cowboy seated on a stunning white horse with brown spots in the middle of the road. The cowboy, his beautiful horse and his herd of massive brown cows crossing the interstate were in her way. Literally. They blocked traffic in both directions.

Traffic was a stretch. Paige's rental car was the only vehicle visible for miles on either side of the road.

Her stomach rumbled again. A hunger headache pulsed behind her temples. Careful to approach in the horse's line of sight, Paige paused within easy conversation distance. No shouting required. "What are you doing?"

The cowboy nudged his hat up his forehead and regarded her. His half grin etched a dimple into his cheek. "I'm working."

Paige worked on reining in her frustration. Hunger was never her best look. She wanted to get to her cousin's house. She wanted to eat fried eggs, slather two thick slices of toast in butter and pretend she was in town for a two-week vacation with her family, not a forced administrative leave from her veterinarian job.

Paige put her hands on her hips and eyed the long line of cows waiting to cross. "Will this take long?"

"Well, that depends on your definition of long." The cowboy settled into his saddle as if he was settling into a lazy morning of his own.

"There's more than one definition?" And of course, more than one dimple. His full grin revealed the pair and fully captured Paige's attention. As if she'd never seen perfectly carved dimples on a man before. Now she knew exactly what devil-may-care—one of her grandmother's favorite terms—looked like. Her grandma Opal would've warned her about him.

The warning wasn't necessary. Paige was in Texas to figure out how to get her job and life back on track in Chicago. She wasn't there to get distracted by handsome cowboys and their horses, no matter how beautiful and well-mannered.

"Sure. Long can be a lot of things." The cowboy looked toward the sky, then returned his attention to Paige. His sunglasses covered his gaze, but not the appealing timbre in his voice. "If you mean long, like the many hours it takes to get a brisket smoked just right, then this won't take that long. But if you keep your watch set to city time, then this might take a bit longer than your barista needs to make your fancy whipped-milk-and-vanilla-flavored extra tall coffee."

She'd already been staring at the cowboy too long, wondering if his hair was darker than his deep-charcoal-colored hat. Wondering if his eyes were the color of a singing blue jay or a protective gray wolf. Perhaps she should heed her grandmother's warning after all. "You know. In some places, they have bridges over highways and roads specifically designed for animal crossing and their safety."

"This is Texas." He leaned into his Southern drawl for his next words. "We use what we have. And here we have a perfectly good road."

"This is an interstate." And one meant for

driving on. It wasn't meant for cow crossings and cowboy meetups.

"No. The interstate is that way." The cowboy pointed over the line of cows. "This is the by-pass."

Paige sighed. She wasn't even on the right road. Her grandpa Harlan would've cautioned her that sometimes even the wrong road could turn out to be right in the end. But Paige had already taken several wrong turns in her life and had vowed not to lose her way ever again. "What exactly am I bypassing? More cattle crossings?"

"Can't say exactly." The cowboy shifted in the saddle. "If you ask me, it was the first name they came across that they hadn't used yet."

Bypass or interstate. This road took her to her cousin's house. The one spot she really wanted to be. The cows, walking two by two, streamed across the pavement, spilling through the open pasture gate on the other side. The herd waiting to cross hardly seemed to be thinning. "Can you pause the cows and let me pass? It's a compact car. I don't need much room."

"I'm afraid I can't do that." He shook his head and his frown dropped into place. "Can't risk spooking them and sending the herd running down the road instead."

She considered the disagreeable cowboy. She was a veterinarian of small animals. Knew full well that the tiniest sudden movement could startle a timid cat or frighten a pet rabbit. She had no idea if cows spooked that easily. But she wasn't going to test it. The cows' well-being mattered. And right now, the entire herd was calm and orderly. "What am I supposed to do?"

He rubbed his chin again as if considering her options. "You could go back the way you came."

She narrowed her gaze. He sounded as if he was suggesting she should go back to where she came from. Everything she'd read about Texas said that Texans embraced hospitality. This wasn't the Texas welcome she'd expected from a cowboy who looked as much a part of the landscape as the tumbleweed and plains surrounding her. Paige pointed toward the cows and smiled. "But I really need to go that way."

"Nothing to do then but wait." He touched the brim of his hat. "Now I need to get back to work. It's already been a long morning and not the good kind either."

"What's the good kind?" Paige smashed her lips together too late.

He stilled and his head tilted to the side. His smile started and stopped. Another surge of that devil-may-care.

Warning bells sounded. Paige's heart raced. *Never mind.* Her voice never gained traction.

"I can think of a few things." That tempting drawl returned.

The one that hinted of a different kind of long morning. One reserved for couples and the private moments only they shared. Paige blinked, certain her prescription sunglasses were fogging up from the heat radiating off her cheeks.

"Since the good kind of morning isn't rushed," he continued, more of his Texas roots coming out in his voice, "it always starts with your favorite thing and leaves a promise that the day will only get better from there. What's your favorite thing?"

Not unexpected cattle crossings or attractive cowboys with all-too-appealing accents that made her want to linger. Paige blurted, "Breakfast." And once she had breakfast, her day would certainly improve. Courting a cowboy wasn't part of her two-week agenda. "What about you?"

He picked up the reins in one hand. "Has to be watching the sunrise with a large cup of regular coffee. No flavored sugars. No fancy creamers. And definitely no surprises."

He disliked surprises? Well, she disliked delays in her schedule like the very one he was causing. "Maybe tomorrow's sunrise will give you exactly what you want. Plain coffee and an ordinary, routine day."

He chuckled and guided his spotted horse

across the road. He glanced back at Paige and grinned. "Used to be the best breakfast in town was at Autumn's Bed and Breakfast. But it closed several years back. Now you can find it at one of the local ranches, but it's by invite only."

"I'm not here for all that." Paige shrugged. "Besides, I know my way around a kitchen well enough to make my own breakfast."

"I'm not surprised." He pressed his hat lower on his head. "Hope you find what you came here for."

She was there to visit her sister and cousin. And "cool off." That was the exact term one of the senior partners had used yesterday morning at the emergency animal clinic where she worked. *You're going to cool off, Paige. We don't want to see you in this building for two weeks. Then we're going to come together and discuss this.* Paige had agreed. Until her ex-boyfriend and current colleague had interfered again.

And she'd lost her cool. *Again.*

She'd then launched her ultimatum and walked out. Now she had two weeks to decide how to fight for a job she loved in the practice she'd helped build in the city she'd called home for more than a decade. And finally have the life she always wanted.

Another cowboy rode into the empty spot in the middle of the road and nodded at Paige.

She left the ranch hand to his work, returned to her car and texted her sister and cousin to tell them she was stuck in a cow jam. Then she searched her purse for a forgotten mint or stale piece of candy. Anything to distract herself from watching her cowboy's every move in the pasture. As if she was fascinated by him. As if she suddenly welcomed unexpected surprises.

The only thing she was interested in was getting to her cousin's house before nightfall, eating and getting a lot of sleep. Otherwise, how else was she going to come up with a decent strategy to convince the partners to make her one in the practice?

Still, she unwrapped a forgotten mint, stuck it in her mouth and scanned the pasture. She could count cows. Instead, she watched her cowboy and his horse. The pair moved as if they were one. Natural and smooth. The ideal team.

And one Paige could fully believe in. The cowboy's horse was reliable and trustworthy and everything he would need in a good partner. Paige was her own personal team of one now. She'd been a solo team for the past year. She was determined not to change her dynamic. Her past relationship had been a doomed detour, but she'd found her way out and herself in the process.

The last pair of cows walked across the road. Paige waited for the ranch hand to close the empty pasture gate, then ride across to the other pasture and close that gate before joining the herd. Then she started her car, stepped on the gas pedal and headed down the bypass. Putting her cowboy in her rearview mirror.

Twenty minutes and two stale mints later, Paige parked in her cousin's driveway and stared at the front yard. More specifically the explosion of Christmas that spread from the sidewalk to the front porch. Not even the mailbox had been spared. Thick green garland with sparkly ribbon, lights and pine cones had been draped over the mailbox. Snowflake lights lined the pathways from the driveway and sidewalk to the porch stairs. Giant gift boxes were stacked in the yard. Colored ornaments in all different shapes and sizes swung from every branch of every tree. More garland wrapped the porch and thick pillars. Large silver bells hung over the windows. Her cousin's Christmas decor could inspire the North Pole itself.

Paige inhaled around the discomfort in her chest. She hadn't participated in Christmas for years. Christmas hadn't been her favorite time of year ever since she'd been a kid. When she was only seven, her father had died just days before Christmas and the joy had dwindled. Her older sister, Tess, had jumped into the holidays after they'd lost their dad. Paige had withdrawn.

She'd posed for the customary family photographs, hung ornaments on the tree and woken up early to open presents every Christmas morning. She'd smiled and laughed, but mostly she'd simply endured. Counting the days until the New Year began and she could pack away the lingering sadness. Her father had put the magic into the season and without him, she'd never seemed to find it again.

More recently, her ex had claimed commercialism for his dislike of Christmas celebrations and Paige had gone along. After all, she'd stopped looking for the joy—that magic spark—in the holiday years ago. She'd chosen work over festivities and skipped the expensive gifts to save money for their joint practice. The one her ex had vowed they'd open together. But that was merely one more broken promise.

Paige got out of the car, pulled her suitcase from the trunk, and gathered her secrets close. Now she had one more secret to keep from her family: Paige disliked Christmas.

She walked up the stairs to the front porch. Plump pillows on the porch swing pledged joy, love, and peace. Two thick red-and-black plaid blankets offered warmth. Red ornament balls and lights filled the hanging flower baskets. A vintage sled wrapped in more colored lights offered lightness and fun to the intimate space suited for a magazine spread on how to decorate for Christmas.

Twin wooden toy soldiers, their tall hats reaching Paige's shoulder, stood guard at the triple-wreath-bedecked front door. Paige clutched her suitcase and rang the doorbell.

The front door swung open, and her cousin flung her arms wide in welcome. "Paige. You're finally here."

Abby James glowed from the spark in her gaze to the color in her cheeks to her brilliant smile. Even the threads in Abby's silver, blue and white color-blocked long cardigan sparkled. And the smallest flicker of Christmas spirit shimmered inside Paige. But she wasn't there to rekindle some misplaced holiday magic. This was about cooling off, resetting, and focusing on her career. "Abby. It's good to be here."

Abby wrapped Paige in a hug. The embrace all the more awkward given Abby's protruding belly. Her cousin's baby was set to arrive in March. Meanwhile, Paige still held on to her suitcase as if she hadn't yet committed to staying.

"Tess will be here soon. She got caught up with customers at the store." Abby released Paige, took the suitcase in a quick move to set it aside, then motioned Paige indoors. "That gives us time for a tour and to get you settled."

Abby's Christmas decor outside looked more like a snow flurry compared to her indoor decorations. Christmas had arrived inside Abby's house like a blizzard. There wasn't one corner, one shelf, one wall that didn't reflect the Christmas spirit. Paige knew only one other person who'd achieved Christmas on such a grand scale: her dad. A familiar catch tangled inside her chest. "Abby, this is…"

"A lot." Abby laughed and cradled her stomach. "I know. It's not all me. It's Wes's fault too. We can't seem to stop decorating."

Her dad had been the same. *One more strand of lights, Paigie. More tinsel on the tree, Paigie. We've got to see it to really feel it. That's the magic. Can you feel it yet?* Paige rubbed her neck and cleared her throat. Nothing cleared her father's fun-loving voice from her thoughts. Or the ache in her heart.

"It's like Wes and I are kids again." Abby adjusted one of the embroidered stockings hanging on the fireplace. "And it seems we both want to re-create the Christmases we never really had, but always wished for."

Abby had spent most of her childhood overseas. Traveling from one of her mother's archaeological dig sites to another. Paige had always envied her cousin's adventures. If Paige had been able to up and move from one city to another, surely then she'd have outrun her pain. "I think you've accomplished your goal."

"Wait until you see the guest room." Abby grinned. "I added a few special things for you."

It's special stars for your ceiling, Paigie. Now you can always wish upon them. The stars had been the last special present her dad had given her. "You didn't have to go to so much trouble, Abby."

"You're no trouble Paige." Abby returned to Paige's side. "You're family."

Maybe it was Abby's soft touch on Paige's arm or the honesty in her cousin's gaze that eased the tension inside Paige. Whatever it was, Paige welcomed the reprieve. She pressed her palm against the sudden rumble in her stomach and inhaled. "Is that bacon I smell?"

"Fresh out of the oven." Abby linked her arm with Paige's. "The tour can wait. Let's eat instead while everything is still hot."

Christmas in Abby's kitchen tapered back to a snow-flurry level. Still more than Paige had been surrounded by in a long time. But at the square kitchen table nestled in the window nook, Paige could once again withdraw and observe. The way she preferred to spend her holidays.

"I thought you might be hungry." Abby picked up a piece of bacon from the cookie sheet on the stovetop and took a small bite, then motioned to the dishes arranged on the counter. "I wasn't sure what you'd like so I made a few of Grandma Opal's favorites. Her spinach-and-cheddar quiche. Her overnight oats. Her biscuits. The zucchini bread and cranberry-orange muffins are from Ilene, who is a baking wizard. You'll meet her later. There's yogurt. Fresh fruit. Coffee and assorted tea."

"Abs, you could be a bed and breakfast hostess." And her cowboy thought the best breakfast was on a ranch in town. Clearly, he hadn't been invited to Abby James's house. Paige lifted a muffin from the basket. "You won't judge me if I take a sample of everything, will you?"

"I'll join you." Abby laughed and lifted a vintage coffeepot from the stove top. "Coffee or tea?"

"Coffee, please." Like her cowboy, Paige drank her coffee straight. No added creamers or sugary syrups. As for surprises, he was one she didn't seem inclined to forget too quickly. "Point me to the mugs and I'll get it. You should be sitting down with your feet up."

Abby frowned at her. "Now you sound like your sister and Wes."

Paige paused and considered her cousin more closely. "You are feeling okay, aren't you?"

"Better than I would've imagined." Abby handed Paige a candy-cane-striped coffee mug.

"I thought the morning sickness wouldn't ever let up, but it did. And now I'm finally getting the hang of this pregnancy thing."

Abby all but sparkled. The last time they'd seen each other had been at the funeral for Tess's husband. That had been in March and the trip was a short one, only lasting two days. Paige had been given the weekend off. There had been tears and goodbyes given too soon. Little time for catching up. Even less for reconnecting.

Regret pinched inside Paige. She should've been there longer for her only sister. Paige sipped her coffee. She was here now. Her sister would be by soon. She had time to make it up to her. Meanwhile, she concentrated on her cousin. "Well, it looks like you got a serious handle on Christmas too."

"I couldn't wait for Thanksgiving to be over to get started." Abby cut open her biscuit and slathered butter on it. "I was desperate to decorate this year and there's so much more to do. There's just so much to celebrate this year."

Imagine if we celebrated every day like it was Christmas, Paigie. What a kinder world it would be. But it could also be a lonely world too. Paige glanced out the wide kitchen window. "Abby, you even decorated your backyard fence. You might be ready to just enjoy the season now."

"I'm more than ready for that." Abby dunked

a tea bag into her cup of hot water and smiled. "I'm in love, Paige. Can you believe it?"

Paige could see it. That was Abby's sparkle—love lit her from the inside out. Her cousin had fallen in love with Wes Tanner, who was by all accounts a really good man. Paige was happy for her cousin—truly happy. After everything Abby had been through, Paige wanted her cousin to have her very own happily-ever-after like the one their grandparents had shared. As for Paige, love had derailed her once. And she'd vowed it wouldn't happen again. "Love suits you, Abs."

"I won't be one of those lovesick people who tell you that you should try it again." Abby grabbed Paige's hand. "I'm just glad you're here. It's been too long."

There was that word again: *long*. Was it ever long enough when you had secrets to keep?

"What should we do first?" Abby wiped her hands on a napkin and picked up the *Three Springs Tribune*. She opened the thin paper to the activities page. "Here's a full list of December's Holiday Happenings. The events are all mine, as is the article, to keep the locals in the know."

Abby had not only fallen in love in Three Springs, but she had also landed a job as the assistant to the town manager. And she was clearly passionate about her work, which included planning local events. Paige scanned the events list.

"This is your vacation, so you get to choose what we do." Abby sprinkled sugar into her tea, her voice sweetened. "I want it to be everything you envisioned."

Her sister and cousin believed Paige was there for a much-needed, past-due vacation. They had no idea that Paige's leave had been mandatory.

After a heated argument between Paige and her ex-boyfriend in front of staff and a patient's owners. All Paige knew was her work. She'd never been banned from the job she loved. That she blamed on her ex. And rather than risk another altercation with him, she'd booked the first flight to Three Springs.

Paige hadn't even considered ice skating, cookie swaps or tree lightings in the town square when she'd boarded the plane. But that was about to change, if she could pull herself together.

Abby and Tess believed Paige had it all together from her successful career to her life in the big city that she always desired. Paige wanted them to keep believing in her. Then she would keep believing too. After all, once she secured an equal partnership in the clinic, she'd be back on track to having everything she'd ever dreamed of. "Right now, we should eat this delicious food and savor this coffee."

"It's the best coffee you've tasted, isn't it?" Abby asked.

"In the top three for sure." Paige took another sip. She'd worked nights quite often at the emergency animal hospital and had drunk a lot of coffee during those shifts. She considered herself to have gained something of a refined coffee palate. "This stuff rivals some of the best coffee houses in Chicago."

"Maybe you can get Wes to reveal his secret." Abby shook her head. "It's his blend. He serves it at the Feisty Owl, if you can believe it."

Wes owned the Feisty Owl Bar and Grill in town and sure knew how to brew a good cup of coffee. Her own cowboy had mentioned a ranch served the best breakfast in town. Still, it was possible she'd found it. No invite needed. "Does Wes serve breakfast at the Owl too?"

"No. His mornings are spent out at the horse rescue." Abby blew on her tea. "The Owl serves lunch and dinner."

So, Wes wasn't the cook of the best breakfast in town. Her search would have to continue. Paige bit into her cranberry-orange muffin and sighed at the burst of flavors. "I need to meet Ilene. I want to take dozens of these muffins home with me." And have her own best breakfast in town. No cowboys required.

Abby peered out the bay window and smiled. "You're in luck. She's here now."

Paige brushed the crumbs off her hands.

The back door opened, and a young red-haired little girl burst into the kitchen. Tears dampened her pale cheeks and dripped onto her ginger-bread man and candy-cane-printed scarf. The little girl beelined for Abby. Her pink flower em-broidered cowboy boots thumped on the floor. "Ms. Abby, guess what? Macybelle is laying down and not wanting to get up."

"I didn't think a storm was coming." Abby folded the little girl into her side and glanced at Paige. "This is Riley Bishop, Ilene's grand-daughter."

"Sorry for interrupting your breakfast." A thin woman with a salt-and-pepper chin-length bob and warm smile set a wicker basket on the coun-ter and introduced herself to Paige. "I'm Ilene Bishop."

"Please, don't apologize." Paige rose and shook Ilene's hand, then turned her attention to the upset little girl. "Who is Macybelle?"

"Macybelle is Riley's pet cow." Abby pulled several tissues from the box on the side counter and handed them to Riley. "Macybelle likes to sit down before a rainstorm to keep her spot dry."

"But it's not gonna rain." Riley wiped the crumpled wad of tissues against her freckled cheek. "It's worse. She doesn't even want to eat. She's sick like daddy's other cows."

Alarm shifted through Abby's words. "There are more sick cows at the ranch."

Riley's distress ricocheted inside Paige. She knew firsthand the little girl's bond to her pet. Paige had been about Riley's age and scared when her own pet cat had stopped eating and drinking one night. Dexter had been her one constant companion after her father's death. Her buddy on the nights she couldn't sleep. Her dream keeper. Her confidant. She'd been terrified of losing Dexter too. Like Riley was now. She wanted to draw Riley into her own arms and comfort her. Promise Riley her cow would be fine. But those weren't words she could freely give. False hope could be even more detrimental.

"We have more cows sick than we'd like of course." Ilene clasped her hands together and dropped into one of the kitchen chairs as if exhausted. "Our family runs a beef cattle ranch."

And every cow mattered to the family's livelihood. One sick cow was one too many. "Isn't there a veterinarian in the area who can examine them?"

Paige had found Dexter limp and weak right before bedtime. Her mom, a nurse, had been at work. Grandpa Harlan had called the neighbors for help. Within the hour, Dr. Lawrence Trevino had rung their doorbell. Dr. Trevino had been the first veterinarian Paige had met. He'd saved Dexter that night during his special house call. And Paige had discovered her own calling to do the same.

"Dr. Gibson broke his leg real bad." Riley hiccupped. "And his assistant up and moved to Oklahoma City without tellin' no one. Right, Grandma?"

Ilene brushed her silver-and-gray-tinged bangs off her forehead. "Unfortunately, that's what happened. It hasn't been a very good week for Dr. Gibson."

"There has to be more than one animal doctor around." Eighteen certified and licensed veterinarians worked at her emergency clinic alone, including Paige's ex-fiancé.

"Three of the closer doctors are already booked at the larger ranches." Ilene accepted a cup of coffee from Abby. "It'll be days before they can come out."

And with the weekend approaching, their availability shrank even more. That was time the ranch couldn't afford. An infection could spread quickly. Kennel cough could close a canine boarding facility within days. A sick herd of cattle could have devastating effects on a ranch.

"What can we do?" Abby sat again and rubbed

Riley's back. "I can call other veterinarian clinics too. There has to be someone who can visit."

Abby avoided meeting Paige's gaze. Paige tapped her fingers against her coffee mug. Even if she wanted to help, she wasn't qualified. She'd rotated briefly through a large-animal clinic during her internship. But she'd completed her residency on small-animal emergency and critical care. Cows were not considered small animals.

"Evan has left messages all around the Panhandle." Despair crossed Ilene's face, dimming her voice.

"I'm sure someone will call back soon." Abby took Riley's hand. Her voice lifted, her tone positive. "You know what always makes me feel better?"

"One of Daddy's big bear hugs." Tears clung to Riley's eyelashes.

Paige smiled. The little girl's obvious love and adoration for her dad warmed her. She very much wanted one bear hug to make Riley's world right again.

"I was going to say hot chocolate, extra marshmallows and a swirl of a candy cane." Abby stood and pointed to the family room. "But we have to pick the candy canes off the tree. Want to help me?"

Abby and Riley walked into the family room.

Paige stared into her coffee mug, searching for the right words to ease the family's worry.

"This is not how we wanted to end the year." Ilene cradled her coffee mug and frowned. "It's Riley's favorite time of the year. Her dad works so hard to make it perfect for her. My son is a single father. I'm a widow. We're all Riley has, along with her pets. If she loses her cow…"

Ilene's voice drifted off. The older woman's pain and fear wrapped around Paige. She'd learned years later, after Dexter had lived a full, extended life, that Dr. Trevino had never made house calls. He'd gone to Paige's home to help a frightened little girl who'd lost her father unexpectedly months earlier. That one simple house call had given Paige hope again and a direction for her future. She'd always vowed to pay it forward one day. Still, she was hardly trained for this. "I'm a veterinarian, but only for small animals in Chicago."

Abby appeared in the walkway to the kitchen as if she'd been listening. And waiting for Paige to make the offer. "But Paige, you treat animals all the time. You heal them all the time."

Ilene shifted, set her folded hands on the table, and considered Paige.

Paige scrambled to retreat. This was not paying it forward. She could do more harm than good. Besides, she was a licensed veterinarian in another state. How could she possibly help here, even if she wanted too? "I have no experience with cows."

"But you might be able to offer an observation or something Evan has missed." Ilene's voice was calm, her gaze imploring. "Something that might lead him to figure out what's wrong with the cattle."

"Think of it as being another set of eyes," Abby suggested.

"You could do that, Abs." There was much less risk to Abby lending support than Paige.

Besides, Paige's career was already hanging in the balance. Practicing in another state could be the reason the partners would decide not to give her a formal stake in the clinic. She couldn't be reckless again. Her lack of professionalism in front of witnesses was still too fresh for the partners.

"My eyes aren't trained like yours," Abby countered.

Riley walked back into the kitchen. Her fingers were wrapped tightly around four candy canes. "Ms. Paige, you help animals feel better like Dr. Gibson?"

"I try." Paige kept her gaze fixed on Riley's.

"Dr. Gibson talks to our animals when he comes out." Riley tipped her head to the side.

Her voice was watered down and hushed. "Do you do that?"

"I do." Paige leaned in and lowered her voice. "I talk to my patients all the time and as much as I can."

"Why?" Riley edged closer and closer to Paige. Her inquisitive gaze never wavered.

"Because I think it helps my patients feel better." Kind words. Affection. Soft gestures were all meant to calm and soothe the animals. To build a bond. To make sure they all knew they weren't alone.

Riley bumped into Paige's knees. "If you talked to Macybelle, then maybe she'd feel better too."

Paige knew exactly where the conversation had been leading. It was inevitable really, once Riley had fastened her saucer-round, fragile hazel eyes on Paige. Paige had been terrified for her pet once too. And a stranger, who'd later become a mentor, had helped. Now it was Paige's turn to do the same. Perhaps not to diagnose and treat ill cattle, but rather to give a little girl hope and show her that she wasn't alone. "You know what? I think that's a very good idea."

Riley beamed and lunged for Paige. She wrapped her arms around Paige's waist and squeezed. Paige absorbed the little girl's version of a bear hug and melted inside. Paige returned the embrace and held on as if bear hugs really did make everything better. She glanced across the table at Ilene. "Can you give me the address for the ranch? I'll head out there, as long as you know this isn't an exam. I can't offer a diagnosis or treatment plan."

Riley lifted her head. "But you can talk to Macybelle and the other cows. And even my dad. Then he might feel better too and be happy again."

Paige chewed on her bottom lip. Cats and dogs were her specialty. She wasn't sure she had the right words for a single dad and his happiness. Those she was certain belonged to someone else. "Let's start with Macybelle and go from there."

Riley grinned and handed her candy canes to Abby. "Can we have hot chocolate now and go to the hardware store? Mr. Rivers has reindeer as tall as me. And they light up."

"Sure we can." Abby walked to the refrigerator and opened the door. "I want to find more outdoor ornaments. Maybe you can help me find some."

Riley cheered. "You should put reindeer in your yard too, Ms. Abby."

"Evan is at the ranch now." Ilene wrote on a piece of paper and handed it to Paige. "This is the address. I'm sure he'll be glad to see you."

Glad or not, Paige was more than pleased to

let Riley join her cousin on a hunt for more holiday decor. Paige took the paper from Ilene and looked at her cousin. "Can I take my hot chocolate to go, please?"

CHAPTER TWO

EVAN BISHOP CLOSED the stable door. He brushed his hands off on his jeans and eyed the silver compact car kicking up dust and pebbles on the unpaved road leading to the Bishop family home. He recognized the four-door hatchback from the traffic stop he'd caused earlier that morning on the bypass.

Evan adjusted his hat and walked to the edge of the roundabout in front of the farmhouse. He'd returned from the southern pasture to grab a quick bite of last night's leftover meat-lovers pizza. Cold pizza was all he had time for. He needed to get back to the cattle corral and his ill cows. Every hour, another cow seemed to be added to the quarantine pen.

He had no time for interruptions. Especially ones that had hair the color of roasted chestnuts and smiles as refreshing as a springtime rain. And who looked like everything he wasn't interested in. But his traffic stop encounter had left an impression. One he hadn't been able to completely dismiss. Even now, the smallest twinge of anticipation skimmed through him.

The silver hatchback rolled to a stop. The engine cut off and the driver's door opened. A familiar brown-haired woman appeared. He caught the flash of that smile. The one etched in his mind. Her hand lifted as if she intended to wave.

Evan crossed his arms over his chest and widened his stance as if preparing to block her charm and curb his own reaction. He was borderline excited to see her again so soon. Three Springs was small. He'd expected to run into her at the gas station or the Owl. He had not expected to find her on his property. He waited for recognition to hit.

She didn't disappoint. Her smile dissolved as her mouth curved into an O shape. Her brow furrowed above her trendy glasses. Her eyes widened behind the clear lenses. She hadn't expected to see him either. If she was slightly like him, all the better. That put them solidly on common ground.

Her hand did a slow drop that matched the bewilderment in her words. "You're my cattle crossing cowboy."

He liked her use of *my* despite her obvious wince over her verbal slipup.

She stammered, "I—I meant the cowboy from the cattle crossing this morning."

He preferred *my cowboy*. But now wasn't the time to consider the why behind that foolish thought. The same as it wasn't time to contemplate all the highlights the afternoon sun revealed in her long brown hair. "Welcome to Crescent Canyon. I'm Evan Bishop."

"Paige Palmer." She stepped forward as if she meant to shake his hand, then paused. Her arms remained firmly at her sides.

And Evan remained completely still and not quite as indifferent as he wanted to be.

Paige Palmer wasn't a complete stranger he'd met on the road. She was Tess Palmer's younger sister and Abby James's cousin. Abby was dating one of Evan's best friends, Wes Tanner. He'd been hearing about Paige's impending arrival for several days from his own mother and the locals at the Feisty Owl bar, and from her own family. He wondered if Paige would like to know she'd been the talk of the town for the past few days. "Well, Paige Palmer, did you get lost on the bypass again?"

"Actually, your mother sent me out here." She loosened the lightweight scarf around her neck.

Unease loosened inside Evan. What was his mother up to? His mom had been quite vocal about encouraging him to date again. But she hadn't gone so far as to arrange any blind dates or awkward meet and greets. Until now. "Why would she do that?"

"I'm a veterinarian." Paige watched him from behind her glasses. The round frames only enhanced her all-too-observant gaze.

Her job was a detail he already knew. Thanks to the town chatter. Now he also knew her eyes were a whiskey-brown color, upturned at the edges and entirely too expressive. What he didn't know was if she was a morning person or night owl. Or if she preferred salty snacks or sweets. Not that he really cared. Just plain curiosity. "Yet you aren't licensed to practice here in Texas."

"No, I live in Chicago." She tucked her hair behind her ear. "I work at an emergency animal hospital."

More details he'd already learned from the gossip about her visit. That explained her irritation at the cattle crossing. She was a city girl, accustomed to a fast pace and high-stress situations. Quiet country walks, unrushed dinners and watching for shooting stars would most likely not appeal to her. Not that he wanted to do any of that either. He was dedicated to his daughter and his work. And had a full plate just like he wanted. "Don't suppose you treat many cows in the city."

"Not a one. I treat dogs and cats mostly. Sometimes rabbits and birds as well as the occasional hamster." She patted her hand against her leg. A small smile twitched across her mouth. "But I have colleagues I can consult. And I'm good at observations others might miss."

Evan noticed Rex, one of his pure white Great Pyrenees, watching them from beside the farmhouse. Rex was a timely reminder that Evan had work to do. Cows to tend. A ranch to run. A family legacy to establish. "I'm sorry you came all the way out here, but I have everything in hand."

The slightest chill, like whiskey poured over ice, flashed in her gaze. Annoyance flashed in her words. "So, you don't want me to even take a look at your sick cows."

He shook his head. Not to tell him things he'd already observed himself. It was more than clear he had sick cattle on his land. What wasn't clear was why and how he was supposed to treat them before he lost most of the herd. And a city veterinarian with no experience wasn't going to have the answers he needed. "I appreciate the offer, but you should be enjoying your vacation with your family, not caring for my cattle."

"I'm here at a request from your family." Paige tipped her chin up, seemingly unmoved by his suggestion to go and relax. "Your daughter specifically. Riley wanted me to talk to Macybelle."

"What exactly are you going to say to Macybelle?" he asked.

"That's between Macybelle and me." Paige patted her leg again.

Rex's thick tail swished against Evan's jeans as he trotted by to get closer to Paige. Evan might've envied the dog. If he'd been interested in Paige. In wanting a connection. He had his land and Riley and his friends. He considered himself well-connected already. No more were required.

Paige knelt and greeted the large dog. Her fingers sank into his dense coat. Her gaze lifted to Evan's. "I gave Riley my word and I don't want to break it. She was already pretty upset."

Evan winced. His voice sounded too thin. Riley's tears always cut through him, sharper than any knife. "She wasn't crying, was she?"

"What would you rather hear?" Paige countered.

He'd thought he'd shielded Riley. He'd told her it was nothing to worry about. Hugged her that morning until she'd giggled. He'd laughed over their misshaped pancakes and matching chocolate-milk mustaches. Pretended it was just another routine morning. Yet somewhere inside the laughter, Riley had sensed his concern. His own alarm. He had to do better. Be better to protect his daughter. "You don't actually believe talking to Macybelle is going to heal her, do you?"

"I believe all animals, big and small, respond to kindness and considerate care." Paige framed Rex's massive head and pressed a kiss between his large ears. "After all, everyone wants to know they matter."

Riley mattered. He made sure his daughter felt that every single day. And knew it in her heart. "Rex and I can take you out to Macybelle's pasture."

"That would be great." Paige rose and settled her all-too-assessing gaze on Evan. "I'm not here to cause any problems. I just gave Riley my word."

He'd made his own vows too. Six years ago, standing alone at the altar with his five-month-old daughter in his arms. He'd vowed Riley could always count on him. That he would keep Riley from getting hurt. That his daughter would know unconditional love.

Evan nodded and headed toward the UTV parked outside the stable. Rex jumped into the bed of the vehicle. Evan dropped into the driver's seat, started the UTV and pulled onto the dirt road. "Do you always keep your word?"

"My grandpa Harlan taught me to never give my word if there was a chance I'd break it."

Paige wrapped her hair into a low ponytail. "So yeah. I keep it."

"And if I refused to let you see Macybelle?"

"I would've called your mother for directions to Macybelle's pasture." Paige grinned at him.

He believed her.

She added, "Grandpa Harlan also taught me there's more than one way to shoe a horse."

Evan laughed. "He's not wrong, you know."

Minutes later, Evan opened the pasture gate and motioned Paige inside. He latched the gate and pointed to the nine-hundred-pound brown cow in the far corner. "That's our Macybelle. And her friend Annabelle is the other one. Both belong to Riley."

"Is Annabelle sick too?" Paige asked.

"Her symptoms are mild," he said. "And she's seeming to respond to the antibiotics. I thought it'd be more stressful to separate them. They've always been together."

Paige walked slowly toward Macybelle.

"Both were rejected by their mothers," Evan explained. "Riley declared herself their mom."

His daughter had insisted, actually. Insisted the pair of calves would be scared if they were alone. Insisted they couldn't be abandoned. She'd been young, but fierce and determined. "Riley visits every day before and after school. This pasture is the first place she goes when she gets home in the afternoons."

"Can we approach her?" Paige asked.

Evan agreed.

"Anything I should know?" Paige's attention remained on the cow.

"Rule of thumb, if you can see a cow's eye, then she can see you." Evan walked beside Paige, unhurried. "No loud noises. Nothing that would startle her."

Paige remained in Macybelle's line of sight and lowered to her knees near the cow's head. She offered praise for her soulful eyes and apologies for her unwell state.

Evan guided Paige through taking Macybelle's heart rate from her tail. Checking dehydration by pinching the skin behind her ear, then finally getting a respiratory rate.

Paige listened, followed his instructions with ease and heaped more praise on the young bovine.

"The symptoms are the same for the others." Evan crouched beside her. "The usual treatments for colds and mild pneumonia aren't working."

"What have we missed?" Paige checked Macybelle's ears and leaned in closer. "What aren't you revealing to us?"

Us. They weren't a team. He and Riley were

the only team. Evan rubbed his knuckles under his chin, but his frown remained fixed in place.

Besides, Paige wasn't supposed to know what ailed Macybelle. But Evan should. The cows were his responsibility. So, what had he missed? "There's been no rashes. No drainage from the nose or eyes. Nothing that makes it definitively one disease over another."

Paige rested her hand over Macybelle's ribs. "Yet it's clear she's unwell."

Frustration rolled over Evan. He wanted Paige to possess those magic words. The ones that would heal his herd. But that would've been good luck. And Evan subscribed to hard work, determination and resilience, not luck these days. He pulled out his phone. No missed calls from the clinics he'd left messages at. "I have to get to the handling facility." And also find someone with those answers.

"Thanks for letting me see her." Paige stood and walked with him toward the gate.

Evan nodded and secured the pen. "I can take you back to your car."

"I can walk," she said. "It's not far."

"Are you leaving, or are you going to follow me to the cattle corral?" His smile teased, yet his tone was serious.

He wasn't certain himself if he wanted her at the handling facility or not. He wasn't as against it as he should be. That was surprising. Still, she wasn't trained. He couldn't watch over her and give his full attention to the herd.

"I was going to…" She stopped and rolled her lips together as if catching her words. One beat. Then another. "I was going to meet up with Abby, Riley and Ilene in town at the hardware store."

Evan eyed her. Nothing in her calm voice or neutral expression warranted his doubt. Still, he wondered what she was really going to do. And what it was about her that made him so darn curious to know more. "Riley has been trying to convince me to buy the life-sized reindeer Gordon has for sale there."

"I wish I could be more help," she said.

She'd already helped. He was calmer being with her. And that allowed his focus to return to his cattle. Now it was his turn to bite back his words. "Enjoy the rest of your stay."

"I can give you my phone number in case you need me," she offered.

"That's not necessary." He had everything he needed already. As far as a large-animal doctor went, he'd find one of those soon.

She pulled back as if his dismissive tone bruised her feelings.

"I know where to find you," he rushed on. He disliked the tempered caution in her gaze that he'd put there. "The general store. The apartment above the general store or your cousin's house. All those places are within walking distance of each other."

"Okay." The wariness dimmed.

"It's a really small town." Evan grinned. "I imagine someone will tell you I'm looking for you before me. That's how it works around here."

"Do you like that?" Surprise filtered through her words as if the lack of privacy bothered her.

"When I was a teen, not so much." But as a single father, he'd changed his mind. "Now, I prefer it that way. Riley will have a lot of people watching out for her when she's a teenager."

"Speaking of Riley," she said, "tell her the truth about Macybelle and the others."

And break his daughter's spirit? How was that protecting her? "I don't want to disappoint her. Or risk making her a promise I can't keep."

"I'm not asking you to give her your word, only be honest about the situation," she countered. "Sometimes that's the best we can do."

"That's all I'm trying to do. The best for my daughter. For my family. And for this ranch." And he had to make sure it was enough. He touched the brim of his hat. He had more work to do.

CHAPTER THREE

PAIGE WASN'T HAVING a good morning.

It'd started with a large cup of Wes's delicious coffee and one of Ilene's pumpkin streusel muffins. Two of her current favorite things. But there hadn't been a promise that the day was going to get better.

Instead, there'd been the coffee she'd spilled on her leggings. The realization that she'd forgotten to pack deodorant. And a restless frustration inside her that seemed to have been recycled in the morning sunlight.

She'd even fallen asleep frustrated last night. Frustrated by the realization that a detailed list of her achievements wouldn't result in her owning more shares in Windsor Haven Animal Clinic. It wouldn't make her a partner with a voice in its management. She wasn't going on a job interview in two weeks. She'd worked there for five years. The partners were fully aware of her skill set and talents. How did she convince them she deserved to be their equal when one of those four partners was her ex-fiancé who never treated her as such?

That frustration knotted inside her.

She took the outside staircase leading to her sister's apartment above the Silver Penny General Store. The general store had been established by one of the Palmer ancestors and passed down through the family. Their grandparents had been the last owners. Now, Tess was running it.

Paige adjusted her grip on her to-go coffee cup and the container of Ilene's muffins, then knocked on the door.

Tess greeted her. Her bulky heather-gray turtleneck sweater only accented her too-thin cheeks and round eyes. Eyes that used to be a vibrant green and now were the shade of wilted grass. Grief shadowed her widowed sister. Paige hurt for Tess's loss. Wanted to draw the shine back into her sister's gaze. But she wasn't certain where to start. Or if her sister would welcome or resent her interference.

"Morning." Paige dipped her voice into upbeat and handed her sister the container. "I brought you pumpkin streusel muffins delivered fresh this morning by Ilene."

"Thanks. I already ate." Tess set the container down beside her and held tight to the door as if warning Paige not to intrude.

Paige caught a glimpse of a small entryway and stacked moving boxes. Nothing more. Her sister hadn't extended an invitation to come inside. To sit down and relax. Catch up.

They'd had dinner at Abby's last night. Abby had gone to bed early. Tess had gone home, and Paige had retreated to the guest room. They'd been polite. No one had pried. No one had stepped across the imaginary privacy boundaries they'd set. The conversation had circled around their chicken-cornbread casserole dinner, one of their grandmother's favorite dishes. Paige's retelling of her airline delays and Abby's growing list of Christmas events for the town. All of which Paige was expected to attend.

Paige should be thrilled. She hadn't wanted to share too much about her past relationship or her current career crisis. Still, more of that frustration coiled inside her. Tess and Paige used to share everything from clothes to their fears and dreams. They used to be each other's rock. Now they were more like strangers, balancing on eggshells. "You know, I could stay here."

"Abby's house is better." Tess tucked her hands into the pockets of her jacket and moved down the stairs. "It's bigger. You get your own bathroom and it's more comfortable. What more could you want?"

More time with my sister. Paige trailed after

Tess and tiptoed across those eggshells. "I have to say the queen bed is quite nice. You know how much I like to stretch out and sprawl across the mattress."

In grade school, the sisters had always slept in the same room. Tess had always complained Paige was a bed hog. Paige had accused Tess of stealing the covers. Despite their grievances against each other, they'd still crawled into the same bed night after night. If their mom had suggested they sleep in their beds alone, they'd acted as if she'd suggested they sleep in different states. Between the giggles and the fun, the sisters had shared secrets and crafted their friendship. Built their bond. It should've been indestructible like her grandparents had taught her to believe.

Tess said, "I figured you'd have outgrown that habit."

Had Tess outgrown Paige? She skimmed over the kink of sadness in her throat. "Guess not. I also haven't outgrown my sweet tooth."

"Then Ilene's baked goods won't go to waste," Tess offered. "Ilene is one of the best bakers."

And her sister used to be one of the best candymakers Paige knew. Paige slipped on the last stair and more of those eggshells. How had their relationship fractured to this? Where she was too afraid to ask if her sister created her candy concoctions anymore. Where she was too afraid to pry.

How did she pick up the pieces? Put it all back together. Selfishly Paige had assumed it would always be there. When she was ready. On her terms. They reached the sidewalk, but not common ground. Paige touched Tess's arm, tentatively and gently, as if testing their connection. "Tess, are you okay?"

Tess turned and blinked at Paige. Two slow sweeps of her long eyelashes and she widened her eyes as if seeing Paige for the first time. "Fine. Good. I'm just distracted by some things for the store."

"Anything I can help with?" Paige asked.

"No." Tess stepped toward the front entrance of the general store and away from Paige. "I got it handled."

Those were the very same words Evan had tossed at Paige yesterday. Dismissed by her cowboy and her sister.

Only when they'd examined Macybelle yesterday, Evan hadn't been curt or abrupt. He hadn't rushed her. He'd been patient and attentive to both Paige and the animals, but mostly with Paige. Those were simply his good manners showing. And if she'd been interested in more than his cattle's welfare, she might've been affected. Might've been tempted to ask her sister for more details about Evan Bishop.

Would talking about a boy reconnect Paige and her sister?

The past few years, they'd exchanged more text messages than phone conversations. And those text replies had been short and brief. Neither her nor her sister revealing too much. As if they'd quietly agreed to not intrude on each other's lives. As if they were satisfied with the expanding distance. As if that was enough. Except right now, Paige missed her sister. The one she'd grown up relying on. The one who'd used to rely on her. She missed her sister a lot.

Paige stared at Tess's thin shoulders and straight back. Uncertain how to reach her. Scared she'd lost her sister—her onetime best friend. Terrified she was already too late. "What's the plan for today?"

Tess pulled a key ring from her pocket. "I have to work on finding several special orders this morning. They're going to be Christmas gifts if I can get them to my customers in time."

"What should I do?" *Where do I fit in?* At the clinic, she'd always known her role. Her place. Now she wasn't certain about that either. She suddenly felt lost and very out of sorts. There was a chill in the air, nothing teeth chattering, yet Paige shivered.

"Abby is putting together a wall of forgotten Christmas traditions outside city hall." Tess unlocked the tall doors. "I thought there might be something in Grandma and Grandpa's boxes in the basement for her to add to the display."

One of her grandparents' favorite traditions had been their sugared-cranberry-and-popcorn garland. Paige hadn't thought about that garland in forever. "Let me explore the store first. I can't wait to see all that you've done. Then I'll search the basement."

Tess hesitated. "The store isn't finished. It's a work in progress."

Perhaps that was how Paige could approach their relationship. "Of course, it is. It has been closed for decades."

"The alcoves aren't opened yet." Tess pulled the twin doors open and flipped the sign from Closed to Open. "But the main storefront is coming along. I'm really proud of it."

Surely Tess didn't think Paige wasn't proud of her. Her sister had lost her husband at the beginning of the year and the life she'd envisioned. One month after the funeral, Tess had packed up and moved to Three Springs by herself. Her sister was one of the strongest women Paige knew. She started to tell her, but Tess had already gone into the store. Lights began illuminating the space.

Just then, Abby arrived wearing a long-sleeved maroon shirt with the words Future Elf on Board printed in bold silver lettering and her usual bright smile. She held a cup carrier with four cups of coffee in it. "Refills are here. Now, I have enough time for our Friday box challenge. Then I need to get my workday started."

Paige followed Abby into the store. Her gaze had skipped from the boxes marked Victorian Village stacked against the wall near the massive front window to the towering yet undecorated Christmas tree in front of the two-story-high brick wall with an archway on each side. She was working her way toward the ornate book exchange box when the shopkeeper's bell chimed.

"What's this about a box challenge?" A gravelly voice boomed from the front of the store.

Paige spun around. An older cowboy wearing a brown faded cowboy hat, a large bronze-and-turquoise belt buckle and a warm expression underneath a battleship-gray beard ambled inside.

"Can't have the Friday box challenge without us." This from the cowboy's partner. He wore a black onyx bolo tie, an even larger silver-and-gold belt buckle and an infectious grin under an impeccable white beard and handlebar mustache that even Santa would envy. Santa's rival hollered. "Morning, Abby, Morning, Tess."

Tess laughed, revealing a rare smile, and

moved to embrace the two older gentlemen. Her welcome warm and sincere. The sisters' hug had been all too brief yesterday. And blaringly impersonal, given the embrace Paige witnessed between Tess and the two cowboys now. Regret stirred inside her.

Tess linked arms with the two older gentlemen and guided them toward Paige. Her sister's grin almost reached into her gaze. "Paige. This is Boone Bradley and Sam Sloan. Grandpa Harlan's best friends."

"Don't forget Opal," Boone said. "Your grandmother liked us too."

"More like tolerated us. She was a very kind lady, your grandmother was." Sam, Santa's thinner double, wrapped Paige in a warm hug, which she returned.

Perhaps that was it. Sam had never hesitated, never paused to reconsider. Simply treated her as if she were one of his own family and deserving of such a hearty welcome. And for a brief moment, Paige felt like she fit in. She'd felt it yesterday with Evan in the pasture. But that made sense; she'd always been more comfortable with animals.

"Okay, everyone." Abby clapped her hands together and caught the group's attention. "You have to share Harlan and Opal memories and anything about treasure hunts later. It's Friday and time for our weekly box challenge. I'm supposed to be in my office. Christmas is coming and there's still a lot to do."

Boone shifted a stack of papers and a yellow notepad out from under his arm and held his other arm out for Paige. "Sam and I are the official historical committee for Three Springs."

"We are the authority on all things McKenzie sister and Herring Gang related." Sam moved to Paige's other side. "That's the history about stolen silver and gold that really matters round here. We'll get to all that later. What you need to know right now is that we're looking for a silver coin in a frame, and a treasure map."

Boone tapped his cowboy hat higher on his forehead and lifted his eyebrows. "We believe the silver coin is in a box somewhere inside this store."

"We just need to find the right box." Sam's mustache twitched as his frown settled into place.

"Grandma and Grandpa had packed up the entire store before they moved." Abby handed coffee cups to Boone, Sam, then Paige. "Boxes now fill the back storage room and the entire basement."

"We've been helping Tess sort through the boxes for several months." Boone sipped his coffee. "We discovered all kinds of interesting things too."

"Everything except the coin," Sam said.

"But it's fine because we've turned the hunt for the coin into a weekly game." Abby's smile brightened.

"Let's get to it then." Sam adjusted the onyx clasp on his bolo tie. "I'm feeling lucky today."

"Okay. Tess has opted to take care of some business and sit this one out." Abby cast a frown at Tess. But Tess was already immersed in her special-order request search on her computer. Abby added, "We need four boxes from the basement. Any shape. Any size. The only condition is each box has to be completely sealed."

"And to be clear, the goal is to find the elusive silver coin that will lead us to the treasure map for the missing loot." Boone grinned at Paige. Excitement sparked in his gaze. "Ever been on a real treasure hunt?"

"Never." Paige shook her head and chuckled. But she was starting to think she'd like to join this pair for theirs. "You really believe if you find this silver coin, you'll find a treasure map too?"

"Absolutely." Conviction framed Sam's words.

"Every opened box gets us closer to the coin and the map." Boone pulled a stool out from behind the counter. "We can't give up now."

The pair's certainty and earnestness energized Paige. Five minutes and two quick trips to the basement later, Paige set her hands on her unopened box at the end of the long counter. Doubt flared inside her. "What happens if we don't find the box with the silver coin?"

"Then we vote on who has the best box," Abby answered. "There isn't any set criteria for best."

"We just know which one is the best when we see it." Boone grinned.

"When Riley is here, the winner gets to pick the dinner theme for Monday night's family gathering." Abby considered her box.

"Last week, Evan and Riley chose dessert for dinner." Sam chuckled and scooted his box closer.

Paige hadn't seen Riley since she'd agreed to talk to Macybelle. If Evan was half as attentive to his daughter as he had been with Paige, and she suspected he was, the father-daughter pair was probably irresistible. Not that she was the least bit interested in learning more about Evan as a father or a man. She had her own family dynamic to concentrate on.

"I chose soup and sandwiches when I won." Abby picked up her scissors and cut into the air as if testing the shears. "I still have a container of broccoli-cheddar soup that Boone made stashed in my freezer. I'll take it out for us, Paige. It's delicious."

"Don't think compliments are going to sway the vote." Boone frowned, but the spark in his gaze gave away his delight at Abby's praise.

"Do we open one at a time?" Anticipation spread through Paige, tingling all the way into her fingertips and toes. She'd felt the same sensation as a kid on Christmas morning. But somehow this was better. More exciting. Or perhaps it was simply that she hadn't felt this way in a long, long time. She leaned into the feeling. "Or do we open them together?"

"Together." Boone tested his own pair of scissors. "We're too old for the added suspense."

"On three, then." Abby counted down quickly.

Paige cut the tape sealing the lid and lifted the flaps. Bubble wrap filled the top of the box. Paige rolled up onto the balls of her feet like an eager kid again. "This one is well packed. It's going to be good. I can feel it."

"I got inventory." Sam closed the flaps on his box. Disappointment slowed his movements even more. "Tinsel. Garland. Artificial flowers. This one goes to Tess for the shelves."

"Same here. Gift bags, boxes, tissue paper and ribbon." Abby pushed her box away and slid a plastic container of biscuits toward Sam. "Although the metallic tissue paper is quite pretty. And the snowflake ribbon too."

"Unless that silver coin is hiding among all that shiny tissue paper, we're not interested." Sam opened a jar of strawberry jam and smeared a dollop on a biscuit.

"Too bad Riley wasn't here." Boone repacked his box. "This one is full of brand-new games."

"More inventory." Abby deflated on her stool and rested her chin in her hands. "What about you, Paige? More inventory too."

"I'm not sure." Paige unwrapped a palm-sized wreath ornament and lifted it by the red velvet ribbon holder. "These look handmade."

"They sure do." Boone settled his fingers under the wreath to hold it steady and examined it.

"There's a note card attached." Paige turned over the note card and read the hand-printed message out loud. "'When we remember how it all began, we're reminded that we are always stronger together.' Then there's a Christmas wish. And the date."

Abby took another bubble-wrapped ornament from the box, unwrapped it and peered at the attached note card. "This is Grandma's handwriting. I'd recognize it anywhere."

Tess peered over Paige's shoulder. "That's definitely Grandma's handwriting."

"What are they made of?" Sam asked.

"Looks like tree boughs and herbs." Paige dabbed her fingertip over the dried leaves and the silver birch twigs. "Maybe thyme, sage and lavender."

"How do you know all that?" Abby searched Paige's face. "Do you have a garden in the city? Are you a secret gardener along with being a top-notch veterinarian?"

"I don't know about my sister being a secret gardener." Tess bumped her shoulder against Paige's. "But Paige's favorite book growing up was *The Secret Garden*."

"I used to make Tess read it to me every night." And Tess had without grumbling or skimming. It'd been one of Paige's favorite parts of their bedtime routine.

Paige was encouraged that Tess remembered such a small detail. "I've always wanted an English garden. I've done my share of research and designing on paper."

"Then you can help me." Abby brightened. "This spring will be my first attempt at a garden, and I don't have high hopes."

"Gotta start with cherry tomatoes," Boone said. "They're easy growers."

"Add lettuce if you don't want to fuss much. And marigolds to keep the pests away," Sam said. "The rest you can learn from the Roots and Shoots Garden Club."

"Or buy from Five Star Grocery Depot." Tess lifted her eyebrows up and down. "Like those of us who don't have green thumbs do."

"I'll give you some tips I've learned," Paige offered.

"It'd be better if you were here in person then to help me in the garden." Abby grinned at Paige. "I'll just let that idea float out there for you."

A return trip? Paige hadn't considered staying more than these two weeks before going back to her job in Chicago. Work had always come first. Work had always fulfilled her. The place she'd felt the most at home. "Why don't we talk about your garden while I'm here."

"Let's do that." A dare framed Abby's smile, yet she added nothing more.

Paige relaxed. Abby hadn't challenged her to commit one way or the other. More vacations, like so much else in her life, would simply have to wait until later. Disappointment tweaked the back of her neck.

Eventually, she'd stop putting things into the *later* category. But that wasn't today.

"What's the year on that ornament?" Boone scooted his box to the side and reached for Paige's wreath.

Paige glanced at the note card and handed the ornament to Boone. "It says 1962."

"That was the year we suffered a drought, then a once-in-a-century cold snap. Hasn't been that cold since." Boone rubbed his hands over his arms. The cheer receded from his voice. "Rough times. Folks were forced to close up their farms and leave town to find work elsewhere."

"So many days, we weren't sure our family's ranch was going to pull through." A bleak shadow shifted across Sam's face as if recalling those days renewed the gloom and discouragement.

Paige touched Sam's arm, wanting to ease his distress. Her grandparents had never mentioned a historic drought. They'd only ever talked about the general store and the good people in Three Springs who had made their work not feel like work.

Paige had always loved being a veterinarian. And with her grandparents' willing support and investment, she too had always found her work rewarding. Yet lately, the work had come to feel like work. Would that change if she became an equal partner? She hoped to find her personal satisfaction again. "How did you make it through?"

"Together." Boone laid the wreath ornament on his palm and pinched the note card between his fingers. "We leaned on each other that year. Fought together to keep what we had."

"Helped each other as much as we could." Sam loosened the black onyx clasp in his bolo tie. "No use pulling through if you're the one standing alone at the end. No one wants to live in a town of one."

Paige counted on having her own clinic one day. She and her ex had planned to open a practice together. Paige had believed she'd had a partner in both life and business. She'd believed she had everything she'd ever need. That she would never be alone again. But time had revealed a different man beneath the veneer of the polished and well-respected veterinarian she'd fallen in love with. Too late, Paige had realized everything she'd believed had been nothing more substantial than a smoke screen.

"You know, centuries ago, our families also banded together to kick the nasty Herring Gang out of town." Abby studied her wreath. "Even though Victoria McKenzie never turned up in Three Springs with the missing loot, it doesn't mean the community ever lost hope."

Boone touched Paige's arm. "We'll fill you in on the history this afternoon."

"My grandmother always put a wreath on her front door every holiday." Sam smoothed his fingers through his beard. "Never paid it much attention."

"Maybe there's more to the wreath and Three Springs's history?" Tess said, sounding thoughtful.

"I can do some research on these herbs." Distract herself from the thought of leaving. How could she already miss her family? Now wasn't the time to get twisted up in emotions. She had a sensible path for her future. She had time and money invested in Windsor Haven and she couldn't give up on her dream. "I'll figure out what they are and their meaning."

"We'll go through our official historical records." Sam set his palm on the committee folders as if swearing an oath. "And ask around town. Someone else might remember Opal's ornaments and if there was a link to the past."

"Speaking of research, your light was on late last night, Paige." Abby eyed Paige. Her smile wobbled and blossomed into place as if she couldn't hold it back any longer. "I wasn't spying. I was getting crackers from the kitchen. But I heard you on the computer. Were you researching cow illnesses for Evan?"

No. Maybe. Paige concentrated on wrapping up the wreath ornament, not on the heat inflaming her skin. Yet she could feel the weight of the group's attention trained on her.

"We heard you were out at the Crescent Canyon yesterday." Sam's voice was mild. "How are those cows faring?"

"I only saw Macybelle for a few minutes." Paige picked up Abby's ornament and tucked it into the box.

"Evan giving you grief, then?" Boone's gravelly voice rumbled across the counter.

Only if slipping into her thoughts unannounced and trespassing on her dreams was considered grief. Then yes, Evan was giving her grief. But it was nothing she couldn't manage. "Evan had it all handled or so he claimed."

Sam shook his head and frowned. "You should know there isn't a person more stubborn than a cowboy."

"I'm sure Evan's veterinarian will help him."

"Not from the operating room, he can't," Sam charged.

"Operating room," Paige repeated.

"Yes." Sam checked the time on his watch. "Dr. Conrad Gibson is having surgery on his ankle in less than an hour."

"He needs to have his bones reset." Boone winced. "Or his ankle won't heal proper."

"That sounds painful." Abby shuddered.

And like an injury that would require an extended recovery. Dr. Gibson wouldn't be making a house call to Evan's ranch anytime soon. But that wasn't Paige's problem. It couldn't become her problem. She had her own career to deal with back in Chicago. She was only there for twelve more days. How much could she really offer in such a short time? "I'm sure Evan will be fine."

"But will you be fine?" Tess watched Paige from her stool at her computer.

"What does that mean?" Paige was fine right now.

"You could never stand aside when you knew an animal was injured and hurting." Understanding was clear in Tess's words. "Grandma and Mom finally arranged for Paige to volunteer at the local animal shelter, so she'd have a place to bring her rescues."

Paige pictured Riley's tearstained face again. Heard again that faint rattle in Macybelle's chest. She had been looking up bovine diseases and viruses late last night. She could send Evan her findings, suggest he talk them over with his veterinarian. That was enough. The cows weren't rescues. The stakes were higher. This was Evan's livelihood. "Evan knows where to find me if he changes his mind."

"You could change his mind for him," Boone suggested.

Sam nodded. "That's what Opal did with her mother-in-law one recipe, one Sunday-night dinner at a time. Until she finally won the woman over."

But Paige wasn't looking to win Evan over. It was about his livestock and making sure every animal was properly cared for. And looked after to the best of her ability. She couldn't give her best when she herself had so much to learn. "I would only be in Evan's way."

"That's not always a bad thing," Boone said.

"Wouldn't hurt that boy none to look in a different direction every now and then either." Sam folded his arms over his chest.

Tess's phone chimed. Her sister grinned at the screen. "I finally have a solid lead on an early edition of *A Christmas Carol* that Lynette Kinney wants for her granddaughter."

"I have herbs to research." *And ranchers to stop thinking about*, Paige reminded herself.

Besides, the odds of finding a lost Christmas tradition from centuries past seemed better than the odds of changing one stubborn cowboy's mind about her.

CHAPTER FOUR

THE SHOPKEEPER'S BELL chimed an hour after lunch. Things had been quiet in the general store since Abby had gone back to her town hall office. And Boone and Sam were poring over notes for their historical committee of two at the end of the counter. It was the corner they'd claimed as their own. And where Paige gravitated to again and again.

All morning she'd interrupted the two men with questions about things like a glass butter churn and brass mortar and pestle she'd discovered in the basement. Paige brushed her dusty hands on her jeans and waited to greet the store's latest arrival.

"Hey, Riley!" Tess called out. She leaned around her computer screen to smile at the little girl. "Shouldn't you be in school?"

"I went to the dentist and Dad said I didn't have to go back, since the day's almost over." Riley cradled a large silver tabby cat against her chest. When her eyes locked on to Paige, relief washed over the girl's face. Riley didn't waste a

second as she beelined toward Paige. Her words
and footsteps never slowed. "Ms. Paige, something is wrong with Felix's paw."

Paige had no time to respond before Riley
plunked the plump cat into her arms.

"Can you fix him, please?" Riley pleaded.
"Mr. Gordon says Felix is his favorite shop cat
ever. He's caught so many mice, then delivers
'em to Mr. Gordon."

Paige sat on one of the empty stools and adjusted Felix on her lap. She stroked the cat's
back, drawing out a deep purr. "Riley. Where's
your dad?"

"He's next door with Mr. Gordon." Riley's
eyebrows lowered. "What do you think is wrong
with Felix?"

First, Paige was about to examine a cat that
belonged to a Three Springs resident she hadn't
met. Second, the rancher who'd rejected her
yesterday was next door. Third, said rancher's
daughter was impossible to refuse. Yet her father had no trouble refusing Paige's help. Paige
readjusted Felix until she located the hurt paw.
"I'm not sure yet. Does your dad know you're
here?"

"I told him I was going outside to find Felix."
Riley bumped into Paige's legs as she twisted
around to ask, "Mr. Boone, did you find the silver coin today?"

"Afraid not." Boone tapped one of their committee folders. "But we're gonna find it. Mark my words."

"Have you heard about the legend, Ms. Paige?" Riley looked at her expectantly.

"I have not." Paige shifted Felix, trying not to hurt the cat.

"Can I tell it?" Riley bounced up and down. "Pretty please."

"I can't think of anyone better." Sam reached for a trio of pale blue retro mason-jar-style canisters on the counter.

Boone took a candy-cane-shaped cookie from the shortest canister, then a gingerbread man cookie from another. He offered both to Riley. "The telling is always better with our super special treats."

Riley accepted the gingerbread man cookie and swayed beside Paige. She held up her cookie as if preparing to tell her tale to the gingerbread man. "There's bad guys who took gold and silver a long, long, superlong time ago. And the three McKenzie sisters got it all back. 'Cause they were mad. And they were brave too. Then they got hurt. But one sister, she hid the loot in the cave in the canyon not far from here. And now we're going to go on a treasure hunt and find it. The end." Riley grinned and bit triumphantly into her gingerbread man's leg. Within seconds her cookie was gone and only crumbs clung to her shirt.

"Finding a hidden treasure will be very exciting." Paige spread Felix's front paw gently and immediately saw the problem. Felix squirmed, but quickly settled as if he recognized she wanted to help. "I'm going to need a towel, tweezers and witch hazel. And a warm, damp cloth."

Around her, Boone, Sam, and Tess dispersed to collect the items she'd requested.

"What's in there?" Riley whispered and pointed at the paw as if she feared making things worse for the cat.

"Looks like it might be glass." Paige examined Felix's paw. "We have to take it out."

"Is it gonna hurt?" Riley chewed on her lip. Worry pulled her freckles up toward her eyes.

"Just for a minute." Paige accepted a warm washcloth from Boone and set it gently on Felix's paw. "But it'll hurt worse if it stays in his paw."

"My dad took a bee stinger outta my foot." Riley knocked the crumbs from her shirt onto the floor. "He told me the same thing. Is it like a bee stinger?"

"It is." The rest of Paige's supplies landed on the counter within easy reach. "Exactly like that."

"Let's wrap him in this." Tess unfolded a large

bath towel. "I'll hold him. You deal with the paw."

Paige studied her sister. "Are you sure?"

"It's like old times." Tess smiled at Riley. "I used to help Ms. Paige when she brought home injured rescues. And when she wanted to trim her cat Dexter's claws."

It wasn't exactly like old times, but Paige was determined to find a way to get back to that place for her and her sister. Tess bundled Felix into the towel like she'd been a vet assistant not a librarian all her life.

"I got a sparkly bandage for my bee bite." Riley climbed up onto the empty stool for a better view of the patient. She rested her elbows on the counter. "Felix needs one too to make it all better."

"We'll see what we can find for him." Paige glanced at Boone. "Do you have a flashlight you could shine on his paw for me?"

Seconds later, Boone settled the beam of a flashlight directly over Felix's injury. He held the light completely steady as if he too had been more than a cowboy his whole life.

"Felix also needs a kiss." Riley tapped her fingers on the counter. "Dad says those make everything better."

"Riley Rose." A stern voice tracked across the storefront.

Paige looked up to see Evan, hands on his hips, frowning at his daughter. His cowboy hat was pulled low over his forehead.

Unfortunately, not low enough to block the firm set of his mouth. Or Paige's off-the-rails train of thought. Would a kiss make her rancher feel better?

Evan said, "Riley, you're supposed to tell me when you leave to go somewhere."

"I had to bring Felix to Ms. Paige real fast." Riley jumped off the stool, sprinted over to her dad and grabbed his hands. "He's got glass in his paw. It's bad."

Evan approached the counter. His expression was guarded, but there was a quick flash of concern in his gaze. There and gone. "Do you need any help?"

"I've got it handled." That wasn't a boast. Or a false claim. It was a fact. Also a fact—something about her rancher unsettled her. And she didn't much care for the feeling. She concentrated on her patient, his injury and not the flustery sensation inside her.

Evan swung Riley up into his arms. "Can we get you anything, doc?"

"I'm good. Thanks." The tweezers brushed over the splinter of glass. She just needed to find the right angle. Same as she needed to find the right approach with her rancher. She was too aware of him and that she had to change. "Tess, Boone and Sam are here to pitch in. I don't need anyone else."

Her assistants had gone completely silent. Paige never lifted her attention from Felix's paw. But she was fairly certain their audience was switching their focus back and forth between Paige and Evan like a tennis match. Paige wanted to yell, *There's nothing to see here, folks. Just two people who have everything handled as two adults should.*

"Riley, we still need to stop at Country Time and the grocery store." Evan tapped Riley on the nose. The little girl giggled.

Paige curbed her smile and doubled down on pinching the edge of the glass shard.

"If everyone is good, we'll be on our way," Evan added.

Paige would be good when he did just that. Got on his way. So she could get on hers.

Riley waved goodbye and blew a kiss to Felix. "Don't forget to kiss him too, Ms. Paige."

The tweezers slipped again. Paige offered a silent apology to the cat and concentrated harder on her patient. As for that kiss, she feared she might not forget that idea soon enough.

The store doors opened and closed. The vintage clock on the wall ticked. Finally, Paige pulled the shard of glass free. "Got it."

Boone turned the flashlight off and frowned at the entrance of the store. "Paige, I don't mean to be critical. But that's not how you change a man's mind."

"Not at all." Sam shook his head. His handlebar mustache dipped down. "We might have to lend a hand with these two, Boone."

No. No lending of any hand was required. Hadn't they heard her with Evan? Paige pressed a witch-hazel-soaked cloth against Felix's paw to stop the bleeding and latched on to a distraction. "Seems Riley left out a few details about the legend. This would be a good time to fill me in."

"Great idea." Boone took a sip of his coffee as if settling himself into his best narrator's voice. "I'll start at the beginning. The McKenzie sisters, Vera, Violet and Victoria, were part of a caravan that had traveled here from back east."

Paige cuddled Felix on her lap. Tess, Boone and Sam swept her into a tale about a notorious gang called the Herrings who robbed the newly established town. One night three intrepid sisters, the McKenzies, were brave and bold enough to save the loot. The sisters had planned to return the gold and silver, but the Herring gang pursued the sisters. At the river, the three sisters split up. One sister was killed by the Herrings, and another passed away later from injuries she'd suffered during her escape.

The tale continued into the eventual love story for the only surviving McKenzie sister, Victoria. But Victoria declared that the loot was cursed and with her new husband, she buried it in a cave in Silent Rise Canyon. And that was the cave Boone and Sam intended to find once they located the missing treasure map.

"One of our great-great-uncles found a silver coin in the river." Tess stretched her arms over her head and flexed her fingers. It was the most animated she'd been all day. "He believed it was part of the lost treasure and a sign from Victoria not to give up hope."

"So, he built this general store right here in town." Boone opened the last cookie canister, took out a pale square and bit into the shortbread. "As a sign of hope for the community."

"And a gathering place for the locals," Sam added.

Her grandfather used to say, *Welcome to the Silver Penny. We have what you need, and the gossip is free.* Except this felt like more than a tale. More than a fireside story. "The silver coin exists, doesn't it?"

Boone aimed his thumb at Sam. "We've both seen it more than once. Used to hang on the wall right behind where your sister is working right now."

"Since you're here and we only have two

weeks..." Sam tapped the round face of his watch. "It's not much time to get a treasure hunt formulated, organized and completed."

The closest Paige had ever been to a treasure hunt had been in sixth grade. Her best friend had a scavenger hunt for her birthday party. The winning team had received gift cards to a nail salon. The preteen girls had acted as if they'd been on a quest for fourteen-karat gold, not acrylic nails. Paige had been eager back then. Now she was more than intrigued.

"We still have to locate the original silver coin." Caution muted Tess's voice. "And we need to find the map as well."

Maps and silver coins. It was sounding more and more like a legit treasure hunt. "And the silver coin was only ever in this store? On that wall."

Boone and Sam nodded.

"It has to be somewhere inside the store. We never saw it at their house while we were growing up." Tess collected the used supplies and waved her arm in a circle over her head. "And now we're hoping a map is with it."

"Details!" Sam stroked his fingers through his beard and looked thoughtful. "Those are all details that will sort themselves out eventually."

"We've been searching for the silver coin for months with no luck." Tess glanced at Paige.

"Fortunately, our enthusiasm hasn't dwindled so we haven't given up yet."

"But we did find a typewriter from the thirties and a working record player." Boone smiled at Paige. "Can't deny those were exciting finds."

"Don't forget the 1950s world globe we found tucked inside the traveler's chest in the front alcove," Sam added. "Harlan and I used to spin that globe, close our eyes and drop our finger on it. Wherever it landed was where we were going to travel when we grew up."

"Harlan ended up traveling the farthest when he moved north to be near his granddaughters." Boone lifted his hat and ran his fingers through his gray hair. "He told us it was the best decision he'd ever made."

Their grandparents had closed the general store, packed up a small moving truck and relocated to Wisconsin weeks after the funeral for Paige and Tess's dad. Paige had been seven.

Their grandparents had lived in a cozy house across the street until Paige had finally left for college. They'd been a constant source of support and their home one of Paige's favorite places to spend an afternoon or an entire weekend. Then her grandparents had moved in with Paige and Tess's mother during their mother's lengthy battle with cancer. For Harlan and Opal

Palmer, everything had always started and ended with family.

Paige would be forever grateful for their sacrifices. Many of which she was only now beginning to fully understand. She couldn't thank them, but she could honor them.

She could honor their memory and give her sister a piece of their family's history. A gift. The shadow of sadness around her sister had always lifted when Tess had talked about history. She'd seen it earlier during the retelling of the legend. Seen it when her sister had thrown herself into Christmas after their dad's death. As if that had connected Tess to their dad. But Tess wasn't throwing herself into anything these days. Even the store felt like it was missing something. Or maybe waiting for something.

The silver coin had once given an entire community hope. Perhaps it could do the same now for Tess.

And if she was searching for the silver coin, she wouldn't be thinking about a certain rancher, worrying about his cattle or him.

Paige rose and kept Felix bundled in the towel. "I'm going to return Felix to his owner."

And then she was going to find that silver coin and give her sister a Christmas to remember.

CHAPTER FIVE

"HOW LONG HAVE you been up? Or should I ask, have you been to bed yet?" Evan's mom stood in the kitchen archway and watched him.

Evan nudged his empty plate aside and frowned. "I've slept. Sort of." The sun had barely started to rise.

"Then you're probably in need of sustenance." His mom picked up the stainless-steel bowl with bread dough and dumped it out on the wooden cutting board, then tied an apron around her waist. "We've got milk, apple cider or good old-fashioned water."

"Got anything stronger?" Evan rubbed his hand over his face. "And before you ask, yes, it's that kind of a day already."

"More cows are sick, then." Worry threaded through his mom's voice.

"Yeah. More are sick." Despite having culled the sick ones from the herds into quarantine pens like Dr. Conrad Gibson had advised. Evan worked to keep his words even as if he could hide his own concern from his mother. "I still haven't heard back from the three vets I called. And Dr. Gibson had his surgery yesterday afternoon." Now Evan had to factor in the effect of pain meds when he spoke to the veterinarian.

"Did you do what Conrad suggested?" His mom adjusted the straps of her apron around her neck.

"That and more. His suggestions aren't helping." Evan handed Riley's hand-written letter to his mom. "And there's this too."

"What's this?" His mom unfolded the paper. Smiling suns and plump clouds filled the margins. Neat, bold, rainbow-colored block letters covered the rest of the page.

"That's Riley's wish list for Santa." Evan paced across the floor, trying to still his sudden urge to run. But not even a marathon would be enough to escape his unease.

His daughter had five wishes on her Santa list. Only one wish, the very last one, was something he could grant: the purple bicycle. How could it be a perfect Christmas if he couldn't give his daughter everything she wanted? If only she wanted a dream house for her dolls and more stuffed animals. "Is Riley ever going to like her red hair?"

Number four on the list: "Please turn my red hair brown like my best friend Claire's hair."

"One day, but I don't expect that will happen for a while." Ilene read through the letter, refolded it and handed it back to Evan. "That sweet child has always wished for her father to be happier."

Number one on Riley's wish list: "I want my daddy to be really, really super happy." Riley had been asking Evan if he was happy since she'd learned to talk. It'd started as a simple "Happy daddy" followed by the lightest of taps of her little palms against his cheeks. And somehow his happiness had progressed to an item on her Santa wish list. Evan touched his cheek as if his daughter's kindness was imprinted into his skin. "I can't seem to convince Riley that I'm already happy."

His mom's mouth shifted to one side. Her doubt dropped between them like one of Riley's water balloons bursting all over him.

"I can be perfectly happy as a single father, Mom," he argued. He stressed the word *single* like he did in all their conversations about dating. He was content being single. Casual dating wasn't an option. He brushed aside an image of a certain brown-haired city veterinarian. Paige Palmer wasn't the answer. Not for his sick cows or anything else for that matter. Besides, he had more than his own heart to protect now.

"Yes, you are proving how very happy you are." His mom squeezed his shoulder and then began kneading the dough. "But I won't apologize for wanting to see you blissfully in love too."

His mother would forever be a romantic. She wanted Evan to have what she had shared with his father—a love story that she still talked about even years after his father's passing. But Evan had tried love before.

Nothing about falling in love had fit right. It'd been like wearing snakeskin dress boots to herd cattle. The snakeskin looked stylish, but the material was too delicate for hard work. Hardly durable in the elements. That had been his relationship with his ex—hardly durable in the most stressful of times. And their love, well, even that lacked true endurance. He'd leave love for everyone else.

As for a certain city veterinarian, she probably never owned a pair of good, reliable cowboy boots. And most likely wasn't the least bit interested in trying on a pair. He had his daughter and his ranch. "I'm happy in life, Mom. Let that be enough. And instead tell me how I'm supposed to dye my daughter's red hair brown."

Ilene laughed, then aimed the rolling pin at him. "You won't dye a single red hair on my granddaughter's precious head."

"But it's what she really, really wants for Christmas." And Evan really, really wanted

Riley to have a perfect Christmas this year especially. Then just maybe he'd believe he was getting this parenting thing right too.

"She also really, really wants a mom. That's second on her wish list," Ilene challenged. "I don't see you rushing out to find her one of those."

"Hair dye and finding a mom are completely different things." And truthfully, neither was going to come true for Christmas. Evan wasn't very enthusiastic about changing Riley's red hair brown. He liked it as it was. Her red hair made Riley even more unique, and he considered that a good thing. He loved his daughter just as she was: red curls, freckles and equal parts challenging and adorable.

"Yes, hair dye eventually fades out," Ilene said.

"And the best moms stick." Evan stood. Sticking was why the position for mom wasn't open in his house. He couldn't risk another woman not sticking. Riley was too young to remember the first go around. She'd only been five months old when his ex-fiancée had walked out. But he remembered. And he'd vowed to protect himself and Riley from pain like that again.

Besides, they had each other and his mom. They were as complete as they needed to be. Their family worked as is. Why would he want to change that? Even if a big happy family was number three on Riley's wish list.

Evan filled the coffee maker. At his mother's raised eyebrow, he shrugged. "I haven't had one cup yet. After this, I'll switch to water. I promise."

"Don't promise what you don't intend to do." With the warning issued, his mother went to work flattening her dough.

His parents had been repeating that cautionary advice since he'd been a teenager and bargaining for one more hour of TV, a later curfew and his own cell phone.

Evan turned toward the kitchen sink and stared out the window. He'd made an impossible promise to Riley last night. Riley had zipped her footed pajamas under her chin, climbed into her bed, then thrust her Santa wish list at Evan. She'd bounced on her bed from excitement as she'd recited her short list and ticked each item off on her fingers. She'd announced to her stuffed animals that she'd been good all year and Santa would hopefully give her exactly what she'd wanted.

Evan had assured Riley he'd mail the letter to the North Pole in the morning. Then asked his daughter for clarification on several items. First, did she want the purple bike with the daisy-print seat? Or the rainbow-colored bike with the sparkle seat? Riley had requested more time to consider. It was an important decision and those shouldn't be rushed, according to her grandma.

Evan had eased into number two: "I want Mommy." He'd explained Santa might need further information about finding her a mommy. Riley had blinked, and her long eyelashes had swept downward to tickle her freckles before lifting. Her gaze had lit like the sparklers she liked to hold on the Fourth of July. "You know where to find my mommy, Daddy. You can help Santa."

Evan had forced his jaw not to unlock and drop open.

Unfazed, Riley had rattled on. "So Santa can bring my mommy here for Christmas morning."

Words had stuck in his throat, but he'd stammered, "I'm not sure where your mommy is."

Riley had smiled, innocent and precious. Her heart intact. "If you call her, she can tell you. And Santa can get her in his sleigh."

Evan had kissed Riley's forehead, wrapped his arms around her and lifted her off the bed for a good-night bear hug. But nothing had lifted his unease.

Riley had squeezed him, then whispered, "Promise you'll call her, Daddy. That way she can come home for Christmas."

And Evan had promised. Promised his little

girl because he'd wanted to keep her heart unscathed a little while longer.

Riley had cheered and shouted, "Best Christmas ever."

But there was nothing good about it. Evan already knew his ex-fiancée and Riley's biological mother wasn't coming back. He doubted Marla would even answer his phone call. Still, he'd promised Riley.

All to keep from telling his daughter the truth and truly breaking her heart. Riley was old enough now to understand what silence meant. Riley understood even without using the right words what hurt and abandonment felt like. His old anger and resentment toward his ex's choice shifted inside him. Not that he'd ever trade away any day spent with Riley now.

Yet he had traded an impossible promise for avoiding an even harder conversation.

That was nothing he'd confess to his mother. His mom would be more than disappointed once the truth came out. His stomach soured. He poured his unfinished coffee down the drain and set his cup in the dishwasher.

His phone vibrated on the kitchen table. Evan tapped the answer button and greeted Dr. Conrad Gibson.

His mom waved at him. Flour drifted from

her fingers and dusted the air. "Put Conrad on speaker. I want to hear too."

Evan put the phone on speaker and told Dr. Gibson that his mother was listening in.

Pleasure smoothed Dr. Gibson's usually gritty voice. "Ilene. Always wonderful to hear your voice. I'd rather see you in person, however."

"Then listen to your doctor and do your therapy." Quiet laughter softened his mom's orders. "And we'll be seeing you here at Crescent Canyon sooner than you think."

"Will you have cinnamon-roll coffee cake when I come out there, by chance?" Conrad asked. "Your cakes are the best I've tasted."

"Certainly." Color splashed into his mom's cheeks. "And I'll see about getting apple spice muffins to you in the hospital."

"You're an angel, Ilene Bishop." Conrad's content sigh was easy to hear.

"Now, we need your expertise to save our livestock, Conrad." His mother's voice swung into lemon-curd-tart mode.

There was a beat of silence, followed by beeping and muffled voices over the speaker. Finally, Conrad's voice boomed over the line. "Sorry, the nurse came to record my vitals. I'm back and listening. Evan, talk to me."

Evan ran through everything he'd done the past several days. Listing every symptom he'd observed regarding the mood and appetites of the sick cows as well as their temperatures and breath rates he and his ranch hand had recorded. Then he paused to wait for Dr. Gibson's assessment.

"Sure do wish I could get my hands on those poor babies." No matter the size of his patients, Dr. Gibson always referred to his patients as his babies. "Only way to truly know what's going on is to be there in person." The vet's frustration came through loud and clear.

"What else can we do?" Evan heard the plea in his own voice. But he hadn't wanted to state the obvious. The farthest Dr. Gibson would be walking was the hospital wing the next few days.

"I need eyes," Dr. Gibson demanded. "Experienced ones. Can you get me those?"

"We had a pair of those," Ilene chimed in. "Evan sent her away."

"Who's this Evan sent away?" A scratch rustled over the phone as if Dr. Gibson had moved the microphone closer.

Evan frowned. He hadn't sent Paige away. He let her examine and talk to Macybelle first.

"Her name is Paige Palmer," Ilene continued. "She's a veterinarian too."

"Never heard the name before." Suspicion clouded Dr. Gibson's tone.

"Because she lives in Chicago." And because

Paige was not the remedy to his problems. Evan rubbed the back of his neck. Nothing budged the tension tightening his muscles. "And she only works with small animals."

"What were you doing in Chicago?" Dr. Gibson asked, obviously confused. "Awful cold up there this time of year."

"Paige is in Three Springs." Ilene elbowed Evan aside to get closer to his phone. "Her cousin and sister live here. But Paige came to see Macybelle at Riley's request a few days ago. Then yesterday when I dropped off pumpkin streusel muffins for her, Paige told me that she had heard a small rattle in Macybelle's chest."

"Paige thought she heard a rattle, but wasn't sure," Evan corrected. Just as Evan wasn't sure Paige wouldn't be more of a complication than a help. And Evan didn't need any more of those.

"How long has this Paige Palmer been a vet?" Conrad asked.

Evan glanced at his mom and shrugged. "I'm not sure. She works at an emergency veterinarian clinic in Chicago."

"Then she knows a rattle." More rustling scraped over the speaker. "Now, let's see if I have this straight. You've got a veterinarian in town, and she came out to see Macybelle, correct?"

"Paige is only visiting for a few weeks," Evan called out.

"But she's in town right now," Conrad clarified.

"Yes." Ilene aimed a satisfied grin at Evan. "Yes, she is."

"Then we've got trained eyes and ears." Dr. Gibson's voice sharpened into a command. "Evan, listen up."

"Yes, sir." Dread and caffeine made a poor combination in his gut.

"You need to get that vet back," Dr. Gibson ordered. "Promptly. You hear me?"

He heard. Dr. Gibson was practically shouting over the speaker. "I'm not sure she's available. She's on vacation."

"If she's like the rest of us veterinarians who are worth our salt, she doesn't take vacations," Conrad stated. "Especially not when animals are in need."

"She isn't licensed in the state," Evan countered.

"I certainly am. I'm writing the prescriptions and devising the treatment plan." Dr. Gibson's firm voice offered no further opening for an argument.

Still, Evan didn't need Paige on his property. She didn't know the first thing about cows or ranch life, and he had no time to teach her. Or any inclination to. Despite her gentleness with Macybelle the other day and what seemed to be a natural compassion for every animal, her safety while she was there would be another responsibility of his. "I can give you the details you need."

"How many temperatures have you taken? How many rattles inside chests have you heard? How many different bacterial and viral respiratory disease strands have you come across?" There was a brief pause and Conrad charged on. "Not enough—that's how many. Get me the vet, Evan."

Evan's shoulders drooped as he accepted the task. Like his dad had always taught him to do. "I'll call her."

"Be quick about it," Dr. Gibson launched the last of his instructions. "I'm off to physical therapy later this morning, but I'll have all afternoon and I'll expecting to hear from you."

Dr. Gibson quit the call. Evan shoved his phone in his back pocket and grabbed his cowboy hat from the hook near the back door and his truck keys.

"It's a bit early to call Paige," Ilene said.

"It doesn't matter. I don't have her phone number."

"You can call the general store later." Ilene waved to the old-fashioned rotary phone still hanging on their kitchen wall. It had become a conversation piece that neither his mom nor Evan had wanted to remove. More flour dusted the air and drifted to the floor. "Or you can call Abby's office."

"Don't worry, Mom." Evan stepped over to the butcher-block island and kissed his mom's cheek. "I'm off to the stables to get the guys organized for the day. We've got range checks to make, more stock to observe, and brakes on the tractor-trailer to repair. After that, I'm going to do you one better than a phone call to Paige."

"What's that?" She eyed him.

"I'm going to go get the vet." Evan grinned. "Like Dr. Gibson told me to."

CHAPTER SIX

"THE LAST ONE is free." Abby raised her arms over her head and cheered from her spot outside the general store.

Paige and Abby had been untangling dozens of strands of sparkly globe lights for the past few hours. Paige had her pumpkin muffin half-eaten and hadn't even started her search for the silver coin when Abby had burst into the store. Her cousin had announced a major Christmas light fiasco and pleaded for immediate backup.

Tess's list for last-minute special-order gifts had been steadily growing the past few days. Paige had left Tess at her computer and followed Abby outside. Tangled bunches of lights had been dropped like breadcrumbs along the sidewalk, extending the full block.

Now Cliff and Roman, Abby's town maintenance duo, picked up the strands Paige and Abby had unraveled and carried the lights to hang in the town square. The globe lights were an essential piece of the Christmas wonderland her cousin envisioned for downtown.

Abby draped the last strand over her shoulders like an untied scarf. The lights dangled across her stomach and settled near her boots. "How do I look?"

"Like you're all caught up in Christmas." And it suited Abby. Her cousin seemed even more energized than yesterday.

"I really am." Abby laughed and touched her stomach. Delight sparked in her eyes and broadened her smile. "We've got a baby kick of approval. I think the baby likes all this Christmas too."

Paige liked knowing her cousin was happy. Truly, soul-deep happy. Paige wanted the same for her sister. And for herself. Unfortunately, hanging glittery globe lights and singing along to the holiday music Abby had Tess turn on inside the store wasn't going to get Paige to her own personal happy place.

That place was Windsor Haven Animal Clinic in Chicago. Her grandparents had given her the money to invest in her dream, allowing her to own a small stake in the clinic. Now she wanted an equal share. She'd earned it. Thanks to her, in part, the clinic had become one of the leading pet-care providers in the city. She just needed the other three partners to agree. Then she would have what she wanted. Then she would be happy.

"I'm off to get this last strand hung so that

Cliff, Roman and I can move on. There's so much to do before the Christmas tree lighting in the square next weekend." Abby gathered the ends of the light strand in her arms. "You should head over to the Owl, Paige. And tell Wes that your lunch is on me."

"I can't believe it's that time already." The day was half over.

Calling and pressuring the partners wouldn't benefit her and most likely irritate them. That left two items on her agenda: identifying the herbs in her grandmother's ornament and locating the silver coin.

The silver coin was supposed to be her gift to Tess. An apology, an olive branch and a new start for the two sisters. It was also the very same silver coin no one here had located after months of searching. She refused to be deterred. Besides, the distraction would do her good. At home, she always worked. And never quite understood what to do with her free time other than fill it by working more.

Paige watched her cousin stroll toward the town square. Cliff and Roman met up with Abby and took the last light strand. Abby pressed her hands against her back and continued her slow walk. The trio's unrestrained laughter drifted back to Paige, tempting her to follow and join in. Instead, Paige reached for the door handle of the general store. She could be carefree and merry later.

Once her career was rerouted for success.

Paige checked on Tess, got her sister's lunch order and headed over to the Feisty Owl Bar and Grill. She opened the heavy door and stood inside the entryway. A handful of diners were already seated in the dining room, which filled half the space. An impressive bar, an empty dance floor and an idle mechanical bull completed the other side of the interior.

Wes greeted her first. He sliced lemons on a cutting board in quick succession, set the wedges in the condiment tray, then handed her a menu. "I can guess what Tess wants, but I'm not sure if you're going to try Boone's special potato-and-bacon soup, the grilled cheese with avocado, tomato and bacon. Or the bacon-wrapped onion rings."

Paige grinned. Last night over dinner, they'd debated the best recipes for bacon. The conversation had been lively and entertaining. The consensus was that bacon deserved to be its own food group. The one recipe that showcased bacon in all its deliciousness was still up for grabs. Paige scanned the menu. "There's also the Texas chili and the loaded chicken nachos."

"Tess wants the chili, doesn't she?" Wes typed the order onto a computer screen.

Paige nodded. "I'll take the chicken nachos."

"That's a customer favorite." Boone stepped through a swinging door behind the kitchen and smiled at Paige. He set individual bowls of guacamole and salsa on the bar top. "It'll become one of your favorites too."

Boone and his buddy, Sam, had quickly become two of Paige's favorite people. The pair of cowboys had endless stories and boundless enthusiasm. They'd spent yesterday afternoon beside Paige, digging through boxes in the general store basement. They'd added color commentary to many of the stories her grandpa Harlan had told her about his own childhood growing up in Three Springs alongside Boone and Sam. Paige would've looked to her sister for a friend like that. And she would again. She just had to find that silver coin.

As it turned out, every item Paige uncovered had its own history attached to it. She'd unwrap an item. Boone would smooth his fingers through his beard. And one or the other of the guys would say, "Did you know, that's a…" And her history lesson would begin. Fascinated, Paige had wanted to hear about the antique oil lanterns and the cast-iron well-water pulley. As a result, they hadn't gotten through too many boxes. But somehow, she'd left feeling even closer to her grandparents.

Sam came through the doorway, carrying two baskets of chips. "We're having appetizers while we wait for Nolan to finish the samples of his newest item for the menu."

"Does this new menu item involve bacon?" Paige glanced at Wes.

He shook his head and laughed. "I'm not taking your bacon-wrapped jalapeno popper recipe in exchange for my secret coffee blend."

"It was worth a try." Paige had badgered Wes last night about his coffee, then changed tactics and tried to bargain. He hadn't budged. She slid onto a stool near Boone and Sam at the end of the bar. "How can I get Wes to tell me what makes his coffee so good?"

"Not sure you can." Sam scooped salsa onto a chip.

"You have to find Wes's weakness," Boone suggested. "Everybody's got one."

Paige eyed Wes across the bar. She wasn't sure he had one. Wes was clearly devoted to her cousin Abby—he'd held her hand most of the evening. Watched over Abby and checked on the baby—just a soft press of his palm against Abby's stomach. Wes wasn't the biological father, but he was already the baby's dad. Wes was one of the main reasons Abby was soul-deep happy. Paige would've claimed love was a weakness. But for Wes and Abby, their love made them stronger. "Sam might be right. There might not be a way to get the secret coffee bean blend from Wes."

"You can't just throw in the towel that quickly." Boone squeezed a lime wedge, sprinkling the juice over his guacamole. "Your grandfather raised you to have more resolve than that."

She'd boasted to Evan the other day that she would've found a way to Macybelle's pasture with or without him. She'd been serious. And he'd believed her. Then he'd dismissed her. Too bad his stunning blue-gray eyes and slow but charming smile weren't as easy to forget.

Paige drummed her fingers on the bar. "Grandpa Harlan would've purchased different coffee beans and already started blending them to figure it out himself."

"That's not a bad idea." Boone nodded, approval in his voice.

"Hey, Wes," Sam shouted. "Paige here is going to blend her own coffee beans and discover your secret herself."

Wes grinned. "I've got extra coffee beans in the back if you want to start now."

"You don't think I can figure it out, do you?" Paige leaned across the bar.

Wes lifted one shoulder in a small shrug. "I think that you are just like your cousin. Abby doesn't know how to back down from a challenge either."

Paige accepted that as a compliment and grinned.

Boone slapped the bar top and laughed. "Cousins got that trait straight from Harlan."

One more trait the cousins had gotten from Harlan—when they accepted a challenge, they usually won. Paige opened her mouth, ready to agree.

"You're hard to track down, Paige Palmer." Evan lifted his cowboy hat off his head, ran his fingers through his short hair, giving the black strands a rather appealing disheveled look.

Speaking of challenges. Her cowboy was certainly one. And Paige wasn't certain if she was glad about that or not. "I can't believe I was that hard to track down. After all, it's a small town. You said it yourself."

Evan tapped his cowboy hat against his leg. "Can we talk?"

Wes came closer to wipe down what Paige was convinced was a permanent stain not far from her. Boone and Sam scooted their stools toward hers. Paige kept her smile in check and patted the empty stool beside hers. "Sure. My nachos should be ready soon. I have it on good authority they're going to become my favorite."

"Any chance you'd be willing to take those

nachos to go?" Evan's voice skimmed the edges of a plea.

She spun and faced him fully. That was her first mistake. "Where are we going?"

"Back to Crescent Canyon Ranch." Doubt disrupted his confidence, pitching his tone slightly higher.

Her brows lowered. The second mistake: locking her gaze on his.

How was it possible his eyes looked even more piercing blue inside the bar? No one should have eyes that color. His were the kind of blue that haunted. That invited her to dive in. That hinted at unknown depths. Ones she wanted to discover. The shock of attraction she absorbed and acknowledged. He was entirely too handsome.

Yet it was the connection she felt to him that rattled her. Connections weren't immediate. Trust wasn't instantaneous. She and Evan were all wrong. From two different worlds. A rancher and a city veterinarian. She drank instant coffee, rarely took breaks, and thrived when her already fast-paced workload pushed her to think even faster. He watched the sunrise, preferred unrushed mornings, and moved leisurely and gracefully as if there was enough time for everything.

The longer she held his gaze, the louder one single whisper became inside her: *Trouble*. But she already had enough trouble without being attracted to this guy.

"I'm sorry about the other day. Really sorry." Evan's words rolled together. "I don't have a good excuse for my behavior. Stress and worry aren't always a good combination."

Neither was an appealing cowboy and a sincere apology.

"You should ask for a do-over," Sam suggested and chomped down on another salsa-loaded chip.

"That's exactly what you need." Boone waved a chip over the bowl of guacamole and dunked it in. "Fresh start."

Evan's gaze, deliberate and gentle, swept over Paige's face. "Can we have that?"

Paige broke the link, glanced over Evan's shoulder, then back to his chin. Anywhere but his intriguing eyes. "That depends. Are you still worried and stressed?"

"Even more so." His cowboy hat tapped an agitated beat against his leg. "More of the herd has fallen ill."

Not more sick cows. Evan was supposed to have gotten help by now. Supposed to have been following a treatment plan for his cattle.

Sam and Boone quieted as if taking in the grim situation. Even Wes's face shuttered into neutral. Their worry for Evan surrounded her, joined her own unease.

The cowboy hat stilled against Evan's jeans. When he spoke, his words were calm and serious. "Dr. Gibson had surgery yesterday, but he wants your eyes and ears."

"Excuse me?" Her gaze snapped back to Evan's. That immediate connection snapped through her again. She ignored it. Elusive emotions were nothing she put her trust in these days. Besides, sick animals took precedence. Always had. Always would.

"Mine apparently aren't as qualified as yours." A trace of disbelief and hint of surprise crossed Evan's face.

"I'm a small-animal doctor," she stressed. And a bad bet for a relationship.

"But you're experienced and trained." Evan moved closer to her. "And in Dr. Gibson's opinion you are the perfect choice to act on his behalf."

"That sounds about right to me," Boone agreed.

"Me too," Sam added.

It sounded all wrong to Paige. Even a provisional license took two weeks to obtain. She learned that last night while researching bovine diseases. Evan required assistance now. And in ten days, she flew home to Chicago. "Still, I need to be licensed to practice in the state."

"Those are details Dr. Gibson seems to have figured out." Evan braced his hand on the bar top. "Claims you aren't prescribing, diagnosing or setting the treatment plan. He is. You're simply relaying information and carrying out what he would do if he were here."

Doubt worked through her, weaving around her own bewilderment that a part of her wanted to jump right in. Agree, despite the potential consequences. Because sick animals deserved to be cared for. And worried cowboys deserved to be helped. "Dr. Gibson knows I'm going to have opinions and observations?"

A faint grin passed over Evan's mouth. There and gone, but a lightness lingered in his words. "I'm quite certain Dr. Gibson is counting on that too."

Paige rubbed at her forehead. She shouldn't be considering this. Her reputation was in a precarious place in Chicago. Any allegation about her practicing unlicensed in Texas could damage her partnership chances completely.

Sam cleared his throat. His voice boomed across the bar. "For a proper do-over for this couple, this isn't very eventful."

"What's supposed to happen in a proper do-over anyway?" Wes draped his cleaning cloth over his shoulder and glanced between Evan and Paige. Amusement flashed in his eyes and tipped one side of his mouth up.

Paige glared at her cousin's boyfriend, silently urging Wes not to encourage the cowboy pair and the conversation about do-overs.

"Fresh starts should be something like dinner on the patio, just the two of you." Boone pushed his empty bowl of guacamole aside and accepted a full soda glass from Wes. "Candles on the table. The fireplace lit. That sort of thing."

"A walk through the million-light display at Haystack Hills Farm," Sam suggested. His eyebrows lifted. "It's supposed to be something special."

"Wes, I will take those nachos to go, please." Paige stood to address Sam and Boone. Her shoulder bumped into Evan. Phantom butterflies bumped in her chest. Nerves were reserved for tricky abdominal surgeries, not attractive cowboys. "As for the kind of fresh start you're referring to, gentlemen, Evan and I don't need that. We're all good. Great, in fact. And now we have cows that need us."

Boone tapped his chin and eyed Evan. "When you finish with the cows, do something extra nice for Paige."

"Show her our Christmas spirit, Evan." Sam's smile was unapologetic, his tone casual. "Thanks to our Abby, there's lots of Christmas things for couples in town this year."

"I'm… Dr. Gibson's eyes and ears…not Evan's date," Paige stammered. Cows, not connections, were her only focus.

"There's no rule stating you can't be both." Boone watched Paige as if he too saw that imaginary connection between Evan and her.

Evan stepped beside Paige as if he intended to join her team. "Boone and Sam, you need to aim Cupid's arrow in another direction. Paige and I have cows to heal. Nothing else."

Boone slapped the bar top and laughed. A deep rumble of pure joy. "Then you two best be getting on with the healing."

Wes handed Paige a to-go bag and told her he'd walk Tess's lunch over to her at the store.

Paige accompanied Evan to his truck, climbed into the passenger seat and set the to-go container on her lap.

Evan stole a cheese-soaked chip from the container. "You'll have to excuse Boone and Sam. They helped a runaway bride last summer and brought the couple back together. Now they consider themselves some sort of matchmakers."

"Was she really a runaway bride?" Paige chose a chip loaded with sour cream and shredded chicken.

"She ran from the historic church in the

square." Evan pointed down the street, toward the spot. "Turns out her groom, suffering cold feet, was already inside the Owl."

Paige glanced at Evan. "Did the couple ever get married?"

"They did." Evan started the truck and switched on the heat. "Whatever Boone and Sam told them worked."

"That's sweet." And another reason she liked the cowboys.

"Boone and Sam are good people," Evan said. "They mean well and have big hearts."

"But?" Paige asked.

"But being in love isn't the answer for everyone." Evan tossed his cowboy hat on the back seat and scrubbed his fingers through his hair.

Paige studied her nachos. "You don't believe in love?"

"Sure, I believe in it." Evan flicked his hand toward the bar. "Look at Wes and Abby. How can you not believe in love when you see them together?"

Abby and Wes shared what Grandma Opal and Grandpa Harlan had shared. A real-deal love story. The precious kind of love that required care and attention. Paige's energy was directed at her career and always advocating for animals.

Besides, Paige had a list of everything she did not want in her next relationship. Although, right now, she was too selfish about her single status. And not the least bit eager or excited about another relationship. "I believe in love too, but that doesn't mean I want to fall in love myself."

"Exactly." Evan helped himself to another chip. "But it's hard to explain that to some people."

"I get it." Yet she wanted to know if he'd ever been in love before. And what exactly had happened to change his views on love? But that required trust, both to ask and answer. And opening up cued that relationship chatter. It was enough to know that they both agreed on love—neither one of them wanted to find it. "Tell me about Dr. Gibson and your cows."

"Dr. Conrad Gibson is hard to describe." Evan wiped his fingers on his jeans and picked up his phone. "He's one of the best I've seen with the animals. Thinks outside the box. Actually, he lives his entire life outside the box. He makes a lasting impression."

"I like him already," Paige said.

"Let's jump right in, then." Evan waved the phone at her. "Dr. Gibson is waiting for our call."

Seconds later, Dr. Gibson's face filled the screen. "Ryan, my nurse this afternoon, showed me how to turn on this video thing."

"Now you can see what we see too." Evan adjusted the phone on the dashboard.

"I can see now, but I still can't get my hands on my sick patients. That matters, Evan." Dr. Gibson sat up straighter in his bed. "Now, tell me you got the vet."

Evan glanced at Paige. "She's right here beside me."

"Put her on," Dr. Gibson hollered. "Put her on."

Evan handed the phone to Paige and completed the introductions.

"Paige, we'll get to the specifics about you later, I promise. I want to know more." Dr. Gibson's finger tapped the screen, blurring his face. "But for now, we need to focus on the cows. This thing is spreading too fast, and we have to get ahead of it. Do you have a pen and paper? Write this down."

Evan handed Paige a pen; she handed him the phone. She folded the paper to-go bag flat. "I'm ready."

Dr. Gibson listed off vitals he wanted and at what times. Symptoms he wanted verified and double-checked. And other nuances he wanted her to look for on every part of the cow from the head to hooves to throat. Paige finished her notes and glanced at the phone screen. "How did you get hurt, Dr. Gibson?"

"A bull stomped… Never mind all that. What's important is getting you out to those cows real quick like. I need you recording and reporting." A shuffling scratched over the speaker and the camera view became that of Dr. Gibson's hospital ceiling. "I can't see you anymore. Now, go get me the information I need to diagnose and treat. You know what I need. Call me back when you have it."

The screen went blank. Evan dropped his phone in the console. Paige buckled her seat belt.

Evan pulled the truck away from the curb and headed out of town. "I've got a clipboard and paper in the house. Where do you want to start?"

"With Macybelle." Paige worked on finishing her lunch. "Then we move on from there."

Several hours and two dozen cows observed and examined later, Paige realized several important things. Evan had a really good eye for what was happening with his cattle. He managed a sizable cattle ranch with skill, competence and passion. She really liked working with him. And it was the first time since she'd arrived in town that she'd felt truly at ease.

Paige climbed out of the UTV and nodded toward the small bungalow behind the main farmhouse. "Does your mom live there?"

"No, Mom lives in the main house with us." Evan whistled. Rex slipped through the fence posts and ran toward him. "She has her own wing. The guesthouse is empty."

"Do you rent it out?" Paige took in the small front porch, with the rocking chair and side table. Perfect to sit and savor that first cup of coffee. If a houseguest was into that sort of thing.

"We used to rent it out when I was a kid." Evan knelt and rubbed his hands over Rex's back. "Hasn't had a long-term tenant in years, only guests every so often. Friends and family of neighbors who don't have enough room at their own places."

"Would you be open to a guest now?"

"Who?" Evan asked.

"Me. It makes sense." Probably only to her, but she'd started down this path and had to see it through. "I need to be close to the cows. It's not a short drive from Abby's place downtown."

Evan looked both thoughtful and resistant to the idea.

"What if you have an emergency?" Paige pressed. "If I'm on the property, I can react faster."

"It's not a big place."

"I'm one person," she countered. "I don't need much room." But she wanted a reprieve. Even a small one from Christmas. It wasn't too much to ask, was it?

"It's real simple," he said. "Nothing fancy."

"That's how I live in the city." She spent most

of her time at the clinic. It was more of a home than her town house.

"The heat isn't always reliable," he warned.

"I'm from Chicago. This isn't cold." She pointed to the chimney on the bungalow. "And besides there's a fireplace."

He tilted his head and studied her. "Don't you want to be with your family?"

Yes. No. She felt disloyal even considering staying with Evan and not her cousin. "I'll still see them every day. And they know I'll worry less if I have quick access to the cows. And I won't intrude on your family time either. You have my word."

"Did you always want to take care of animals?" he asked, neatly pivoting the conversation.

"Dr. Lawrence Trevino came to my house and healed my cat. After that, I only ever wanted to be just like him." She crossed her arms over her chest. "I used to make my grandparents stop for every injured animal on the side of the road. I had to know if there was something I could do."

"They always stopped?" He tapped his hat farther up his forehead as if he wanted to see her better.

"Every single time." She smiled and welcomed the memories of her grandparents. "Grandpa Harlan even put together a first aid kit of sorts for me. I added to it over the years. They never complained, even on long car rides when I made the trip that much longer."

"What about your parents?" His voice was curious, but not pushy.

"My father died when I was a little older than Riley." Paige touched her chest and the ache anchored between her ribs. "My mom worked two jobs as a nurse. She cared about her patients the way I care about animals. She understood me."

"Sorry about your dad." Sympathy was easy to spot in his gaze. "My father passed away five years ago. They say time heals, but it still stings."

"And at the most unexpected times." Like inside Abby's house, surrounded by so much Christmas. Abby lived Christmas the same way Paige's dad had: all-in. Over-the-top. And bursting with cheer. Paige wanted her cousin to never lose that light inside her. And Paige didn't want to risk casting any shadows. Abby should have the Christmas she always wanted. If Paige could stay at Evan's, maybe then the memories of her dad wouldn't still hurt.

"Paige." Evan watched her. "You can stay in the guesthouse."

CHAPTER SEVEN

PAIGE OPENED THE front door of the guesthouse and gaped at the tall ladder filling her view. She crossed the small porch and squeezed around the ladder. Her gaze lifted from the scuffed work boots on the lower ladder rung to the pair of jean-clad legs, past the thick winter jacket to a familiar pair of intense blue eyes.

She wanted to rub her own sleep-filled eyes and climb back under the comfy down comforter in the inviting and charming guesthouse bedroom. "Evan."

"Good morning." His voice was entirely too cheerful. His gaze entirely too alert.

The sun had risen less than ten minutes ago and was still struggling to turn up its brightness dial. At the first scrape against the roof and the shuffling noises outside the bedroom window, she'd stumbled out of bed and down the stairs to investigate. She'd been expecting one of the ranch dogs to be on the porch or even a brave ground squirrel. But not Evan.

She wasn't sure what she required to face the

disarming cowboy at dawn. But she was quite certain it was more than her fuzzy slippers and flannel pajamas. She crossed her arms over her chest. "What are you doing?"

"I'm decorating." He reached up and clipped a strand of icicle lights to the hooks attached to the gutter.

"Why?" Paige ran her hands up and down her arms to warm her cold palms. Clearly, she couldn't escape Christmas.

"Riley." Evan stepped down several rungs and leaned his elbows on the top of the ladder. Closer now, his gaze was less direct and more thoughtful. He spoke with affection. "Riley would light up the pastures if I let her. My daughter believes Santa cannot find us all the way out here in the country unless we are lit up brighter than the galaxy."

Riley had already been in bed when Paige had arrived last night with her suitcase and laptop. The kind little girl had left her unicorn stuffed animal on the queen bed in the guesthouse to keep Paige company. Paige tipped her chin toward the guesthouse. "What about the new wreath on the front door? Is that a Santa requirement too?"

"That's a welcome from my mom with Riley's approval." Evan studied her from beneath the brim of his cowboy hat. "Christmas decorations are much more than simply lights. And Riley lives by the rule more is always better."

Exactly like Paige's cousin. Paige was several miles removed from downtown and Abby's Christmas-bonanza house, but clearly the Christmas spirit wasn't willing to be left behind. But Paige was on the property to be Dr. Gibson's eyes and ears. To collect and record bovine data. Not decorate guesthouses, cuddle with neon-colored unicorn stuffed animals and get involved in the Bishop family's traditions.

She should go inside, get dressed and get to the cattle. Instead, she watched Evan finish hanging the strand of faux icicles, as if he was the one she was supposed to be putting her eyes and ears to.

"You aren't allergic to the smell of fresh-cut fir, are you?" Evan rubbed his gloved hand under his chin. Worry colored his expression.

She could sneeze and nod. End all of this with a falsehood. But the idea settled poorly within her. Much like eating raw bell peppers always hurt her stomach. She shook her head. "No tree allergies."

"Are you allergic to Christmas in general, then?" Evan continued to string up more lights along the porch roof.

"No, it's not that." She wasn't allergic to the season. She just rarely participated in it.

Evan stepped off the ladder and almost into her. His gaze skimmed her face, intense and perceptive. "You told me your father passed when you were little. You never mentioned when."

"December." Paige's voice faded in the chilly morning air. "My dad would've loved all this. Christmas was always his favorite time of the year."

"But it's not yours." Evan nodded and ran his hand through his hair.

Evan was the one person who'd recognized that in her right away. He was little more than a stranger, yet he looked at her as if he already knew her. Already understood her. Already cared about her. That wasn't possible.

She gathered her hair into a ponytail. Put herself back together. Surely her thoughts would fall in line now too.

"We can take the lights down." Evan held out his arm as if reaching for a solution. "I can tell Riley there's a problem with the outlet."

"You would do that? I'm…" Not family. Not even an invited guest. She'd persuaded Evan to let her stay in the guesthouse. She wasn't there to participate in their family life. But she wouldn't ruin anything for them either. "No. You can't do that. How many more icicles were you going to hang?"

"As many as Riley wants." An apologetic

wince worked into the edges of his gaze as he said, "She's the boss."

The boss shouted a good morning, waved to Paige and pulled a red wagon behind her. Riley wore candy cane-striped fleece pajamas, fur-lined pink boots, and a sunburst smile. That warmed Paige faster than a steaming cup of hot chocolate.

"I got lots more lights from the garage, Dad." Excitement spilled from the little girl like an overflowing park fountain.

Evan slanted his gaze at Paige. Hesitation slowed his words. "I'm not sure Ms. Paige wants more lights."

Riley pulled her wagon to a stop and rubbed her nose. "Don't you like the lights, Ms. Paige?"

"I do." Paige touched her forehead as if rummaging for the right words to help the little girl understand. It shouldn't be so complicated. In fact, she shouldn't have gotten involved. "I just don't want you and your dad to go to so much trouble."

"It's no trouble, right, Dad?" Doubt tempered the hope in her subdued voice.

Paige cringed. She was about to disappoint this precious little girl who loved her pet cow. What she really wanted was to celebrate Macy-belle's full recovery with them. Still, she felt slightly queasy, watching Riley's enthusiasm deflate over holiday decorations.

"Can't think of anything else I'd rather be doing than spending the morning with my favorite girl." Evan swept Riley off her feet and into a bear hug. Within seconds, Riley's giggles erupted into the cool morning air.

The little girl laughed wholeheartedly with every part of her. The genuine sound swirled inside Paige and drew her closer to the pair as if she wanted to take part. Paige set her hand on the ladder and kept herself in place. It wasn't her moment to share. Still, she couldn't quite look away from the adorable father-daughter pair.

"Now, about these lights." Evan held Riley in his arms and turned toward the guesthouse. "We don't want to blind Ms. Paige with too many. That wouldn't be very nice."

Well, bringing a bah-humbug attitude to this family would be more than not nice. Mean wasn't something she ever wanted to be. Paige picked up an icicle strand from the pile on the porch. "But Santa has to be able to find us out here so he can drop off all those presents he has. And I heard it's a lot of presents."

That sunshine returned to Riley's face. She wiggled out of her dad's arms and dropped to the ground. "Then you'll help us hang more lights, Ms. Paige?"

Paige zipped Riley's puffy jacket under her chin and smiled. "I need five minutes to change into warmer clothes."

"I'll watch over Dad," Riley announced. "And make sure he hangs the lights right."

Evan chuckled. "I think I'm handling this part just fine."

"But it has to be perfect, Dad." Riley's hands landed on her hips. "Then Ms. Paige and I can have the best Christmas ever."

That was a tall order. Paige wasn't sure she could claim she'd ever had the best Christmas ever. She had great ones and not so great ones. And she was leaving soon. She'd miss out on seeing what Riley's best Christmas ever looked like.

A sliver of regret poked at Paige. She dismissed it and concentrated on the real reason she was at the ranch. And it wasn't to have holiday fun with the Bishop family as if she belonged. "I'll be quick."

Paige hurried toward the front door. The cinnamon sticks, pine cones, and berries tucked within the fresh branches of the wreath caught her attention. She stopped and inhaled. The scent of cinnamon, citrus and pine reminded her of Grandma Opal's simmering homemade potpourri that used to infuse every room in their house. She inhaled again, more deeply this time.

Her shoulders relaxed and her tension unraveled as if she'd stepped inside her grandmother's welcoming embrace.

Behind her, Riley asked her dad if he had called "her" yet. Then quickly asked if "she" had called back already. Evan's brusque response, a simple, succinct "not yet," caught Paige off guard. It was at odds with the doting dad who'd woken up before dawn to continue decorating the entire property for his daughter. And it was a reply, but not a clear answer.

Upstairs in the bedroom, Paige pulled on a pair of fleece-lined leggings, added several layers that she could remove if she got too warm working with the cows and puzzled over Evan's reply to Riley. She couldn't help it—she was curious. Paige wanted to know who the mysterious *she* was. She wanted to know why Evan had evaded his daughter's questions. It was so unlike him.

Unlike him? Now she was behaving as if she knew him better than she possibly could. Her relationship with Evan had to remain professional, even if Evan had been beyond considerate. Even if Evan could be someone she might've been interested in. Her energy belonged to her furthering her career now. Another personal relationship would only drain her. And she couldn't afford that.

She had to get on with her business at the ranch. The cows.

Paige stepped outside, determined to finish decorating quickly.

Almost immediately her attention was diverted. First it was Evan and Riley trading possible reindeer names. Then it was the debate over what to put around the porch posts: garland, tinsel or more lights. Paige inserted herself into the conversation as if she was a vital part of the decorating crew, not just an assistant. Finally, it was watching Riley hug her father as if he was her world.

Before Paige knew it, the precious child had wrapped Paige in the same enthusiastic embrace. A hug from Riley was delightful and heart filling like her grandmother's had always been. And Paige discovered she wanted to linger. Stretch out the moment with Evan and Riley as if hanging lights was her best morning ever.

Riley scampered back to the main house, calling over her shoulder, "Don't stop now."

Too soon, the posts were wrapped in garland, the door framed in tinsel and a red bow tied on the rocking chair. Paige stood beside Evan and surveyed their work. "It's not bad."

"We'll let Riley decide if we're finished when she gets home from running errands with her grandma." Evan folded the ladder and carried it toward the storage shed. "Now we get breakfast and head to the cattle. We have a lot of ground to cover today."

Great. Paige could put her eyes on the cows and work on keeping them off Evan.

Paige and Evan took their time with the quarantined herd, recording temperatures, breathing rates and any changes in disposition and appearance. Paige took their clipboard of data, her phone and stepped outside to call Dr. Gibson. The veterinarian asked for Paige's thoughts and input, then shared his treatment plan and his reasoning. His tone switched from gruff and impatient to agreeable and pleasant in a natural rhythm. Which she was recognizing was just his way. He told Paige he'd call Country Time Farm and Ranch Supply to order the medications he wanted administered as soon as possible.

Paige wrote down Dr. Gibson's instructions, reminded him to follow his physical therapist's instructions and hung up.

She walked back inside the cattle handling facility and located Evan. "Dr. Gibson wants us to check all your herds. Or in his words, 'Put your eyes on every last cow, Paige. Every last cow.'"

"We should get going, then." Evan glanced at the time on his phone. "It's going to be a long afternoon."

"How many cattle do you have?" Paige followed Evan outside to the UTV.

"Six hundred and thirty-two head. That includes the handful of bulls we keep for breeding." Evan tossed his phone on the driver's seat. "I'll be right back."

Paige sat concerned in the passenger seat. That was a lot of cattle. Cattle required a lot of land. And a ranch required a lot of organization to keep the operation functioning. Not to mention the responsibility for so many staff. Evan seemed to have accepted the pressure and discovered how to thrive. She shouldn't be surprised. He seemed to have conquered being a single parent as well. She smiled, she was impressed.

Evan returned, set a cloth bag behind his seat and whistled. Rex dutifully appeared from the side of the handling facility and jumped into the bed of the UTV. Evan drove away from the ranch and out onto the open plain.

Paige asked, "Where do you keep so many cattle?"

"Pastures we own and some we lease." He swung the UTV onto another dirt road. "Every generation of our family slowly increased the number of cattle and added acres here and there. I got a degree in ranch management and returned, determined to grow the ranch in a more intentional, efficient way."

Paige had been determined after graduating from veterinarian school. *Don't ever give up on your dreams, Paige.* Her grandparents had always told her that and she'd believed them. She hoped she always would. "It looks like you have accomplished a lot."

"My dad preferred shoebox record keeping and honoring what generations before him did. That worked for him." Evan slowed the UTV on a curve. "I've done things differently."

"Is it working for you?" Sitting next to Evan, driving across open pastures, and learning about her rancher was surprisingly working for her. If she wasn't more careful, she'd need to start doing things differently too. Like limiting time spent with Evan. Otherwise she might forget she and relationships were not a good fit, especially at this point in her life.

"It will be once the branding program with a local grocery store chain is official." Evan slowed the UTV and scanned the pasture. "I can't lose any more cattle. Otherwise I risk losing the branding program too. We can't afford that."

She heard the disquiet in his voice. She caught a stray piece of hair, tucked it behind her ear and tucked away her urge to take his hand. She was

Dr. Gibson's ears and eyes—a collector of scientific and medical information. Emotions were not to be charted, observed, or examined. "Let's make sure you don't lose any cattle."

"The herd is up ahead." Evan parked the UTV and pointed across the pasture. "We can watch from here and eat lunch."

"You made lunch?" Paige pressed her hand against her stomach to stall the slow rumble. "Was that what you were doing earlier?"

"Yeah." Evan picked up the cloth bag he'd set behind his seat, reached inside and handed her a sandwich container. "It's a to-go lunch today. Nothing fancy."

"I'm used to eating on the go." Paige opened the lid, picked up half of a triple-layer BLT sandwich and examined it. Her mouth watered. "Is this homemade bread?"

"Mom's recipe." He took a large bite of his sandwich.

"And you just threw this together in under a minute." There were fresh tomatoes, lettuce, and layers of bacon.

Evan grinned. "I've had a lot of practice with Riley's lunch. I pride myself on my speed and keeping it nutritionally balanced."

Paige took a bite and savored the crunch of the crispy bacon. The basil-lemon mayonnaise was a tasty surprise. But not as much as the man beside her or the fact that she could sit there for the rest of the day and be satisfied learning more about him. Like where was Riley's mom. And why was someone like him single?

She concentrated on finishing her lunch. She already knew enough: Evan was a talented rancher and dedicated father. It wasn't like she wanted to take their relationship beyond anything work related. As for her curiosity, she could control that. She picked up the other half of her sandwich. "This is a gourmet lunch. Do you eat like this every day?"

"You'll have to join me for lunch tomorrow to find out." He grinned and popped the last of his sandwich into his mouth.

"I just might do that." But only if it was cattle related.

"It's a lunch date, then." He swallowed, then coughed as if the word *date* had become wedged in his throat.

Paige cleared her own throat, wanting to deny it was any kind of date. Yet not wanting to draw any more unnecessary attention to the harmless comment. Her curiosity spiked again. What would a date with Evan look like? As if she had time to go on one.

Evan chugged water from a bottle, then glanced at Paige. "What kind of to-go food do you eat back home?"

"The typical." Would he take her out to dinner like a typical date? There was nothing too predictable about him.

"That's very nonspecific," he teased.

"You know those crustless peanut-butter-and-jelly sandwiches for kids—well, I eat those." She snapped the lid on the empty sandwich container, clipped her curiosity about dates, but not her sudden chagrin. "I also eat granola bars of every kind. Yogurt, with the unhealthy toppings. I'm all about the real kind of to-go foods—processed and packaged and rarely homemade." She shrugged.

One more thing to fix when she got home, which was scheduled to happen in less than ten days. Paige focused on the cows in the pasture. The animals were clustered together. None had separated and moved away from the others—a telltale sign, according to Dr. Gibson, that something was amiss with the cows.

"Crustless sandwiches. You really eat those?" Evan rested his hands on the steering wheel and watched the pasture.

"They are quick and easy," she said.

"But not always tasty," he countered. "Don't you crave more?"

"I'm usually too busy to think about it." Like now, she was too busy concentrating on the cattle to even consider all the things, expected and unexpected, she wanted to tell Evan. She slanted her gaze toward him. His intense frown startled her.

"What's wrong?" Paige brushed her hands on her pants and followed his gaze toward the herd. Nothing appeared to have startled the cattle.

"TJ, one of the ranch hands, commented on Luna not being her usual self yesterday. That's Rex's partner." Evan frowned. "She should've already been here, her tail wagging in greeting, waiting for a sample of my lunch. It's part of our routine."

"That doesn't sound great." Paige scanned the cattle, hoping for a dog to appear.

Evan held the dog's gaze. "Go find Luna. Go get her."

Rex jumped from the UTV bed and ran across the pasture. Sniff checks completed on the cattle, the white Great Pyrenees dog disappeared over a small hill.

Paige climbed out of the UTV.

She and Evan set off after the dog and found Rex sitting beside his littermate as if protecting her. Luna was lying down, her head on her paws, her tail wrapped tight against her body.

Evan called her name. Rex whined and scooted into Luna's side.

Paige set her hand on Evan's arm. "She's in

pain and hurting. Her left eye is swollen shut. The right one is barely open."

Paige kept her voice low and even. "That makes her reaction to you unpredictable."

"We have to help her." Worry threaded through his words.

"We're going to." Paige checked Luna for any other visible injuries or obvious trauma. "But we're going to take it slow."

"I've got dog treats. I'll go get those," Evan suggested. "She likes those."

Evan jogged off toward the UTV. Paige wanted to wait, but the dog's distress demanded she do something. She talked to Rex first, detailing what she planned to do. Then she switched her attention to Luna, promising she was only there to help. Luna bared her teeth, but her growl was more bluster than anger. Paige lowered onto her knees, kept up her steady stream of conversation and held out her hand for Luna to sniff. The dog licked her palm. Paige took that as an invitation and sat down beside the massive dog. She sank her fingers into the dog's thick coat and stroked her back. Luna's heart raced. She panted and whimpered. Finally, she lifted her head and rested it on Paige's leg.

"You must speak dog fluently." From several feet away, Evan watched Paige with something close to awe. He held up the container of dog treats. "It doesn't look like you need these after all."

"We'll use those when we get her loaded into the UTV bed." Paige kept stroking the dog's back.

"Can you treat her at the ranch?" Evan asked.

"With the right supplies, I can make her more comfortable." Paige leaned closer to peer at the swollen eyelids. "But she needs an ophthalmologist for a thorough exam and diagnosis."

"How bad is it?" Evan asked.

"Bad." Paige relied on the sedate tone to keep herself and her patient calm. "But I don't want to speculate on the cause or the outcome yet. We have to know one to predict the other."

Evan shook his head. "She's been one of the best dogs I've owned. Protective and loyal to her herd and family."

Paige glanced at him, noted his obvious concern. "And now, we're going to protect her."

"I'll get the UTV." Evan pivoted but then looked back at her. "Paige, I'm really glad you're here."

"I am too."

AT THE GUESTHOUSE, Evan and Paige guided Luna inside. She flopped onto the floor in front of the fireplace and refused to move any farther. "Looks like this is where she wants to stay."

"The light is better in the kitchen," Evan said.

"But she's happier here," Paige told him. "We'll work it out."

And they did, over the next hour. Together. As a team. Evan never left Paige's side, followed her every instruction, and proved his easygoing nature shouldn't be confused for indifference. Paige had called Dr. Gibson and he'd phoned in the referral to an ophthalmologist. Luna appeared to have a bacterial eye infection. Both Paige and Dr. Gibson agreed the sweet dog required a thorough exam to determine if Luna also suffered from an injury on her eye. Thanks to an over-the-counter pain medication, Luna finally fell asleep, stretched out across the carpet.

Evan handed Paige a bottle of water and followed her outside onto the porch. "You know if this rancher thing doesn't work out, you'd make a good veterinarian," she said.

"Thanks." He twisted off the water bottle cap and toasted her. "I'll keep that in mind, but I hope I won't need a career change anytime soon."

Paige needed to change her focus and now. She said goodbye and scooted into the guesthouse. She needed to remain cow focused, not rancher interested. No matter that Evan had been more a partner, a teammate, with treating Luna than an assistant. She'd never questioned if he'd follow her lead. Never worried he'd stop listening, believing he knew better. He'd trusted her with his dog's care completely. He'd trusted her period.

She was reminded that her ex-boyfriend had never fully trusted her. Not in the clinic. Not in their relationship.

Paige recalled the deep scent of cinnamon she'd caught from the wreath on her way inside. One of her grandmother's favorite spices. *Live in the moment, Paige. The past has already moved on.*

Paige wanted to trust the moment, believe in what she felt when she was around Evan. But her past didn't seem to want to let go. Or she didn't.

Tomorrow, she would be all about her priorities. Remember she was there to assist Dr. Gibson, not discover a team of her own.

CHAPTER EIGHT

"It's going to be another hour before the rest of the medicine for the cows is ready at Country Time." Evan dropped his phone into the console in his truck and drove away from the elementary school pick-up line. "Any ideas what we should do to pass the time, kiddo?"

"Eat ice cream," Riley called from the back seat.

Evan glanced at Paige sitting next to him. She'd ridden along in case there were instructions to go with the newest cattle medicine or any follow-up questions. He asked, "How does ice cream sound?"

"Ice cream always sounds good, especially on a Monday afternoon." Paige laughed and leaned around her seat to fist-bump with Riley. "It's one of my top five to-go foods."

Evan laughed. Paige was unapologetic about her sweet tooth and he liked that. He pushed his sunglasses into place and pushed aside the things he liked about Paige—the list was steadily expanding. He aimed his truck in the direction of

Frosty Dreamer's Ice Cream Parlor and directed his thoughts away from Paige.

Inside Frosty Dreamer's, the trio placed their order. Paige and Riley claimed a table near the front window and left Evan to wait on their sundaes. Inevitably, his gaze drifted to Paige, where it seemed to have been landing more and more.

But Evan's plate was already full. He could handle all of it and make everything work. Like always.

Yet it was his intriguing houseguest and his interest in her that he wasn't sure how to handle. She could be the one woman who'd upset his precariously balanced full plate. If he wasn't careful.

He picked up their ice cream order from the counter. Filed Paige's favorite flavor of ice cream, triple vanilla bean, into the nice-to-know-but-unnecessary column.

Paige was in town for less than two weeks. Surely, he could manage both his interest and his attraction to her in that short time frame. Expectations couldn't be established. Hearts couldn't get involved. It just wasn't possible. He should be more relieved.

Sundaes handed out, he dropped into the metal chair and set his cowboy hat aside. He slid a stack of napkins across the round table toward his daughter.

Riley dipped her spoon into her unicorn sundae, scooping out candy-confetti, marshmallow and birthday-cake flavored ice cream. "What are we gonna do for Christmas?"

"What we always do." Evan watched the frown form on Riley's face. "Is there a problem with that?"

Riley shrugged. "Can we do new stuff too?"

They already were. Paige was new. She was staying in their guesthouse. And now she was eating sundaes with them as if she always joined them for afternoon ice cream runs. "What do you have in mind?"

"My friend Colton and his family have a movie marathon and camp out in front of their Christmas tree." Riley picked a marshmallow off the top of her ice cream with her fingers. "Can we do that?"

"I don't see why not." Movie night could be easily slotted in without too much effort. And too much disruption to his schedule.

"Savannah from my class is going to ride on the Polar Express train." Riley skipped her gaze away from Evan as if she sensed his forthcoming refusal. "Have you ever been on a train, Ms. Paige?"

"Yes, with my grandparents." Paige set her spoon down and wiped a napkin across her mouth. "My grandma Opal always told me she liked to keep her feet closer to the ground. So, we traveled on trains instead of planes."

Paige's happiness at the memories was vivid and clear, untroubled, unlike that morning when he'd been decorating the porch. He couldn't imagine the loss she'd suffered as a child. He hated that even her memories of her dad still caused her pain. Hated even more that Christmas had lost its magic.

Could he help her find the joy in the season again to help balance out the grief?

It was the only way he'd gotten through the period after his ex had walked out and left a bitter darkness in his life. But Riley, with her endless optimism and vibrant energy, countered it. Every day his daughter reminded him of all the good in his world. He'd held on to that and had been grateful.

He watched Paige stir her spoon in her whipped cream. Wanted to know what her good was. Wanted to know how to ease her lingering pain. He stuffed a bite of hot-fudge-covered ice cream in his mouth and dismissed his disappointment that there wasn't enough time for him to find out.

"Did you sleep on the train?" Riley's spoon stood untouched, sticking out of the top of her ice cream. Her fascinated gaze remained fixed on Paige. "Did you eat on the train?"

"We did. They had a special car for dinner and other cars for sleeping." Paige's words were sugar-dipped, her mellow voice all too appealing. "But my sister and I always liked when Grandpa Harlan ordered pizza and it was waiting when we pulled into the train stop."

"Can we go on a train like that and eat pizza? I like pizza." Riley added a lengthened plea to her voice. "Please, Dad."

His daughter had always been hard to refuse. And, he hadn't taken a real vacation in years, but still, he couldn't see one in their near future. Not until the ranch was financially stable. And even then... He stalled by saying, "We'd have to research where we want to go."

"You'd have to plan a vacation like that," Paige offered. "That will take some special effort to put together."

Evan smiled at Paige. A silent thank-you for her support.

"What about riding the Polar Express to see Santa like Savannah?" Riley raised her eyebrows.

Neatly played. His daughter had brought them full circle. The kids' attraction would only be one afternoon. And if Riley rode the Polar Express, she might forget the promise he'd given her about her mom. If he kept his daughter busy with Christmas activities, would it be enough to counter the truth about his ex, Marla, abandoning them?

Evan shifted in the small chair, rolled his shoulders, avoided looking at Paige. Would she tell him a diversion was a bad idea? What could it hurt to try? Riley would have fun. That's what mattered. He nodded. "The Polar Express we could maybe do."

"Really?" Riley clapped. "Like *really* really?"

"I think we should start making a list or we're going to forget all the things we plan to do this Christmas." And Evan had to avoid making any more promises to his daughter. He'd already made an impossible one and that was more than enough.

Paige handed him a pen. He claimed one of his daughter's paper napkins and started their list.

"Can we do other things we haven't done before?" Riley asked.

"So, we're having a Christmas of firsts." Evan grinned and pressed the pen against the napkin. "That's a first. What haven't we done that you want to do? I've got Christmas campout and ride the Polar Express."

"Jump in a frozen pond," Riley declared. "Bryson Mackintosh and his brothers do it *every* year. You gotta jump in, but jump out even faster."

Evan swallowed his immediate refusal. He

wasn't letting his young daughter jump into a frozen pond. That was something reckless his ex would've done. He wanted Riley to have fun, not freeze. What if she got sick too? "You mean you want to take a polar plunge."

"That sounds really cold." Paige gave an exaggerated shiver. "Are you sure you want to take a polar plunge? What about riding an ice slide and walking through an ice maze?"

Evan relaxed, once again welcoming Paige's suggestions. If she kept rescuing him, he was going to be compelled to help her too—like getting her to enjoy Christmas again.

Riley tilted her head and eyed Paige. "Is it a real slide?"

"Made completely of ice." Paige glanced at Evan, offered him a small smile. "I saw it advertised in the newspaper. It's in Belleridge."

"Dad can drive there!" Riley bounced up and down in her chair. "We have to do that. We have to."

Evan added to their list. "We're going to be busy."

"But we haven't put down staying up all night to meet Santa on Christmas Eve. Putting reindeers in the front yard and hanging lights in the big tree. Making gingerbread barns. And getting a Christmas tree for my room." Riley sighed as if exhausted.

"You want a Christmas tree for your room," Evan repeated. He was starting to feel exhausted too. Doubt eased in. Maybe this wasn't the best idea after all. Who knew there were so many Christmas firsts? "We're going to put an extra big tree in the family room that we cut down ourselves," he told Paige.

"We never cut down a tree before. It's another Christmas first." Riley cheered.

Evan sighed. "And now, so is decorating Riley's room."

"This way I can wake up to Christmas every morning." Riley clapped some more. "Ms. Paige should cut down a tree too."

Paige set a crumpled napkin in her empty sundae container. "Oh, I don't need to do that."

"Have you ever cut down a Christmas tree?" Riley asked.

"No." Paige stared at Riley's melted ice cream. She was right there across the table from them, but she sounded miles away. "When we were kids, we went to the tree lot and just picked one. The last few years I worked over the holidays. There wasn't time for a tree."

Or she hadn't made the time. Either way, Paige Palmer wasn't into celebrating like his family. It wasn't fair to thrust their zeal on her.

"You gotta have a tree." Riley pressed her hands against her cheeks as if astonished at

Paige's confession. "Santa puts your gifts under it."

Paige crumpled another paper napkin under her fingers. Her focus remained on the table. "I had a small potted palm tree that I put lights and ribbons on once."

"But that's not a *tree* tree." Riley turned her dismayed gaze to Evan. "Tell Ms. Paige she's gotta come with us and get a real tree."

"Remember, it's not always polite to tell people what to do." Paige was hurting, and although he wanted to help her, he wasn't certain how to do it. "Paige, would like you to come with us and pick out a tree for the guesthouse?"

"Thanks, but I won't be here that long." That cool distance slid from her gaze into her words. "Besides, who will look after the tree when I leave?"

Riley made a scrunched face.

Now his daughter was unhappy too. What happened to the fun they were having? Christmas firsts were supposed to be enjoyable. This was anything but. Evan pushed his unfinished sundae aside and scrambled for a compromise. "What if you came along to the tree farm and picked out a potted tree? Then Riley and I could plant it after you leave."

Her gaze searched his face as if she were

searching for the catch. Finally, she said, "I wouldn't want to put you to that much trouble."

"Don't worry." Riley clutched Paige's hand. "I'd like to help you pick out the perfect pot and Dad's good at planting stuff. And he's fast too, right, Dad?"

He hoped this was the right offer. The right path for Paige. "Of course."

"Now me and Paige each have a Christmas first." Riley pressed her hands flat on the table. "Dad needs to have one too."

"I can't share yours?" He smiled at Riley, hopeful, and waved the napkin list at her. "This is a really good list."

"No." Riley giggled, then stressed, "*You* have to pick something you've never done before, Dad."

"I've got it," Evan said. "But it's a secret."

Riley slapped her hand against her forehead and released an exaggerated sigh. "Dad."

"Okay." Evan leaned in. "I'll give you a hint, but you can't tell anyone."

Riley scooted closer to him. Even Paige leaned forward, the slightest of changes in her posture. Evan claimed it as a win.

"I've never had fruitcake," Evan whispered, then pressed his finger against his lips like Santa. "Not even the smallest, tiniest taste."

Riley wrinkled her nose. "Fruitcake? No one likes fruitcake."

"But *we* haven't tasted it yet." Evan dropped the pen on the table and spread his hands wide as if he'd just successfully brokered an international treaty. He watched the grin twitch across Paige's mouth. Another win. "That's my first—eating fruitcake."

Riley looked skeptical. "Are you sure that's what you wanna choose?"

"Do you have a better idea?" Evan challenged.

"We could play games," Riley exclaimed and thrust her arms out to the sides, even wider than Evan had. "With all our friends."

"What kind of games?" Evan stroked his chin as if considering.

"Fun ones!" Riley grabbed her spoon, dunked it into her sundae and swallowed the giant mouthful of ice cream in one go.

"A vet tech where I work has a board game party once a month," Paige offered. A spark lit in her gaze highlighting a new liveliness in her words. "You could host a board game holiday party with your friends."

"Yes! Board game party." Riley pressed her palm over her mouth, catching her delighted squeal. Suspicion quickly set in. "Um, we don't have a lot of board games."

"You could give the games as gifts to your

friends, then invite everyone over to play them for the board game party," Paige said. That spark flashed again. "It's supposed to be really fun."

Evan was enjoying seeing this Paige, relaxed and candid. "I'm beginning to wonder if it's not your colleague, but rather you who hosts these monthly board game parties," he teased.

"Not me." She shook her head, but the cheerful interest in her gaze remained.

Evan sat back and considered his houseguest. She'd been animated. More animated than he'd seen her all day. He looked from Paige to Riley, then pointed at himself. "I haven't hosted a board game party. Paige hasn't hosted one. Riley, have you?"

Riley giggled from her belly and shook her head, making her red curls sway.

"Then the board game party is on," Evan announced. "It's another group first."

Riley raised both her arms over her head in victory. "Christmas game night."

"Well, we've filled ourselves with ice cream and filled our Christmas-first list." Evan rubbed his stomach and stood. He picked up his cowboy hat and set it on his head. "I think it's time to get that medicine and head home to the cattle."

"I want to see Macybelle." Riley swiped a napkin over her mouth, then tossed it onto the table. "What are you going to do when we get home, Ms. Paige?"

Paige gathered the trash and paused as if she was struggling to find an answer. She looked flustered.

And Evan discovered one more thing he liked about Paige Palmer. Yep, too bad his plate was already full.

CHAPTER NINE

PAIGE SLAPPED A "SOLD" sticky note on one of the vintage board games she'd spotted in the general store while searching for the elusive silver coin. *Priorities*, she repeated to herself. The past couple of days, she'd let things slide, although, to be fair, she was out on a ranch caring for a herd of sick cows. Not to mention trying to keep up with Riley, which was almost impossible. And then there was Evan.

Evan should not appeal to her. Not as much as he did. And not so quickly.

Strong relationships progressed slowly. To see who someone really was required time. Besides, relationships were not a cure for being alone. Love did not cancel loneliness. She knew that all too well. And wasn't willing to compromise either. That alone hardly made her good material for a relationship.

Her rancher might appeal to her. But that was as far as her interest went. Work fulfilled her. She needed nothing more than that.

She put the vintage board game with the others she'd set aside on the counter, then used her phone to research and total the value. With a check written out to the Silver Penny General Store, she left the collection of games and walked over to Tess.

Her sister sat in her usual spot, typing away on her computer. Her phone within easy reach. "I'm close to finding the pocket watch for Mrs. McKee. I just hope when I do that it won't be out of the dear lady's price range."

"You'll figure out how to get it within her budget," Paige assured her. It was one of the things Tess did well. Her sister's personalized service was amazing. She treated each search as if she was adding the item to her own personal collection or closet. As a result, Tess didn't give up until she'd located the exact item and she'd built quite a steady business over the past six months.

Paige never realized there was a market for hard-to-find and rare items or that so many people wanted them. She glanced over at the vintage games. She hoped Evan would agree they were as perfect for his board game party night as she did. She felt slightly guilty for talking Evan into a game night and wanted to make it up to him. Paige handed Tess the check. "Here you go."

"What's this?" Tess's fingers paused on the keyboard.

"I'm buying the board games Boone and I found the other day."

"Paige." A disgruntled note stretched through Tess's tone. "You don't need to do that."

"I do. And I am. No arguments." Resolve stiffened her shoulders and her steady gaze. "I checked their current value online just now and that's what I'm paying."

Tess's frown deepened and she pushed away the check.

"Tess, you could put those games on the shelves right now and sell them before Christmas," Paige said. "Or post them online and sell them that way. This is your business now."

"But you are family. It feels wrong to make you pay." Tess waved at the shelves and pointed at the boxes of inventory. "You have as much right to whatever is in this store as I do."

"No," Paige argued. "You moved here and reopened the store. This is your place now. And I'm more than happy to be a customer."

Tess eyed Paige. Her sister's round green eyes had always been inquisitive and way too perceptive. As kids, her sister had always been the first to know when Paige was holding something back. Tess had also been the first to be there for Paige, quick with a hug and encouraging advice or even offering to fight on Paige's behalf. Paige had always done the same for Tess.

Now they were both holding back. But if Paige pried and Tess pushed her further away, what then? Paige kept her expression neutral and the conversation light. "What? You don't want me to be your customer?"

Tess picked up the check. "I'll accept this if you tell me what you're doing with those board games."

"Would you believe me if told you I wanted them for myself?" Paige grinned and arched one eyebrow.

"Not for a second." Tess's quiet chuckle shook her shoulders.

"I feel like I should be offended." Paige crossed her arms over her chest.

Tess's laughter slipped free. "When was the last time you played a board game? Or cards? Or had any kind of fun? You're always too busy working."

"I have fun." Paige refrained from adding a foot stomp. There was nothing playful about her defensive tone.

"Fun outside of work," Tess qualified.

Paige opened and closed her mouth. Her argument stalled. She couldn't recall the last fun day she had at work. But she loved her career and was passionate about her job. But her ex-boyfriend's presence had eclipsed the enjoyment—and the fun. Now, Paige hoped once she became an equal partner, she'd be able to put her ex and his behavior toward her aside and contribute in more meaningful ways to growing the business. Then work would be fun again. She hoped.

As for fun outside of work, she had fun hanging lights and eating ice cream with Riley and Evan. Proof she could have fun when she chose to.

Still, she sidestepped a direct answer. Not wanting Tess to make too much out of her time spent with Riley and Evan. "Riley and Evan have a list of Christmas firsts for this season."

Tess's gaze narrowed. Paige knew that look. Her sister was already reading between the lines.

Paige rushed on, "Evan is going to give board games as presents and then host a holiday board game party. I thought he could use these games for his gifts."

Tess leaned back on her stool. The speculation in her gaze only deepened. "I don't know where to start."

"There's nothing to start," Paige blurted. She was only in town temporarily. Her visit brief. Even if she wanted to start something—and she didn't—it could only ever be short-lived. Evan deserved more than that. If she ever stepped into another relationship again, she wanted it to be real. Lasting. Not a fling. Not a short-term goal.

"Are you part of these Christmas firsts too?" Tess asked.

The way Tess emphasized *part of* implied there was more between Paige and Evan. Paige bristled. Not at her sister, but herself. She wasn't as against the idea as she should be. She turned and headed toward the other end of the counter. "Yes. No. Riley and Evan have a rather long list and I'll be gone before they finish everything."

"But," Tess pressed and followed closely behind Paige.

Paige relented. She had to give her sister something. Compromise was good between family members. "We're going to cut down a Christmas tree for the main house and get a potted one for the guesthouse. Then there's game night. So, I'm taking part in two things. That's it."

That was her participation limit. No matter how fun and appealing their other adventures sounded.

"What else is on this list of Christmas firsts?" Tess leaned her hip against the counter.

"Trying real fruitcake was Evan's choice. Riley wanted to take a polar plunge, but I convinced her she'd like the ice slides in Belleridge better." Paige rested her hands on top of the games and recited the list. And recalled how Evan had listened to Riley. Had never been closed off. He'd listen to Paige's secrets too. Her dreams. If she shared. If she ever trusted like that again. "There was also camping out in the living room in front of the tree for a movie marathon. Oh, and staying up all night to meet Santa."

Tess laughed and touched Paige's arm. "We did that. Don't you remember?" Tess's smile grew from one ear to the other. Her bright energy infectious. "We brought a pile of books to read into the family room. More than we could carry. We turned on the radio to play holiday music. And hid all kinds of candy in our sleeping bags to snack on. We were going to have a read-dance-candy-eating marathon."

The memory began to take shape. Paige grinned. "We were convinced we had everything we needed to stay awake all night long. Grandpa Harlan gave us a box of cherry candy canes."

"And Grandma Opal made an extra large pot of hot chocolate." Tess sighed. "Her hot chocolate is still my favorite."

"She always told us her secret ingredient wasn't love—it was…" Paige and her sister finished the saying together: "Attention."

Paige embraced the memory, let it fill her.

"We promised to give all our attention to staying awake. But I don't think we lasted much past ten o'clock." Tess chuckled. "Then I heard that strange noise and woke you up."

"I saw the tree branches moving. Then the entire tree started swaying. And we screamed." Laughter bubbled up inside Paige, buoyant and unstoppable.

"Then Dexter jumped from the branches." Tess's laughter burst free, flowing around the store like music. "And we both screamed again and woke the entire house."

"Grandpa, Grandma and Mom all came running into the family room." Tears pooled in Paige's eyes, her cheeks ached, and her laughter rolled on. "Grandma had a rolling pin in her hand."

"How did she get that rolling pin so fast?" Tess wiped at her eyes, but she was still smiling.

"I think she slept with it under her pillow." That earned another round of laughter. The kind they'd used to share. The kind that had brought their mother to their room over and over to tell them to mute it and go to sleep or else. But there had been no muting their laughter or their shared joy. And they never did learn what *or else* had meant.

"Grandpa Harlan stayed with us and read one book after another that night." Tess's gaze softened.

Their grandparents had encouraged Tess's love of books and reading. The same way they'd supported Paige's love of animals. Paige imagined

Evan would do the very same for Riley. Stay up for an all-night reading marathon or encourage her dreams whatever they turned out to be. Evan was part of the good people her grandparents always spoke about whenever they'd mentioned Three Springs. He could be her kind of good, if only.

Paige rolled her shoulders and her thoughts back into place. Evan had only a fleeting place in her life. "Then we woke up Christmas morning in our own beds. Dexter was curled up on my pillow as if nothing had happened and the presents were under the tree."

Tess sobered as if tucking the memory away. "That was the last time we ever tried to wait up for Santa."

But not the last time for them staying up all night. For laughing until their bellies ached and cheeks hurt. For enjoying each other's company. Tess's cell phone started ringing so she headed back to her computer station to answer it. Paige gathered the board games together and collected this moment. It was a start.

THE NEXT MORNING, Paige woke before her alarm. The sun had only barely begun its ascent. She dressed quickly in jeans and more layers and grabbed the games. A quick check of Luna, who'd taken to sleeping on the front porch on the makeshift bed Paige had created for her, and she was headed to the main house. She wanted to surprise Evan and see his reaction. Her knock was followed by a brusque "Door's open. Come on in."

Paige bounded inside and announced, "I brought board games. perfect for your holiday party. They were part of the inventory in the general store."

Evan leaned against the farmhouse-style sink and nodded. He dunked a half-eaten cookie into his coffee, then shoved it in his mouth.

Not exactly the reaction she'd been anticipating. She'd expected something more than disinterest but less than cartwheels. She clutched at the stack of games and her deflating excitement. "I'm sorry about that, by the way."

He set his coffee cup down, took the games from her and paused to consider her.

She rubbed her chilled hands together and tried to decide where she'd gone wrong. Perhaps she should've texted him first and asked if he wanted the games. Assumptions always got her and never in a good way. "I feel like I talked you into hosting the party."

"You didn't." He set the games on a kitchen chair and returned to his position at the sink.

Okay. Should she be encouraged or not? She opened her mouth.

He cut her off. "I'm not that easy to talk into things. It sounded fun and something that Riley will enjoy."

"What about you?" Because he wasn't the least bit thrilled right now.

He tipped his coffee cup toward the pile. "How much does Tess want for those?"

"Nothing." Paige could deflect too. "Mind if I have some coffee?"

Evan took a cup from the cabinet, filled it and handed the mug to her. He didn't offer her cream and sugar. She always took her coffee straight, but she'd never told him that. He'd paid attention. To her. That was a good sign, wasn't it? Not that she wanted him to pay that much attention to her.

"What if these games are worth something?" He brushed by her and lifted several games from the stack. "They're brand-new. Unopened. In great condition."

"We already priced them online." Well, she had yesterday evening, instead of researching the herbs in Opal's wreath for her family. Or working on how to convince her colleagues to include her in their partnership. Although Evan didn't need that information, or he might think she was paying too much attention to him too. "Most of the games are valuable for sentimental reasons."

"Sentimental reasons." He arched an eyebrow at her.

"You know, you played word games or strategy games with your grandfather growing up." She pointed to the board game he held that had battleships. "And now you want to share that experience with Riley."

"It's a Christmas of firsts. We're sharing all kinds of experiences." He set the games down, pulled out his phone and tapped on the screen. A shadow crossed his face. He refilled his coffee mug, grabbed another cookie and retreated to the kitchen sink.

Paige sipped her coffee and kept her voice casual. "Everything okay?"

"Sure." He shrugged and ate his cookie.

There was nothing confident in his one-word reply. She should head to the cattle handling facility and start her day. Do what she was there for: treating cattle, not soothing irritable ranchers. Evan could handle his own issues. It was the dusting of loneliness around him that held her in place. Called to her. Still, she should leave. "I'd pegged you for a healthier breakfast kind of guy."

"Seems like a good morning for a sugar rush." Evan picked up a third cookie and waved it around. "Aren't these supposed to make you happy?"

"I'm not sure about that. Perhaps giddy until

the inevitable crash." Paige leaned against the island as if she intended to stick around. As if he'd invited her interference. "But you don't look happy or giddy."

Evan popped the rest of the cookie in his mouth and chewed.

"Have you already been out to see the cows?" Paige poured more coffee into her cup. More comfortable than she should be inside his kitchen. More at ease than she should be with him. As if they were a typical couple, working together to sort through the day's obstacles.

"Not yet." He placed his coffee cup on the counter, scrubbed his hands over his face and leveled his solemn gaze on Paige. "I have to let Riley down."

Paige stilled. She was Dr. Gibson's eyes and ears, not Evan's confidante. A coworker of sorts. Not a partner. But she lingered as if she wanted to be all those things for Evan.

"It never sits well," Evan continued, his voice serious. "And for some reason it's always worse at Christmastime."

"Maybe because you're doing it all yourself," Paige said. "It's okay to ask for help sometimes."

"I've always done everything myself," he said. "Since Riley was five months old, we've been a team. It's my job to give her the perfect Christmas."

"I'm sure you can still give Riley the best Christmas ever." Look at what he'd done for his daughter already. And there was still twelve days to go.

"Except, it's the official day for tackling the Christmas-first list and we can't do it." Evan rubbed the back of his neck. "I haven't told Riley yet."

That explained his current mood. "What was today's item?"

"Wreath making at Double Rainbow Arts Center after school today. Claire and her mom are going." He rinsed his coffee mug in the sink and set it in the dishwasher. "I have a meeting to discuss the branding program. It can't be re-scheduled. We're so close to having the contracts signed before the New Year."

Paige nodded, intent on listening.

"Mom is working at the Owl tonight," he added. "She's filling in for Violet, one of the waitresses. With the holidays coming, it seems everyone is short-staffed. Riley will have to go to the after-school care instead, until I can get her."

"I can take Riley to make wreaths." Paige pressed her lips together.

"I can't ask you to do that." Evan shook his head.

"You haven't asked. I offered." And it changed

nothing in their relationship status. She was simply keeping a little girl from being disappointed. That her offer also helped the little girl's dad wasn't the point. Even less of a point was how much Paige already cared about the father-daughter pair and wanted them both to be happy. "If it helps, I've never made a Christmas wreath before. It's another first for me."

She was rapidly collecting Christmas firsts. For someone who preferred to linger on the fringes of the holiday season, she should be more cautious. But it was only wreath making. It wasn't as if she'd fallen for her rancher. Then she'd have to admit love at first sight existed. And that was the last thing she'd ever put her trust in.

The back door swung open. Riley raced inside like a whirlwind. Her red hair was wind-tossed, and her cheeks were tinged pink. "Guess what? Guess what?"

"You remembered you weren't supposed to go out to the pasture in your unicorn slippers." Evan's voice was dry. "And you rushed home to put on sensible outdoor boots."

"No." Riley jumped up and down in her unicorn slippers. "Macybelle is eating again."

"That is good news." Evan touched Riley's shoulder. Her bouncing stilled into tiny hops. "But I'd still like you to put on proper footwear."

Riley shuffled in her slippers. "Because you have to protect your feet if you want to walk in your father's shoes one day."

Paige pressed her hands against her mouth, letting her laugh fill her cupped palms.

Evan held up his hand and high-fived Riley. "And you never know what is out there in the pastures or the roads that could injure you."

Riley's eyebrows pulled together. "Aren't you happy about Macybelle?"

"I'm pleased Macybelle is eating." Evan pointed toward the family room and the closet under the stairs leading to the second floor. "And I'll be thrilled when you're dressed properly and ready for school on time."

Paige smiled at Riley. "Your dad and I will head over to see Macybelle first, I promise."

Riley cheered up instantly. "Don't forget to talk to her, Ms. Paige. I think she likes your voice."

"You think so?" Paige asked.

Riley nodded. "I like your voice. It's pretty and soft like the pink and white roses Grandma grows in her garden."

Paige couldn't help but not like this sweet, precious child, who adored her cow, her father and called her voice rose-petal soft. "Riley, would you want to have a girls' day with me, later, after school? We can go to Double Rainbow Art Center, then you can show me around downtown."

"Dad and I are supposed to make wreaths today." Indecision worked across her face. "Can Dad come too?"

Evan's brow rose. "I'm not sure it's a girl's day if a boy is there."

"But what are you going to do?" Riley opened the closet door, pulled out a puffy purple jacket.

"I have an important meeting with the grocery store." Evan guided Riley's arms into the jacket and zipped it up under her chin.

"Work isn't fun." Riley wrinkled her nose, then spun to face Paige. "My friend Claire has girl's day with her mom. They get their nails painted and their hair done. Can we do that?"

"No." Evan's one word denial landed on the floor like a dropped brick.

Riley pursed her lips. "But Ms. Bec is there. And Ms. Paige wants to see all the stores."

"You can go everywhere but there," Evan said.

"That's not fair." Riley pulled off her unicorn slippers and tossed them on the floor.

"That's the deal for girls' day," Evan said.

Riley's hands dropped to her hips. Her elbows jabbed out to the sides. There was something sweetly stubborn in her stance and words. "Santa knows what I want, and you can't stop him."

"Santa may know what you want." Evan's tone

of voice was somewhere between determined and stern. "But Santa only grants wishes to good kids who listen to their dads."

In her socked feet, Riley slid across the floor toward the closet and sank onto the hardwood as if Evan had ruined her entire day. She yanked on a pair of polka dot rain boots and lifted her sad gaze to Paige. "Ms. Paige, we can't go to Ms. Bec's or else Santa will put me on the bad list."

"That's okay." Paige wanted to wrap the little girl in a big hug. She made sure she sounded upbeat when she said, "I'm sure we'll have just as much fun at the art center and maybe we can get in some silver-coin-searching time at the Silver Penny too."

"Really?" Riley jumped up. Her boots thunked on the hardwood.

Paige smiled and nodded.

A car horn honked outside. Riley grabbed her backpack and sprinted toward the door. "Bye, Ms. Paige."

"Riley Rose." Evan's firm voice stopped his daughter in her tracks.

The little girl spun around and looked at her dad.

"Aren't you forgetting something?" Evan asked.

Riley stubbed the toe of her boot into the

floor, then hurried over and hugged her dad. "I'm still mad at you."

Evan kissed the top of Riley's head. "And I still love you."

"Love you too." Riley squeezed Evan harder. "Don't forget to call her today. You promised."

Evan never commented. Only kissed his daughter again and then released her. The back door slammed shut. Silence descended.

And Paige's curiosity spiked. Evan's gaze, distracted and distant, clashed with Paige's. She recognized that look—she'd seen it in her own reflection. Evan hurt and he'd buried it deep. She knew something about that too. She wanted to know who Evan was supposed to call. And why she got the feeling he was forgetting on purpose. But she'd already inserted herself into their lives. After all, she was only supposed to be a cattle observer. "Isn't Bec's a beauty salon?"

Evan blinked as if he'd been expecting an entirely different question. "Yeah. It's Bec's Beauty Spot."

"What do you have against beauty salons?" Paige finished her coffee and placed the cup in the sink.

"I have no problem with the salon itself or the owner." Evan took two stainless steel travel mugs from the cabinet and filled them with coffee. "Bec Ashley is a longtime friend. It's the hair dye I'm worried about."

"Hair dye," Paige repeated.

"Number four on Riley's Christmas wish list— turn her red hair brown." Evan pressed a lid on one of the mugs and handed it to her. "I'm worried someone at the salon will tell her it can be done."

"Riley doesn't like her red hair." The little girl's hair was a stunning shade. Her natural loose curls and prominent hazel eyes upped her adorable factor by a thousand. Her spirited nature made her even more unique. And someone Paige wouldn't soon forget. Much like her father.

"*Doesn't like* is too mild for how Riley feels about her hair." Evan took his cowboy hat off the hook on the wall, set it on his head and held the back door open for Paige.

"What about you?" Paige glanced at him.

"I don't want her to change anything about herself," Evan said. "Or ever feel like she has to."

That only confirmed what Paige already knew. Evan was a good man. And a great father.

Evan added, his voice reserved and detached. "Riley's hair is the same color as her mom's."

That was an opening if Paige ever saw one. She'd have tripped falling into it if she wasn't watching her steps. But they were outside, heading to the UTV. Paige was back on task. Cattle watching came first. No more getting personal with her rancher. "We won't visit the salon, but if it's okay with you, I'll pick up some nail polish and things for a spa night of pampering at home."

"Riley will like that." Evan started the UTV, then rubbed his hands together. "That leaves me with a free night."

"Going to call your friends for a poker session?" Paige teased.

"That's very tempting," Evan whistled and waited for Rex to run from the stable and jump into the UTV bed. "But I've got Christmas shopping to do. I want to make sure I get the exact bike Riley wants before they're all sold out."

"Do you always get Riley exactly what she wants?" she asked. *And does that principle apply to all the people in your life? Would you give me what I want?*

"Whenever possible I give Riley what she wants." He drove the UTV down the dirt road.

But what Paige *could* want wasn't possible. The rancher and the city veterinarian. Two different worlds. Two different states. Two different lives. Impossible situation.

Good thing Paige knew exactly what she did

want. The life she'd invested her time, heart, and grandparents' money in back in Chicago.

Nothing was going to derail her this time. Especially not love.

CHAPTER TEN

"STOP!" PAIGE SHOUTED.

Evan jolted and pressed on the UTV's brakes. "What's wrong?"

Paige never responded. Instead, she lunged from the vehicle before Evan had completely slowed to a stop in the middle of the dirt road leading to the cattle handling facility and the pastures. Rex jumped out, barked twice, and followed Paige. Evan shoved the UTV into park and sprinted after the pair. Paige yanked the gate to Macybelle's pasture open, unraveled her scarf, and ran across the open field. Rex remained right beside her.

Evan scanned ahead. His gaze landed on Macybelle, laying in her same spot in the far corner of the field. Blood covered the cow's entire face from her eyes to her nose. Alarm cut through him. The bovine had just been eating with Riley. She was supposed to be on the mend. Not bleeding. Not injured.

Evan slammed the gate shut behind him, locking his panic firmly inside him. He hurried toward Paige and the injured cow. "How badly is she hurt?"

"I can't tell until I stop the bleeding." Paige pressed her scarf against Macybelle's face. Her focus remained fixed on the cow. "She's cut from under her left eye across her face and into her muzzle."

"What can I do?" He crouched next to Paige. His knees ground into the dirt. Worry pressed against his chest.

"Apply pressure here." Paige guided his hand to the area just above Macybelle's muzzle. She adjusted the scarf and used it to feel further up Macybelle's face.

A steady stream of Paige's encouraging words meant to reassure the cow filled the charged silence. Evan watched Paige. Minutes passed. Her soothing, gentle care continued. A mixture of awe and calm filled Evan.

Paige sat in the dust. Macybelle's massive head rested on her legs as if the nine-hundred-pound cow was no larger than a lap dog. Rex waited nearby, alert and watchful as if he'd accepted guard duty over both Paige and Macybelle. Evan noticed Paige's grey scarf was completely blood-stained under his fingers and most likely ruined. But she'd never hesitated. Never paused to look for something else to use on the wound. Helping Macybelle had been her only priority.

Right now, right beside him, she looked and acted like she'd been a part of Evan's ranch and his life for years, not days. So much for only picturing her in the city.

And yet a city veterinarian wasn't a part of this equation, he thought, as he scanned the pasture and thought of the ranch, all so beautiful, but raw. No matter how comfortable Paige seemed to be with him. Or how much he discovered he liked about her.

"I think the bleeding is finally slowing." Paige peeked under the soaked scarf. The tension in her voice released. "It's not as deep as I feared, but it has to be irrigated and treated."

"I've got bottled water in a cooler in the UTV." Evan stood. He'd expected and prepared for another full day spent attending his herds. He hadn't expected an early morning confession in the kitchen and Paige's quick offer to help. And now this—one more reason to be grateful she was here. With him.

"I'll take whatever you have." Paige adjusted her hands, covering the spot where Evan had been applying pressure.

Paige was doing what she'd been asked: looking after his cattle. He had to stop looking at Paige and seeing something more. She was temporary in Three Springs and his life was here permanently. Time to focus. And not on how much he liked being around Paige.

A quick trip to the UTV and he returned carrying the cooler of water and a portable toolbox.

Paige set about flushing the gash on Macybelle's face, rinsing it clean. She kept up her one-sided conversation with the patient cow. "The past few days certainly haven't been good for you, have they? Ol' Macybelle."

Evan wanted to agree with Paige's assessment. His days hadn't been all that great recently, either. But there had been good moments since Paige's arrival. And he was looking forward to more, if that was possible. He twisted the caps open on several bottles of water, cut off his interest in Paige and then opened his toolbox. "Macybelle hasn't been moving far from this corner. Whatever cut her has to be close by."

Paige frowned and leveled her gaze on Macybelle's soulful big eyes. "I don't suppose you want to make it easy for us and show us what happened and where."

Macybelle's exhale was deep and long and pitiful.

Evan considered the long, curved cut across the gentle cow's face. He shifted his attention to the fence line and scanned the length of the back corner where the ill cow had taken refuge. "She most likely rubbed against something. Probably wanting to scratch her nose."

He stepped over to the fence and began searching the posts. He and his ranch hands had been steadily replacing the fence, removing barbed wire from decades past and updating. However, some of the original posts remained. Several feet away, he examined one of them. Just below knee height on the thick wood, he located a large nail sticking out several inches. Fresh blood covered the rusty nail. He grabbed the pliers and pried the nail loose. "Found the culprit."

"Macybelle will need a tetanus shot." Paige glanced at him. "Got any of those handy?"

"Down at the handling facility." Evan picked up the toolbox and dropped the nail and pliers inside. "I want to check the rest of the fence posts before we leave."

"That's a good idea." Paige let more water flow across Macybelle's wound. "I'll help as soon as I'm done here."

"I got it." Evan turned toward the fence. Hopefully he'd soon get over his fascination with his city veterinarian.

Evan had removed three more rusty nails and had checked half of the fence when Paige knelt beside him. She ran her hands over the outside of the next wide wooden post. "Found one." She grabbed a second set of pliers from the toolbox then worked the nail free. "Got it."

Her smile spiked inside Evan, sparking his own grin. "You're hired. We've got miles and miles of fence lines around here."

Paige walked beside him to the next section. Together they worked their way around the pasture toward the main gate. She paused to look up at the sky and then seemed to study the horizon. "There's something satisfying about being out here."

There was definitely something refreshing about being with Paige. That was both surprising and undeniable. "What do you mean?"

She motioned toward Macybelle, resting in her corner. The cow's long cut was no longer bleeding. Paige examined another fence post. Her eyebrows pinched together. Her words were thoughtful. "Maybe it's just getting back to practicing basic animal medicine. Where what's right for the patient always comes first. It feels good."

"Don't your patients come first back in the city?" he asked.

"I always believed they should." She swung around and inspected the last post. "Looks like we covered the entire pasture."

Evan held open the gate for her and tucked away his curiosity about her life in Chicago. Cows were his business, not intriguing city animal doctors. He dropped the empty cooler and toolbox in the bed of the UTV and whistled for Rex.

Paige climbed into the passenger seat. "Riley and I will check on Macybelle when we get home tonight from our crafting afternoon."

Home. She'd spoken as if the ranch was her home. As if it'd always been hers. He should correct her. Remind himself and Paige that her home was in another state, not Three Springs. Not on his ranch. Not with him. Evan cleared his throat. Ready to face the facts. "That's a good idea. Riley will want to see for herself that Macybelle is okay."

And when Evan got home, he'd face the fact that both his home and his heart were closed to long-term guests and dreams of forever.

CHAPTER ELEVEN

"I want to give my dad a superspecial present this year." Riley skipped alongside Paige outside the art center.

Paige had yet to see the little girl simply walk. Everything Riley did, from singing in the car to cleaning up her craft station, she did with an abundance of enthusiasm. It was refreshing and infectious. Riley reminded Paige to be present in every moment. "I think that's really nice. What kind of superspecial gift are you getting your dad?"

"I want to make his present," Riley hopscotched down the sidewalk toward the general store. "My teacher, Ms. Hayes, says you can put your heart into a homemade gift. And that's what matters most at the holidays."

"I made an ornament for my parents when I was about your age." Paige shifted the bag with the bubble-wrapped wreaths they'd created at the art center to her other hand. She hadn't thought about her childhood ornaments in years, and made a mental note to find her ornaments once she got back to her apartment in Chicago. "I remember all the ornaments my sister and I made were always on the front of our tree."

"What did they look like?" Riley swayed into Paige and took her hand for balance.

"Bells made from egg cartons. Lots of construction-paper loop garland. Oh, and one time I tried to do an elf with felt and glue, but it didn't quite turn out." Paige gripped Riley's hand, settling into an easy connection with the girl. Same as she'd fallen into an easy connection with Evan earlier that day. There'd been no awkward conversational pauses or strained moments. They'd treated cattle, checked the herds and laughed over lunch. They'd been engaged in their work and in each other. It was everything a good working relationship should be. Paige stopped where her thoughts were heading next. "Another one was a pine-cone snowy owl. It was pretty cute. A Popsicle-stick picture frame. A clothespin reindeer. A handprint snowmen family."

"That one. The snowmen family." Riley landed on both feet, released Paige's hand, and jumped around to face Paige. "Can we make that one for my dad's superspecial present?"

"Sure." Paige pulled out her phone and searched for a picture on the internet. She turned her phone screen for Riley to see. "It looks like this."

Riley tucked her arms against her sides and

gave a delighted shimmy. "Yes. How do we make it?"

"Well, we're going to need a few supplies." Paige stuck her phone in her purse and pointed at the Silver Penny. "And I'm pretty sure Ms. Tess should have everything we need."

"I love the Silver Penny." Riley slipped her hand inside Paige's again. "Mr. Boone says it used to have a train inside at Christmas. Mr. Sam looks like Santa. But his belly isn't so big, so he isn't Santa. But Santa used to come to the store. Did you know that? Mr. Boone told me so. Maybe Santa will come back this year. Maybe he can't come without the magic coin."

Paige took a breath for Riley and replayed what the little girl had told her. "Why does Santa need the silver coin?"

"There's no chimney." Riley frowned at Paige as if Paige should've already recognized that problem. "Santa can't get in without one."

"Right." Paige nodded and worked to hide her confusion. "And the coin?"

"Gives people hope." Riley lifted her chin. "That's what Mr. Boone says."

"So, Santa can hold the coin and hope for a chimney," Paige guessed.

"Yup." Riley frowned. "Or he can't go inside."

"Guess we better find that coin, then." Paige stepped up to the general store.

Riley tugged on Paige's arm, stopping her from opening the door. Riley's whisper was more library loud than genuinely quiet. "Remember it's a supersecret present."

"Right." Paige held a finger up to her closed lips. "Then we need a special name for our superspecial Christmas present project, so no one will know what we're doing."

"Gumdrop," Riley whispered. She giggled into her hands and her shoulders lifted to her ears. "Dad eats all the gumdrops off the gingerbread house every year. Most times he eats them before we can put them on."

Paige grinned and filed that information away. Evan ate cookies for breakfast and liked gumdrops. It was possible Evan's sweet tooth rivaled Paige's. She'd finally have someone to share dessert with. Paige backtracked. She was more than fine eating an entire piece of cheesecake by herself. She motioned Riley into the store. "Project Gumdrop has officially begun. Now it's time to shop."

Riley and Paige gathered their craft supplies in a handheld shopping basket. Paige read off the supply list from the DIY ornament website. Then she sent a quick text to her sister explaining the details of Project Gumdrop. "Hmm, we have everything we need. Time to check out."

Tess was prepared for them. She bent down

to Riley's level and looked one way and then the other, as if to make sure no one was going to overhear her. "I got supersecret boxes for Project Gumdrop," she whispered. "No one will know what's inside."

Riley clasped her hands together and nodded. "It's a surprise."

Tess wrapped a plain blue ornament for decorating in bubble wrap and placed it in a box marked Bathroom Tissue. The acrylic white paint, glitter, pipe cleaners and permanent markers went into a box marked Cleaning Supplies. She took out a Silver Penny paper bag and dropped two large bags of gumdrops inside. "Can't have Project Gumdrop without gumdrops."

Riley covered her mouth. Her shoulders shook.

"We can use the gumdrops to distract your dad," Paige added. And if she was lucky, she'd have discovered other ways to distract herself before Evan got home. She'd already thought about her coworker too much already.

Riley exclaimed, "He's going to be so surprised."

"He's going to love it." Tess set the boxes into a plain large bag and sighed. "Makes me wish I had someone to make me an ornament too."

Riley tugged on Paige's jacket until Paige

leaned in. "Can we also make the owls?" she asked.

"Of course." Paige smiled at her sister. "We're going to need pine cones. Big ones. Googly eyes and cotton balls. Orange felt too, if you have it."

Tess laughed and pointed to the craft section. "You already know where to go."

"Can we get another ornament?" Riley paused in the Christmas aisle and touched a glass ball. "I need to make a second one."

"It's probably a good idea." Paige picked up a second blue one from the shelf. Riley had insisted her father's favorite color was blue. "Then you have an extra in case one breaks."

"It's not for that." Riley chewed on her bottom lip. "It's for my mom."

Mom. Paige straightened, swallowed, then pushed her shoulders back again. Still, her throat was too dry. Her words stuck. She managed a weak: "Your mom."

"Yeah." Riley shoved a stray curl off her face. Her certainty, from her stiff chin to her steady voice, was unmissable. "Mom is coming home for Christmas. Dad promised."

Mom was the mysterious *she* who Riley had been asking Evan about. If Riley's mom was returning, why was Evan being so evasive? Paige pretended a sudden rapt interest in the selection of other ornaments. She kept her tone casual, wanting to sound indifferent. "When was the last time you saw your mom?"

"I've never seen her for real." Riley sorted the ornaments into matching color groups. "Only pictures."

Paige's heart squeezed. For Evan and what must be his pain. And for the innocent child beside her. She cleared her throat. "You've never met your mom?"

Riley shook her head, then she popped her eyes wide open and faced Paige. "But this year Mom will be here. And it's going to be the best Christmas ever."

"That will be very special." Paige stuffed her own worry away. She picked up a green ornament and a red one. "What color do you think your mom will like?"

"Red." Riley touched her hair. "She's gotta like me. We got the same hair."

Another squeeze inside Paige's chest that built into an ache. She didn't know Riley's mom and the history, only that Evan never mentioned the woman. Not once. Not even in passing. Neither had Ilene.

Paige set the extra ornament in their shopping basket and smiled at Riley. "Well, I like your hair and you very, very much."

Riley beamed at Paige. "Do you think Ms. Tess has any more candy?"

Paige held out her hand for Riley to take it, which she did. "Let's go ask. Shopping makes me hungry."

Riley skipped beside Paige and they went back to check out. The snowy owl supplies and additional red round ornament had just been paid for when the shopkeeper's bell chimed. A pair of petite older women bustled into the store and made a beeline for the counter.

Tess lifted her eyebrows at Paige. "You're in for a treat. The Baker sisters have arrived." Then Paige's sister stepped forward to embrace the petite pair. "Welcome, Breezy and Gayle. What brings you in today?"

"Hello, dearest Tess." The shorter of the Baker sisters cupped Tess's cheek with a ring-bedecked hand. "So, so lovely."

Gayle had a silver-and-gray chin-length bob, wore jean overalls that somehow looked trendy, and the roundest eyeglass frames Paige had ever seen. Gayle examined Tess as if she were looking through a microscope. "My chicken-and-dumpling stew is good for the heart. I'll bring a pot by."

Tess never missed a beat. "Thank you. Now, what can I do for you lovely ladies?"

"Nothing." Gayle nudged her elbow into her sister's side. "Breezy and I came for your sister."

"Paige?" Tess turned and motioned to Paige. "My sister is right here."

"We know." Breezy said with a satisfied grin. "We've been tracking Paige and Miss Riley for several blocks."

Paige glanced at Tess, who shrugged, looking as confused as Paige felt.

Breezy stepped fully into Paige's personal space and glanced up at her. It seemed like a strong wind could knock the woman over. But there was a resilience to her frame and her expression that said she'd simply get back up and dare the wind to try again. Breezy squinted at Paige. "Dr. Gibson told us you have good eyes."

Gayle adjusted her eyeglasses and blinked at Paige. Her sparkly purple eye shadow was all the more prominent behind the saucer-round lenses. "They're very pretty eyes."

"My dad thinks I have pretty eyes." Riley tipped her head and studied Paige. "I bet he'd think Ms. Paige has pretty eyes too."

"I bet he would, too." Breezy looked rather pleased with Riley's suggestion. A shrewd speculation shifted into Gayle's gaze.

In fact, Paige noticed the gleam in both sisters' faces and it made Paige slightly uneasy. She thought Boone and Sam were the only matchmakers in town. She should tell the cowboy duo they had competition. "Ms. Baker, how can I help you?"

"Breezy. It's always been Breezy since I started crawling. We're not sure where it came from, but it sure did stick." Breezy chuckled, then quickly sobered. "Something is not right with Scooter. We were hoping you could tell us what's wrong."

"I'm sorry," Paige said. And she was. "I'm not seeing patients here in Texas."

"You saw Evan's cows, did you not?" Breezy's penciled-in eyebrow arched high on her forehead. There was nothing easygoing or light about her tone now.

Paige searched for an explanation. "I was just assisting Dr. Gibson while he was laid up on bedrest."

"Of course, you were. Great to have you fill in like that. And Conrad, such a dear man, handsome, too, if you like the older ones." Breezy announced, "Everyone knows love doesn't have an age limit."

Love might not have an age limit, but Paige had taken a hiatus from love and all things love related. She let Breezy's comment breeze by her.

"Conrad mentioned you might consider assisting again, only with our little Scooter." Gayle hooked her thumbs in her overalls.

Riley giggled. Paige wished she could laugh.

Paige wanted to tell her sister this wasn't a treat. It was closer to sabotage. In the form of two entertaining and spry longtime retirees.

"I'd have to call Dr. Gibson and check with him." Paige tried to stall. She wasn't licensed. She was only supposed to observe cattle at Evan's ranch. Dr. Gibson knew that, yet he'd sent the women after Paige anyway.

"There's no need." Breezy opened a sparkly compact mirror she retrieved from her clutch, checked her reflection, then pinched her cheeks. They blossomed pink. "Conrad already vouched for your talented, well-trained eyes."

"Don't forget her ears." Gayle grabbed her own earlobe, pulling off her clip-on earring in the process. "He said Paige also has good ears."

Breezy snapped her compact closed and glanced around the store as if looking for the crowd of customers. "We just need you to peek real quick at Scooter."

"Riley and I have a busy afternoon." Paige was scrambling. Surely if it was an emergency, Dr. Gibson would've sent the women to the nearest animal hospital. She couldn't risk her license any more than she already had. "I promised Riley a girls' day."

"Isn't that lovely," Breezy sighed.

"She certainly needs that." Gayle smiled at Riley, then looked at Paige. "Riley's grandmother is one of the best people we know. But it's good Riley has you now too."

"Women need to pick each other up. Help each other out more. It's the right thing to do," Breezy said. "We won't take up much of your time."

Relief skimmed over Paige. The Baker sisters understood. "Maybe you can schedule a house call with Dr. Gibson. I know he's anxious to get back to his patients."

"That won't be necessary." Breezy hustled into Paige's side and linked their arms together faster than a cheetah on the hunt. Breezy added, "Scooter is right outside for you to see now."

"We pride ourselves on being very time efficient." Gayle walked toward the entrance. "Now you can get right to it with your eyes and ears."

The Baker sisters should pride themselves on the art of the ambush. Paige let herself be escorted outside. Riley kept pace beside them. In her defense, to save her license, Paige would claim she'd been outnumbered.

Breezy pressed a button on her key chain and the lights flashed on an oversize black SUV parked in front of the Silver Penny. One tire was on the curb. The windows were tinted. Reindeer antlers were attached to the front windows and a massive red nose to the grille.

Gayle opened the tailgate. A crate covered with a snowflake blanket filled the back of the

SUV. "Scooter usually likes to ride in the back seat, but not today."

Breezy pulled the blanket off the crate and draped it over her arm like a game show hostess. "This is Scooter, our miniature potbellied pig."

Riley gasped beside Paige. "Scooter is more red than my hair."

The poor pig certainly was. There wasn't an inch of Scooter not Rudolph-nose bright. Paige stepped closer. Scooter was sound asleep on another glittery Christmas blanket, breathing normally and looking very nonstressed. Paige reached for her cell phone inside her purse.

Dr. Gibson answered on the first ring and skipped over any greeting. "Paige, you with the Baker sisters?"

"Yes, sir." Paige stepped away from the SUV and the others to hear better.

"Wonderful." Relief echoed through Dr. Gibson's voice. "I suspect it's another allergic reaction, but Breezy and Gayle insisted on Scooter being seen."

"I can see him right now," Paige confirmed. "He's a very festive crimson shade."

Dr. Gibson launched into an abbreviated history about the Baker sisters and their penchant for decorating everything at each holiday from Valentine's Day to St. Patrick's Day to the first day of spring, the winter solstice and anything else that came up in between. And everything included the pig's area and his bedding. "Every inch is decorated, Paige. Can't seem to convince either sister that their pig doesn't need coordinated bedding for every holiday."

Paige set her hand over the speaker of the phone and called out to Breezy and Gayle. "Did you put anything new in Scooter's bedding?"

"I washed the blankets in a lovely seasonal scented oil," Breezy answered. "Gives the entire house an uplifting scent. Every time we inhale, we're filled with the wonder of the season."

Paige relayed the information to Dr. Gibson. He sighed over the phone. "I'll send over a prescription. And please suggest again that Scooter prefers simple fleece if they must or straw. Good old-fashioned straw. I really appreciate this, Paige."

With that, Dr. Gibson disconnected. Paige returned to the SUV and updated the Baker sisters. Just then, Boone and Sam stepped out of the Feisty Owl and headed across the street. The cowboy duo tipped their hats at the women individually, then moved closer to the SUV.

Boone leaned in and peered inside the open crate. "Looks like Scooter might be allergic to Christmas. That's a shame."

"Add a Santa hat to Scooter here, if he doesn't mind, and snap a few Christmas pictures before all that red goes away. Good for the Christmas card." Sam set his hand on Boone's shoulder, glanced from the crate to Paige. "It will go away won't it, doc?"

"Yes." Paige looked at the sisters. "Antihistamines. Dr. Gibson is calling in the prescription. And you need to get all new bedding."

"You hear that, Scooter?" Breezy spoke into the crate, her voice singsong soothing. "It's just a little rash. We'll find you something festive that won't turn you red anymore. We promise."

Paige warned, "You need to find something hypoallergenic."

"Does this hypo-whatever come in a Christmas pattern?" Gayle tapped her glasses up her nose.

"Scooter likes reindeers and snowmen," Breezy added.

"So do I," Riley offered. "And candy canes, polar bears and Santa's elves too."

"Elves." Breezy hugged Riley. "We need that. Scooter would love to burrow in an elf blanket."

"Why don't you pick up Scooter's medicine and take him home," Paige suggested. "I'm sure my sister and I can find the perfect Christmas blanket for Scooter."

"Well, aren't you sweet in addition to having good eyes and ears. The town needs more folks like you, Paige." Breezy air-kissed Paige on either cheek.

"When you've got the blanket, you can come out to the farm and meet everyone," Gayle exclaimed. "We'll have dinner, perhaps my chicken-dumpling stew."

"And mulled wine. It's an old family recipe. Pairs with anything." Breezy smiled at Boone and Sam. "You gentlemen must join us."

The two sisters bustled into their SUV. Breezy behind the wheel, Gayle buckled in as the copilot and suddenly sporting a Santa hat. Breezy honked the horn and Gayle waved goodbye.

"Ms. Breezy and Ms. Gayle are sweet on Mr. Boone and Mr. Sam." Riley mimicked Breezy's singsongy voice. "That's what Grandma says."

"The only sweets we should be discussing are the red velvet cake truffles I heard Tess has inside." Sam opened the door to the general store and motioned everyone in.

Riley raced ahead, straight to the checkout counter, and announced, "Ms. Breezy and Ms. Gayle asked Mr. Boone and Mr. Sam over for dinner! They're dating!"

"Nonsense." Boone's cheeks turned redder than Scooter's rash. "It's an open-invite dinner. Paige is going too."

"Paige needs a date too." Riley spread her arms wide. "Then everyone will have a person for dinner and mulled wine, whatever that is." Riley wrinkled her nose.

Everyone stared at Paige. She felt her skin heating from her neck to her cheeks as if Scooter's rash had been contagious.

Sam smoothed his hand over his beard. "As it happens, I've got too many single grandsons. Four to be exact."

"Good boys. Every one of 'em." Boone nodded and considered Paige.

Paige wasn't looking for a date. Or anyone to be sweet on. She'd been hustled to put her eyes on a miniature potbellied pig. Now she was being hustled for a dinner date. Three Springs needed a warning in their tourist brochure about matchmaking seniors. "That's a kind offer, but…"

"But Ms. Paige is gonna take my dad," Riley declared.

Evan. As her date. If Paige had to go with someone, she'd want it to be her rancher. No, that wasn't right. She was perfectly fine attending events being single. She preferred it. It was that whole relationship thing again. Dating was the first step. Another first… Better not to even begin. "I may not be here. Finding a hypoallergenic blanket might take longer for Tess to track down and order."

"What are you looking for exactly?" Tess opened her laptop and tapped on the keyboard.

"Breezy wants an elf-print blanket for Scooter. Preferably fleece. And it must be hypoallergenic and suitable for a miniature potbellied pig." Paige exhaled. "Scooter had an allergic reaction to the Christmas oil they added to the blankets."

Tess nodded and studied her computer screen. Two taps and a wide smile took over her face, and she raised her arms over her head in celebration. "Done. It'll be here by Saturday."

"That's rather quick." Paige eyed her sister. Was she part of the dating ambush squad?

"I'm really good at what I do," Tess challenged. "Ask anyone in town."

"Now you can take Dad to dinner." Riley cheered.

"I'll have to see if he wants to go." Paige rubbed her forehead. "I'm sure he's busy."

"He'll say yes to you." Riley was all confidence. "He always says yes when you ask. Remember he was tired and yawning. Then you asked to him to help with Luna and he wasn't tired no more. Remember?"

That was nothing. Paige wanted a hand taking Luna outside before bed. It was a short walk through the front yard. Not a midnight stroll under the stars. Not a date.

Boone and Sam grinned. And Tess looked away, but not before Paige caught her smile. She was going to have to set everyone straight. As soon as she set herself straight. Dating Evan was a bad idea.

"Maybe you could ask Dad if we could go caroling," Riley suggested.

No more Christmas firsts. That list was full. And no more talking about dates and Evan. "I think we should ask Tess if she'll give us some of her red velvet cake truffles for our girls' night tonight."

Riley's eyes lit up. "Truffles are my favorite."

Tess took a tin from under the counter. "I thought unicorn sundaes were your favorite."

"Last week, I could've sworn she said it was peanut butter fudge." Boone reached into the tin for a truffle.

"Grandma says I change my mind faster than a hummingbird's wings flap. But it's okay because I'm a kid." Riley giggled and popped a truffle into her mouth. "These are really good, Ms. Tess."

Paige picked up a truffle and bit into it. Paige hardly ever changed her mind once it was set. And her mind was set. And her heart wasn't going to change things now.

CHAPTER TWELVE

Evan silently praised his mom. Paige looked relaxed as she stood in the open doorway of the guesthouse, bathed in the warm porch light. He held up the twin glass stem mugs he was carrying. "Nightcap from my mom. It's hot buttered rum with apple cider. A popular specialty drink she makes at the Feisty Owl. She figured you could use something after your afternoon and evening entertaining Riley."

Paige accepted a mug and stepped back to allow him entry. "It was a lot of fun."

"Thank you for that, by the way. I really appreciated it." Evan tapped his glass against Paige's. "Riley fell asleep midsentence tonight. She convinced me I need to try your coconut cream face mask so my skin will be supersoft too. And put cucumber slices on my eyes so they won't be so puffy."

"I think I have extra of both I can give you." Paige laughed and sipped her drink. "Did you find the bicycle for Riley?"

"I found the bike and more." Evan wandered into the cottage-style kitchen.

His mom had replaced the curtains covering the open shelves under the sink with an updated fabric. He'd replaced the counters with butcher block and painted the cabinets a pure white. The original floating shelves his great-grandmother had installed still hung on either side of the antique stove. And the cast iron sink remained intact.

The modern and the old blended together as if they'd always belonged.

The same was true of Paige, in her flannel pj pants and deep burgundy fleece hoodie. She looked as if she'd always belonged in the cottage too. As if she was as much a part of his family as Riley and himself. He stared at his drink. He'd only had a few sips, not nearly enough to go to his head. He moved away from Paige and ignored his rum.

Craft supplies covered the kitchen table. He picked up a cotton ball. "What's all this?"

"Project Gumdrop." Paige intercepted him, squeezing between him and the table.

Except he couldn't look away. One more place Paige seemed to fit: close to him.

Paige lifted her chin and kept her gaze locked on his. Laughter danced through her brown eyes. "It's supersecret. On a need-to-know basis."

There were things he wanted to know. Like, was her skin as soft as he imagined? If he lifted his hand, he could brush his fingers across her cheek and find out. If he leaned forward, the smallest of adjustments, he could kiss her. Again, test that softness of her lips. Finally know if their attraction was a simple sparkler or an elaborate fireworks display. All of that was on a need-to-know basis. But Paige was here temporarily, and some heartaches left permanent scars. Love required a change he wasn't willing to make, he admitted. "I'm good at keeping secrets." Even from himself it seemed.

"So am I." Paige's mouth quirked. She produced a bag of candy and held it between them. "I hear you have a weakness for gumdrops."

He could have a weakness for Paige, although he hoped he had more restraint than that. One corner of his mouth lifted, and he plucked the candy bag from her hand, before he forgot his aversion to change. He walked into the family room, set his mug on a coaster on the coffee table and sat on the couch. He opened the gumdrop bag and tossed one in his mouth.

Paige settled on the other end of the couch and tucked her freshly painted toenails underneath her. "What do you think about going Christmas caroling?"

"I think we can fit that in." Evan dug inside the gumdrop bag for a cinnamon one.

"You'll be exhausted by Christmas Day if you keep adding to the Christmas-firsts list." Paige held out her hand for a candy.

"It's all for a good cause." Evan placed several flavors on Paige's palm. "It's for Riley and giving her the perfect Christmas."

"I heard this year is going to be the best Christmas ever." Paige picked up a green gumdrop and watched him. Her gaze, steady and direct, searched his.

"Because we added eight prelit reindeers and a sleigh to the front yard decorations? Or because dozens of paper snowflakes are dangling in Riley's bedroom windows and from her ceiling?" Evan stretched out his legs and set his boots on the edge of the coffee table.

"I'm sure she's thrilled about all that." Paige set her uneaten candy on a coaster and brushed her hands together. "But this was about her mom coming home for Christmas."

The spicy gumdrop glued his jaw together. Evan lowered his boots to the ground and set the candy bag on the table. He worked on swallowing the sticky candy and his surprise. "Riley told you about that."

Paige tugged a blanket from the back of the couch and covered her lap as if she felt Evan's own personal chill. "Part of the supersecret present making includes something for her mom."

Evan rose and paced over to the fireplace. He added another log, picked up the poker and stoked the flames. He could add a dozen logs, stoke the flames into a bonfire, yet nothing would thaw that cold pit inside him. "Have you ever made an impossible promise?"

"No." Paige's voice was thoughtful. "I can't say that I have."

"Well, I have." He jabbed at the pine logs. The wood cracked and popped, throwing sparks. "I promised my daughter her mother would be here for Christmas to avoid telling the truth."

"What's the truth?" Paige's mild voice pulled his focus to her.

That I'm a bad father. And a coward. He set the poker in the stand and looked at Paige curled on the couch. She watched him, her gaze open and gentle. No judgment radiated off her. If he sat beside her, she might take his hand. And he might forget that he was good being single. He might forget that he wasn't interested in finding a life partner. Even if Paige was as close to the kind of partner he'd want in his life.

He braced his hand on the mantel and himself for the truth he'd never put into words. Never spoken out loud. "The only traits Riley shares with her mom are their matching hair color and eyes. Riley is selfless. My ex is selfish. Also, Marla prefers parenting only when it's convenient for her. It hasn't been convenient since Riley was five months old and even then, parenting didn't suit her."

The fire snapped beside him. The bitter memories, spiteful arguments and harsh accusations snapped inside him. High school sweethearts. Reunited during Marla's surprise trip home. Accidental pregnancy. An engagement. A wedding date set for after the birth. Expectations had been met.

He'd so badly wanted to see their future—the one that everyone from the high school principal to the postman had always claimed they'd have— because love conquered all. However, Marla had seen a different future. One where Evan gave up everything to be with her.

Paige picked up her mug and cradled the cup in her hands. "Where is Marla now?"

"Las Vegas." Evan pushed away from the fireplace and paced a small circle. The same as he'd done at the altar six years ago. Only then he'd been trying to soothe a crying infant. "Marla met a wealthy high roller during her bachelorette weekend. He promised a more extravagant lifestyle than a rancher could ever give her." In her mind, he'd promised a better prize than Evan's love.

Paige's gaze narrowed. Her mouth dipped into a frown. "And Marla never came back from her bachelorette party?"

"Marla came home, but never showed up for the wedding." Evan had, with his tuxedo and tie pressed. His hair trimmed. His cowboy boots dust free. And still determined to believe love would win. After all, there was another heart on the line: their daughter's. Evan rubbed his chest. "Marla left Riley and me standing at the altar and a goodbye note in the nursery."

"That's... I have no words." Paige's mug thumped on the coffee table. "That's not true. I have words. A lot of not very nice words for Marla," she sputtered angrily. "I'm sorry that happened to you and Riley. No one deserves that."

"But there's Riley. I'm grateful every day to have her. She's the good that came from the bad." He'd hurt for a long while. None of what happened had been so easily brushed aside. Or dismissed. He inhaled, scrubbed his hands over his face and up into his hair. "My daughter is my reason for everything. And now, I'm going to break my promise and crush her heart in the process."

"Have you spoken to Marla? Maybe this year will be different."

"I've tried over the years." Until he'd used up

the last of his hope. None of it had been for him; it'd all been for his daughter. How could Marla have left Riley? Even now, he didn't fully understand. "I sent reminder texts about Riley's birthday. Left voice mails about big moments in our daughter's life. Milestones Riley reached." All the things involved parents celebrated.

"And Marla never responded?" Paige's expression was total shock.

"Not once." Evan shoved aside the old anger. It only ruined his mood and his days if he hung on to it. And he'd vowed Marla had done enough of that already. "Eventually I stopped trying. Stopped reaching out."

Paige sipped her drink and eyed him over the rim. "What did you tell Riley?"

"That her mom was away. That she was thinking about her, but not able to come home." Evan admonished himself, but nothing released the guilt and regret. He dropped onto the couch across from Paige and stared at the beams exposed in the ceiling, wishing he could right his mistakes now. "Then I signed birthday cards and gave her Christmas presents from her mom."

Paige's eyes went round.

"I didn't want Riley to think badly of her mother." Moms weren't supposed to walk away from their children without a backward glance, like Marla had. Love wasn't supposed to be conditional, but that hadn't been his reality. "I'm afraid when Riley learns the truth, that I've been lying, she's going to hate me."

"I don't believe she could ever do that." Paige set her mug down and touched Evan's arm. A firm conviction seemed to infuse her words. "Riley adores you."

"Riley also likes the image I built of her mother, but it's completely made up." Evan stared at Paige's hand on his arm. Felt the warmth of her touch. The gentle kindness. The simple connection. "I was stupid."

Even more foolish for thinking, even for a second, something good could happen between him and Paige. His love hadn't been enough for a homegrown country girl like Marla; what chance would he have of making Paige happy?

"That's a rather harsh thing to say about yourself. You wanted to protect your daughter." Paige squeezed his arm. "Grandma Opal always told me bad decisions don't make you a bad person."

"And it's how you go forward and grow from your mistakes that matters on this journey of life," Evan added. "That's what my mother would say."

"Growing can be uncomfortable." Paige stretched slightly as if working through those growing pains herself.

"Then you've made bad decisions as well," he concluded.

"One or two," she admitted. "And before you ask, let's just say for the sake of that growth thing that love and I have agreed to a mutual time-out."

"I've agreed to the very same time-out after I went to my wedding reception alone." Evan grinned. "And had more fun than I thought possible for a jilted groom."

"And you've been happy ever since," Paige said.

It was what he told his daughter. Every single day. "Something like that."

"But this is about Riley and her happiness," Paige stated. "That matters more to you than anything."

"Exactly." Evan relaxed into the couch. Paige understood. He stacked his hands behind his head. "How am I supposed to tell Riley her mom isn't interested in being a mother? I don't want Riley to think she did anything wrong. Or that it's her fault."

Paige tucked her hair behind her ear and studied him. "I think you have to start with the truth."

Evan resisted Paige's suggestion. "Riley is only six years old. Isn't she too young for such a hard reality hit?"

"I was about Riley's age when my father died." Paige's fingers twisted in the fringe on the plush blanket. "At the time my mom told me the basic facts about his illness—cancer—and how we were going to have to stick together. We tried to, especially around the holidays. Dad passed only weeks before Christmas. It was his favorite time of the year."

And Paige's worst. Evan reached for her hand, linked his fingers around her cold ones. "No child should lose their parent."

Paige's fingers tightened around his. "Start with the truth. Tell Riley her mom isn't ready to be a parent yet. Then give Riley space to feel whatever she wants to feel. And show her your love is forever."

"Is that enough?" he asked.

"It's what my mother did for me and my sister after our father died," Paige said. "And my grandparents did the same. They always answered any question I had and shared memories of my dad whenever I asked."

"I gave Riley a photo album of her mom," Evan said. "But talking about Marla. Sharing stories about us. About her..."

"Hurts," Paige finished the sentence for him. "And forgiveness, I have learned, is a journey."

"I moved on years ago," Evan argued. "It's

Riley that matters. I'm going to keep on with our Christmas of firsts."

"What about trying to reach Marla again?" Paige asked. "Maybe Marla will answer this time. If not a visit, you could arrange a video chat or phone call."

"That would mean Marla has changed." Evan shook his head. "I doubt it's possible."

"You should try," Paige urged.

"Only to be disappointed again?" Evan said. "If she wanted to be a part of Riley's life, she would've contacted her. She knows where we are." After all, he'd refused to change everything—to give up his life and his family's livelihood—to be with Marla.

Paige nodded. "What about talking to Riley?"

Evan released her hand. "I'll do that."

"When?" Paige pressed.

"Soon." As soon as he figured out when. When exactly would be the right moment to break his little girl's heart? A restless energy, uncomfortable and awkward, seeped through him. He stood and picked up their empty mugs. "I'll let you get some sleep. I need some myself. We've got another full day tomorrow. Thanks for listening."

"Evan…" Paige's voice stopped him at the door. He turned to face her. "The truth comes out eventually, no matter how fast we run from it."

He wasn't running, though. He was preparing. Preparing to protect his daughter as best he could. He would face the harsh facts. And when he did, he intended to be fully equipped for the fallout. He hadn't been ready for Marla walking away.

And that was his error. He wouldn't be caught off guard again by anyone doing the same.

CHAPTER THIRTEEN

EVAN CHECKED THE TIME and smiled. He'd been in his office since the lunch hour, working on payroll and the back-office responsibilities he'd been putting off while acting as Paige's assistant for the past week.

He'd taken a time-out. A Paige Palmer time-out to be exact. He'd swapped in one of his more experienced ranch hands to take his place. Three hours had passed, and Evan hadn't thought about or talked about Paige. He was putting himself back together and finally focused on the right things: his ranch and taking care of his family.

Last night in the guesthouse with Paige, he'd detoured. Shared more than he should have with a guest. Paige was too easy to talk to. Even more, she listened. Always giving Evan her full attention. It was powerful. Irresistible. But that was the problem with detours: they were only a quick diversion. His houseguest would be leaving soon. And that would be the end of that.

He'd woken this morning with new clarity. What he felt for Paige was nothing more than gratitude. He was grateful for Paige's assistance with the cattle and his daughter. But gratitude couldn't be confused with something deeper like love and affection.

Sure, he wanted to spend more time with Paige, but only because Paige had shaken up Evan's routine. One that if he was honest with himself had gotten a bit stale. Paige reminded him that he needed to change things up for himself. If he'd already been doing that, Paige's presence on the ranch wouldn't have been so appealing.

What he needed was a new hobby to freshen up his routine. Not a relationship.

His mom went past the open French doors of his office, carrying a large box. But the new lasso rope he'd ordered last week was still on back order and not expected to arrive until the end of the month. He called out, "What's that?"

"Dr. Gibson had it sent over for Paige. I peeked inside to make sure it wasn't perishable." His mom had stopped and was now grinning over the top of the box. "It looks like a very well stocked house-call veterinarian kit."

"Paige isn't actively treating patients here in town." Evan closed his laptop and stood.

"She's treating your cattle," his mom argued.

"Dr. Gibson formulated the treatment plan. And besides, the cattle are not small animals," Evan countered. Small animals were Paige's specialty. And he was more than sure Paige had her own perfectly fine veterinarian kit in Chicago.

Ilene turned away and walked toward the family room. "Paige helped our precious Luna. Then she examined Scooter, the Baker sisters' miniature potbellied pig. Those are small animals."

"She only looked at Scooter because Breezy and Gayle cornered her at the general store yesterday." And one thing Evan had learned about Paige was that she wouldn't refuse an animal in need. He appreciated her dedication and her compassion. One more feeling he wouldn't confuse with love.

He trailed after his mom. "Paige can't be Dr. Gibson's assistant. She's leaving to go home in five days."

"Interesting you know the exact number of days until Paige returns to Chicago." His mom set the box on the kitchen table and considered him.

There was nothing interesting about it. He knew the exact number of days until Christmas Eve: nine. And he knew the exact number of days until Riley returned to school: eighteen. See, there was nothing special about when Paige was leaving Three Springs. He frowned and pulled the brand new, cream-colored vet kit out of the box. "The number of days doesn't matter. What matters is that it isn't long-term."

"Dr. Gibson is fully aware of Paige's limited time here." His mom tied an apron around her waist and arched an eyebrow at him. "We all are. You and Paige keep reminding us."

"For good reason." They all had to stop relying on her. Evan pointed to the bag for house calls sitting on the table. "Paige isn't sticking around. This makes it look like she's…she's… permanent."

He began to repeat to himself that he would remain on track. *No more detours, no more detours, no more detours.* No more intimate conversations with hot buttered rum, gumdrops and intriguing houseguests.

"Conrad knows she isn't," his mom said. "He just plans to take advantage of every moment that he has such a talented vet on call."

"This feels like something more." Evan opened the clamshell mouth of the bag and stared inside at the fully stocked vet kit. First his mother fixed a nightcap for him to take over to Paige. Now Conrad sent a house-call-ready veterinarian bag as if Paige was establishing herself in Three Springs. Evan knew that wasn't happening.

What did seem to be happening, however, was Paige establishing herself in his thoughts again. Here he was thinking about and worse talking about Paige. He picked up the battery-powered clippers, noticed the bandages and new stethoscope, as well as more items he couldn't name and medications he couldn't pronounce. Was there anything Dr. Gibson hadn't included in the kit?

There were some things that hadn't been included in their conversation last night. Things Evan wanted to know about Paige. Things he wanted Paige to trust him with. The same way he'd trusted her with those details about Marla. He closed the vet kit and filled a glass with water. He'd go to the stables, saddle Clay, his favorite horse, and head out to the pastures. There in his saddle where he belonged, on his land, he'd try to regroup.

"Perhaps that bag is just a simple thank-you from Conrad to Paige for all she's done." Ilene pulled a bunch of carrots from the refrigerator and set them on the island. "Wouldn't hurt you to consider how you plan to thank Paige. She's saving our ranch."

He'd already thanked Paige. On his way out the door after their hot buttered rum. He'd expressed his gratitude. Anything else could be confused with more than simple appreciation for her hard work. And there would be no more with Paige Palmer. His life was fine as it was. Other than needing a shake-up to his routine, his world was good. He was happy.

The back door swung open. Riley raced inside and shouted, "Dad! Paige! Dad!"

"Right here." Evan dropped his glass in the sink and intercepted his daughter. He lowered to one knee in front of Riley. "I'm right here. And you need to breathe."

Riley inhaled, her body swaying backward with the effort to fully fill her lungs. "I knocked on Ms. Paige's door, but she wasn't home."

Paige's home was in Chicago. Details like that mattered. Evan slid Riley's school backpack off her shoulders. "Paige went to the Silver Penny to see her sister. She'll be back later."

"We need her." Riley grabbed Evan's cheek and leaned in until they were nose to nose. "Right now."

"What happened?" Evan asked.

"Puppies happened!" Riley shouted and released him. She spun and raced outside. The back door slammed before he could ask for more information. He followed his daughter outside and pulled up short. Paige, Riley and Mr. and Mrs. Ross, Abby's neighbors in town, stood staring at a smashed cardboard box near their feet.

Evan moved to Paige's side. "What's going on?"

"Not sure." Paige motioned to the couple in front of her. "I just pulled up and this nice couple was already here, waiting for me."

"Doc Conrad told us to bring these little guys to you." Norman Ross touched his bald head and frowned. "We found them just a little while ago out on the bypass."

Evan could say he'd found Paige out on the bypass. Except, she'd been the one to almost run into him and his cattle. "Paige, Alice and Norman Ross have been on the lookout for abandoned animals for years."

Alice nodded and took her husband's hand. "Ever since our first date, when we found a litter of five of the tiniest kittens you've ever seen."

First date. Evan hadn't been on one of those in years. Had he ever been on a first date he'd want to talk about fifty-some years later like Norman and Alice? His gaze slid to Paige. Ideas churned. Paige deserved that kind of first date. But not with him.

Paige kept her gaze fixed on the couple, not the box. "What happened to the kittens?"

"Adopted them all out." Alice smiled and set her head on Norman's shoulder.

"Of course, we kept a pair for ourselves." Norman wrapped his arm around Alice's waist. "Seems we've kept one from every gaggle we've rescued."

Alice slowly shook her head. "It's the first time we can't keep one. We have a full house."

Riley gaped at the couple. "But what's gonna happen to them?"

"We're hoping Dr. Paige can take them for us." Norman pointed at the puppies. "They don't look to be in too good shape. Doc Conrad assured us that you'd know what to do, Ms. Paige."

"Their eyes aren't open yet," Alice fretted. "They don't look to be more than a few days old."

"I don't have a clinic or even an equipped exam room." Paige sounded distracted, as if she was running through a mental list of all the reasons she should refuse. Newborn puppies hadn't been part of the eyes and ears on a herd of cattle, aka the Dr. Gibson deal.

"We have nowhere else to take them." Alice wiped at her eye.

Paige's jaw was clenched shut. Her expression remained neutral, but her tormented gaze was locked on Evan. Her license was at stake, and yet her heart wouldn't let her say no.

Evan cleared his throat. "The puppies can stay here."

Norman, Alice and Riley cheered.

Evan bent and claimed the dented box. "I'll be sure to get them the treatment they need." And if that treatment happened to come from his own houseguest, well, so be it.

Paige touched his arm and squeezed.

Alice sagged against Norman. "We're so grateful."

"Now, if you'll excuse us." Norman pulled his keys from the front pocket of his trousers, "We're late for our weekly dominoes night with the Kinneys."

"We've been winning recently." Alice lifted her shoulders and smiled. "And we'd like to keep the streak going."

Alice hugged Paige, then Norman hugged her. Then the couple each shook Evan's hand. Offered him another round of thank-yous and headed to their car. Several waves and a honk of the car horn and their four-door sedan disappeared down the gravel road.

"We're gonna keep 'em, aren't we, Dad?" Riley tugged on her dad's arm.

"We can't..." Evan started. The same as they couldn't keep Paige either.

"I know." Riley hopped up and down. "Ms. Paige has gotta look at 'em first, then fix 'em."

"And then we'll find good homes for them." Evan steadied his gaze on his daughter and made firm his resolve. "Homes that aren't here on the ranch." Same as how Paige's home was not there on the ranch, either.

Riley's face puckered and darkened like a storm cloud forming.

Paige frowned at Evan and took the box from him. "Riley, I have a lot of steps until the puppies will be ready to go home and I need an assistant."

"Like you're helping Dr. Gibson." Riley looked at Paige as if she was her hero.

"Exactly like that." Paige touched the top of Riley's head. A gentle, soothing caress. "Think you can do that for me?"

Riley straightened her shoulders and lifted her chin. "Yes."

Paige smiled and then knelt and lifted the flaps on the box. "Let's see who we have here."

Riley dropped onto her knees, pressed herself into Paige's side and mimicked Paige's every move. Paige never made Riley scoot over. She simply asked Riley what she saw and what she thought they should do.

"They need a bath," Riley whispered as if she worried the puppies might react badly to that word. Only Luna liked to have a bath. The other cattle dogs ran into the fields if anyone uttered the words, "Time for a bath."

"We can do a spot clean on them. We have to keep them warm, and a bath could make them too cold." Paige reached into the box. Her fingers trailed over the smallest of the pair. A cream-colored puppy stirred under her touch. Its littermate shivered and looked as if it had been dipped in melted chocolate. "Everyone feels better when they're clean."

"We should feed 'em." Riley patted her stomach. "I feel better when I eat."

"That's a good idea," Paige replied.

Evan rubbed his forehead. Now he had to step in as vet assistant again to make sure his daughter wasn't getting too attached to Paige. He needed to remind his daughter that while Ms. Paige was lovely, kind with animals and even kinder with him and Riley, she had a home in another state. They couldn't keep Paige, not to mention the puppies, even if they wanted to.

Paige glanced up at him. "We're going to need more supplies."

"Dr. Gibson sent you a brand-new vet kit. It's inside the house. I'm sure it will have whatever you'll need for the puppies' care. Now, how can I help?"

"I need supplies from the pharmacy and Country Time." Paige cradled the box in her arms and rose. "And I need them fast."

"Text me the items." Evan motioned at his daughter. "Riley, I need you to come with me. You can help with locating all the special things Paige wants us to get."

Riley nodded and looked at Paige. "Will you be okay without us?"

Paige smiled. "We'll be fine."

But would Riley and Evan be fine without Paige?

CHAPTER FOURTEEN

IT OCCURRED TO PAIGE that the Bishops' first annual game-night party had been a success. Only once had they paused their games, as the group headed to the stables.

Cassie Weaver, the local farrier, had demonstrated a new horse shoeing technique she'd recently learned at a ranch in Montana to the delight of the guests.

Most of the happy friends and family had departed an hour ago to put their kids to bed. Riley had been granted an extension of her bedtime since the self-appointed guardian of the recovering puppies had been supervising anyone wanting a peek at the animals.

Now Ilene, Sam, Riley and Evan played snakes and ladders at the kitchen table. While Paige, Abby and Tess battled through a tiled word game at a card table in the family room.

"Sorry." Paige caught a yawn behind her hands. "Last night is catching up to me. I haven't been awake that late with patients in a long time."

In fact, she hadn't been awake all night with a charming, attentive man beside her in an even longer time. Evan had only left long enough to carry a sleeping Riley to her bed in the main house. But he'd returned quickly, intent on staying up with Paige to help her with the puppies.

Nothing Paige said had persuaded Evan to leave. He'd simply dumped his gumdrops into a bowl and her peanut butter chocolates into another bowl, insisting sugar was always needed for an all-nighter. Then he'd instructed Paige to walk him through how to properly care for the newborn puppies. He'd been endearing, patient and funny. Turning the entire night into something both sweet and dangerous. Dangerous to Paige's peace of mind.

Abby placed her letter tiles on the board and leveled her gaze at Paige. "Are you tired from the puppy care or the extra company?"

"Evan seems like a very good partner." Tess counted her score and added it to her current total. "He didn't even need to text me to confirm your favorite candy and snacks. He already knew."

"I'm not exactly subtle about my sweet-tooth cravings." And clearly, she should be less subtle about her determination to avoid romance and all things related to it.

"It's telling when a person pays enough attention to notice the small details about someone else." Abby unwrapped one of Tess's homemade caramels, but speculation had already sweetened her voice.

"It shows they care." Tess pointed her pencil at her and then tapped it on the scorepad. She managed to keep her expression straight-faced, despite the boast in her words. "And if either of you care, I'm currently winning. By a lot."

Paige wanted to ignore both her cousin and her sister. Paige wanted to care about herself, her career, and her future practice. She wanted to care about the promises she'd made to herself. Promises that would ensure no more heartbreak. Financial stability. And being her own true self.

She wanted *not* to care about a certain rancher. Wanted *not* to think about him as often as she did. Wanted to convince herself that she was simply *in like* with Evan. Nothing deeper. Nothing stronger. After all, he was difficult not to like.

"You're going to erase the letters off those tiles if you keep this up much longer," Abby teased and tossed her empty wax-paper candy wrapper at Paige.

The wrapper never reached Paige. It landed intact on the table. Much the same way Paige hoped she returned home: composed, untroubled, and her heart untouched. Paige spelled a two-letter word; it was the best she could do with her mind wandering in so many directions.

"When is the trip to the Christmas tree farm?" Tess scribbled Abby's score on the scorepad.

"Tomorrow, but I'm not going." Paige collected more tiles. The less time she spent with Evan, the less risk to her heart. That was sensible. Preferable, in fact. "I need to stay with the puppies."

"But it's a Christmas first." The corners of Abby's mouth turned down. "Riley talks about the list you guys made together every time she sees Tess or me."

"You agreed to go." Tess arranged, then rearranged her tiles. "You can't disappoint Riley."

Yet Paige had never promised to go. And the Christmas firsts were for a dad and his daughter to share with each other. To make their own memories together. Paige would only be intruding.

Her gaze drifted into the kitchen. Riley sat on Evan's lap. Their heads pressed next to each other's, their attention fixed on the table. Evan moved their piece on the game board, then received a cheerful fist bump from Riley. The little girl snuggled in closer and rested her head on Evan's shoulder. Contentment was there in Riley's relaxed posture. Love was there in the soft kiss Evan pressed on Riley's forehead.

Paige touched her chest as if she could block her heart. Stop her sigh. Silence her wish. "Riley will understand. She knows the puppies can't be alone right now."

The puppies were currently curled up on Wes's lap. He was on the sofa in the family room. He'd used the extrasoft fleece blanket Riley had picked out yesterday at the ranch supply store to form a comfy nest for the pair. Boone sat beside Wes, his shoulder brushing against Wes's as he kept a vigilant eye on the slumbering puppies.

There had been a steady stream of caretakers for the puppies throughout the day. Ilene had taken the morning feedings, Sam had relieved her for lunch, followed by one of Evan's ranch hands in the afternoon, then Riley had returned from school and assisted Paige. The orphaned pups were quickly gaining quite the extended family. Much like Paige and she'd been in Three Springs only a week.

But this wasn't her home. Same for the puppies when they were old enough. And attachments only made goodbyes that much more difficult. Paige dropped her tiles on the board and tallied her score.

The snakes and ladders game concluded in the kitchen. Ilene and Sam cleaned off the kitchen table and moved to the sink and the night's dirty dishes.

"We won," Riley hollered, then covered her mouth. She pressed her finger over her lips and tiptoed to the couch and the puppies. "Sorry, Mr. Wes."

"I don't think there's much that startles these two little ones." Wes chuckled. Still his voice remained hushed. "But I need some help, Riley."

Riley climbed into the recliner and set the chair into a quick rocking motion. "What kind of help?"

"These two little ones need names." Boone smoothed his fingers over his beard. "Do you have any ideas? We seem to be all out of good ideas."

Evan walked in, carrying a paper plate. He stopped in front of the rocking chair. "Remember. One slice of orange for every bite of cookie."

"Got it." Riley crossed her legs and set the paper plate on her lap. "Dad, we need names for the puppies."

"Cookies and Cream. Ham and Cheese. Cocoa and Marshmallow." Evan rubbed his chin and looked around the room. "I can keep going. Fish and Chips. Salt and Pepper. Bubbles and Squeak."

"Dad. Stop." Riley tried to stop her belly laugh.

"I like Bubbles and Squeak." Evan turned to the group, his gaze searching for support.

And Paige liked Evan. She pressed her lips together. Names added another connection. A more personal one. Paige was already getting tangled in too many connections.

"Burger and Fry." Evan's voice lacked conviction. His optimism faded. "Milk and Cookie."

Riley's laughter rolled on, twisting through Paige. Her own smile worked free, and she joined in. "Chips and Salsa. Apple and Dumpling."

Evan nodded, his half smile tipped into his cheek. Appreciation flashed in his blue eyes.

Abby rubbed her pregnant belly. "What about Pea and Pod?"

Paige's focus lingered on Evan. "Hugs and Kisses."

Evan's gaze sharpened into interest. Curiosity crossed his face. Or perhaps that was simply Paige's own interest. Her own curiosity. Hugs and kisses and Evan shouldn't go together. Paige's pulse picked up. She pulled her focus away from Evan, afraid if he looked much closer, he'd see the truth. Paige wanted to know if she and Evan could fit together as easily and naturally as bacon and eggs.

Ilene stood in the archway and dried her hands on a towel. "What about something more Christmasy. Jingle and Holly."

"Those names have a nice ring." Sam sat on the arm of the couch.

"They are Christmas puppies," Boone added.

"Santa's special delivery." Sam touched his nose and winked at Riley.

"Dad, can I add to my wish list?" Riley rocked the recliner and kept her pleading eyes on Evan.

The little girl was hard to resist. Paige assumed Riley wanted to add keeping the puppies to her wish list. She'd asked Paige several times about how to change Evan's mind. She'd even presented reasons why they should keep the puppies forever. Paige could add a few wishes of her own to Riley's Santa list. But she'd planned a different future. In a different state. And her mind, like Evan's, had always been hard to change.

"What about our snack deal?" Evan held up his hand and wiggled two fingers. "That's two bites of cookie. And no bites of orange. No snack deal, no additions to your wish list."

"One slice clementine." Riley stuffed the entire orange slice into her mouth and grinned around her puffed-out cheeks.

Evan glanced toward the card table, revealing the smile he struggled to hide. Finally, he rolled his shoulders and looked at his daughter again. His laughter in check.

Riley picked up a gingerbread man cookie

and bit off his leg. She squirmed in the chair and chanted, "I like gingerbread. Dad likes gingerbread. We all like gingerbread."

"That's it. Riley, you're a genius." Evan snapped his fingers. Riley beamed. Evan added, "We'll call the brown puppy Ginger for gingerbread, a longtime family favorite."

Perhaps Evan's mind was already changing. He'd just claimed naming rights of the chocolate-colored puppy.

"And Clementine." Riley picked up another orange slice and danced it in the air over her plate.

"Ginger and Clementine." Wes picked up the cream-colored puppy and set her on his chest. "I like it. We can call her Tyne for short."

Riley handed her snack plate to Evan and slid off the rocker. She leaned on the couch cushion and stroked two of her fingers over the puppy ever so softly. Just the way Paige had shown her.

"Tyne is tinyyy." Riley kissed her pointer finger, then touched the top of Tyne's small head. Her soft voice was so earnest as she said, "The puppies should know they're loved. You gotta share a kiss until they're old enough to hug, right, Ms. Paige?"

Paige's heart swelled. For the precious child. For two rescued puppies. And their bond developing. She cleared her throat but not the watery sheen in her gaze. "That's right. Love helps them grow."

Riley kissed her finger again and touched Ginger's head. She climbed onto the couch beside Wes and leaned against him to keep her gaze on the puppies. The conversation shifted topics to another arrival for the horse sanctuary. Evan and Ilene disappeared in the kitchen.

"Wes and I can watch the puppies tomorrow." Abby's voice was low and tender.

Paige's attention skipped from the couch to her cousin. "The town tree lighting is this Saturday. I'm sure you have things you need to be doing other than puppy sitting."

"Believe it or not, I'm ready for the tree lighting, and all those unforeseen last-minute crises won't crop up until Saturday. That gives me tomorrow to cuddle with Tyne and Ginger and all that cuteness." Abby set her chin in her hand and tipped her head toward the couch. "Besides, I'm fairly certain it won't be hard to get Wes to agree."

"He spent more time with the puppies tonight than playing games." Tess grinned.

Wes was more than comfortable and confident with the puppies. Handling the dropper of milk replacement with ease and skill earlier that evening. Wes never flinched. Much like Evan last night. From weighing the pups to spot cleanings to two-hour feedings, Evan had remained beside Paige. Never impatient. Never critical. He'd supported and encouraged her in a way she hadn't experienced from someone outside her family. But that was Evan's nature. It hardly made her special.

Paige tightened her ponytail and that hold on her heart. "I'm not sure when we would get back. The tree farm is more than an hour's drive away and Wes has to work, doesn't he?"

"I'll relieve Wes in the afternoon." Tess's frank tone paired neatly with her sharp smile— the one she used whenever a decision wasn't up for debate. "After I close the store, I'll come here to help Abby, if you're not back."

"That works." Abby reached across the table and grabbed each of their arms. "Let's have a sleepover like when we were kids."

"Sleepover," Paige repeated.

"Yes." Abby gave each of their arms a little jostle. "Here with the puppies and the three of us."

"A girl's night." Tess nodded, her smile growing wider.

Abby tilted her head and watched Riley. "Paige, when was the last time you had a girl's night?"

"Riley and I had one two nights ago. Sort of." Paige fluttered her fingers over the table. "We painted nails and put on facial masks, ate popcorn and drank hot chocolate. Danced in our socks. And watched a fun movie about an ice queen and her sister."

Riley's head popped up over the couch. She rested her chin on her folded arms. "But Daddy was here. And he's a boy."

The room plunged into silence and everyone's attention shifted to Paige like a spotlight illuminating its mark. Paige squeezed the hard squares in her hand. Nothing slowed the heat pulsing beneath her cheeks.

"Don't you remember, Ms. Paige," Riley chattered on, not looking the least bit tired or distracted. "Dad brought you Grandma's special apple cider in her fancy drinking glasses."

A slow simmer of laughter spread around the room. That heat speared down Paige's neck to her chest. She saw Evan in the archway.

"I thought you liked Grandma's special apple cider." A line formed between Riley's eyebrows.

"I do very much," Paige reassured her. She very much didn't like the unspoken assumptions shifting around the room.

Riley straightened. Her nose wrinkled, shifting her freckles. "But Daddy didn't bring you any last night when he went back to see you."

Evan pushed away from the wall and finally

came to Paige's rescue. "Riley, you were supposed to be sleeping then."

"I forgot to brush my teeth." Riley lifted both arms and shrugged. "You told me I have to brush my teeth if I want to keep them. Except I can't keep these 'cause I have bigger ones coming."

"Right." Evan squeezed Riley's shoulders. "Good hygiene is important. Thanks for taking care of your teeth. Maybe you can do that and get right back in bed next time."

"Are you going over to Ms. Paige's tonight too?" Riley asked.

"That's enough of the questions." Evan swung Riley up into his arms and tucked her against his side. "I think it's past all of our bedtimes."

No one else made any move to leave. They kept their focus on Paige and Evan.

Paige started packing up the board game. "The puppies and I will be fine on our own tonight."

"Are you sure?" Worry widened Riley's eyes, and she rushed her words. "What if you fall asleep and one of 'em starts crying?"

"I'll wake up then." Paige closed the lid on the game box.

"One night I was crying and crying real bad and Daddy forgot to wake up." Riley frowned at Evan. "I had to go get him."

"What did he do?" Abby stood and set her hands against her lower back.

"He picked me up and told me, 'I got you. I'm not going anywhere.'" Riley wrapped her arms around Evan's neck and squeezed. "And I stopped crying just like that."

Paige imagined she'd stop sobbing too with words like that. To know she was heard. To know someone would stay beside her. That would be powerful. And mind changing. She was glad Riley had her father. The little girl would never question if she was truly loved for who she was. Paige said, "I'll tell Ginger and Tyne the same thing. I won't let them cry."

"But what happens if you start crying too." Looking alarmed, Riley leaned toward Paige.

Paige lost her voice. Forgot her words. How many times had Paige cried alone? Too many. And this precious child acted as if she knew Paige's secrets and wanted her to be safe.

Evan rubbed Riley's back and smiled quietly at Paige. "Then Ms. Paige will come and find me."

But would my heart be safe? What would I lose if I loved you?

Riley hugged her dad, then squirmed out of his arms. She wrapped Paige in one of her all-encompassing hugs. "Daddy says I can go to him whenever and he'll be there for me. No matter what time. Don't forget, Ms. Paige."

Paige embraced Riley and pressed a kiss on the top of her head. Everyone should know they were loved.

Riley worked the rest of the room, gathering sweet-dream wishes and good-night hugs from everyone. Finally, Evan carried Riley upstairs to her bed. Ilene passed out the leftover take-home bags. More hugs were shared. And too quickly, Paige found herself alone in the kitchen with the puppy box.

Evan returned and motioned to the dogs. "Are you sure you guys will be good?"

Paige slipped on her jacket. "I'll set my alarm for their feedings tonight. You should get some sleep."

"So should you." Evan picked up the puppy box and walked beside her to the guesthouse. They greeted Luna who was curled on her make-shift bed on the front porch. Now that the dog's eyes were healing, she preferred to spend her days and nights outside.

Inside, Paige turned on several lamps. Evan set the puppy box near the couch. As if he already knew Paige would sleep on the couch as close as she could to the puppies. She thanked him and showed him to the door.

He turned in the open doorway and faced her.

They stood no more than a candy cane distance apart.

"I know you're used to working nights in Chicago. And you can handle this alone." His intensely expressive eyes searched her face. "But if you need me for anything, I'm right next door. Tears or not, the door will be open."

What about your heart? Paige bit the side of her cheek and opted for the lighter side. "Even if I run out of peanut butter chocolates, I can come get you?"

"Yes." He reached up and freed her ponytail from inside the collar of her jacket. Her hair slid through his fingers. Her heart did a slow free fall. He cupped her cheek in his palm. "I'm here, Paige. For anything."

Something unlocked inside Paige and she understood. He meant what he said. There was no second-guessing. No underlying meaning. No innuendo she had to translate. She'd spent so many years deciphering and decoding her ex-boyfriend's every move and every word. But not Evan's.

She could go to him with anything. How could she not fall for someone like Evan?

Everyone should know they're loved. If Evan loved her, he would make sure she knew it. And if she loved him, would she still be alone? It wasn't a risk she was willing to take to find out. "Good night, Evan."

He pulled away, tucked his hands in his pockets and left.

If only a connection hadn't been made.

CHAPTER FIFTEEN

EVAN FOLLOWED PAIGE and Riley into the log cabin gift shop of Lenox Hill Tree Farm. The trees were loaded into the truck: one nine-foot white pine for the main house and a three-foot potted Leyland cypress for the guesthouse. And another Christmas first was checked off the list.

The debate about a tree in Riley's bedroom continued as it had during the hour-long drive to the Christmas tree farm. It had picked up again during the edible Christmas tree craft—a sugar ice cream cone coated in green-tinted frosting and topped with sprinkles—and during the cutting down of the tree. Riley hadn't relinquished her quest. But one more live tree was one more responsibility that Evan wanted to avoid. Riley had good intentions, but she was six and had an entire world to explore every morning. Evan imagined the tree would be barren and the needles littering the floor in her bedroom within a few days. Some Christmas firsts were more complicated than he'd anticipated.

Even now Riley spun from one display to another like a firefly attracted to the glitter and sparkle, sighing over an adorable knickknack or pretty souvenir. Every exclamation was followed by a version of *Can we get this, pretty please?*

"I think we should put up our ornaments first." Evan eased a glass bowl from Riley's hands and pointed to the look-but-don't-touch sign again. "After our tree is decorated, we can decide if we need more."

"But we should have more bells." Riley picked up a star-shaped ring with a large velvet bow and about a dozen red-and-white bells attached. She jingled the bells and laughed.

Paige touched the ribbon. "These hang on your doors and chime whenever they open and close."

"Like the bell at the Silver Penny." Riley hugged the bells against her chest and swayed to extend the jingle. "Can we get them, please?"

But their house wasn't a store. Customers didn't need to be announced. Evan picked up a palm-sized log reindeer, its legs and antlers handcrafted out of sticks, its body a scrap of round wood. "This is cute." And even better, noise-free.

Paige picked up the reindeer by its hook. "This looks like something my grandma Opal once made."

"Then you should get it." Riley clutched the bells. "To remember her. You can put it on your tree."

Paige's stormy gaze skipped from Riley to Evan and held. And in the deep depths he realized the truth. Paige had agreed to get a living tree for the guesthouse, but she'd never planned to decorate it. Never planned to make it her own. That shouldn't bother him. He'd agreed to plant the tree after she'd left. Ornaments, tinsel and lights would only have to be removed. That was just more work for him. He should be pleased Paige was saving him time. If Paige didn't want to fully participate in Christmas and make new memories, that shouldn't bother him either.

Paige hung the reindeer back on the artificial tree and moved down another aisle.

"Don't you want to remember your grandma?" Riley trailed after Paige. The bells chimed softly around the pair.

"Definitely." Paige stopped and ran her fingers over a snow globe, framed by gumdrops and cupcakes. A ballerina twirled inside the glass globe, her wand scattering glittery snow over cheerful, cuddly woodland animals. Paige added, "I think about my grandmother every day."

Evan hovered near the aisle that resembled the life-size version of the candy board game they'd played the other night. Everything on display was gumdrop colored, oversize and twinkling. A fluffy fake snow flocked most of the items from the waist-high lollipop yard decorations to the pretend peppermint garland to the ceramic gingerbread houses. It was the happiest aisle in the log cabin. But Paige looked as if she was immune to the bright colors and the inevitable sugar rush for the eyes.

Riley reverently touched the peppermint candy tree trimming and peered at Paige. "I think about Christmas every day."

And Evan thought about Paige every day. And every night. Now he'd also think about her being in the guesthouse and then back in Chicago, alone and avoiding the holiday. And something cloying like regret and concern for her made his heart ache.

Paige trailed her fingertips over the smaller collection of snow globes. "My dad told my sister and me that we should always leave a piece of Christmas out."

"Why?" Riley pushed her star door hanger onto her arm, sliding it up to her elbow.

"So when you see it, you feel the joy of Christmas again in your heart." Paige placed her palm over her chest. "Then you spread that feeling to others throughout the year."

She had to allow the joy in first. Yet that

wasn't his problem. He wasn't a holiday fixer. He was a rancher. One with a houseguest who was leaving very soon. If his houseguest wasn't happy, that wasn't his concern, either. He'd given Paige a comfortable cottage to call her own for her stay. He was grateful for her assistance on the ranch. Even more thankful now that his sick stock were improving daily. That was as much as he could care about Paige. Anything more threatened that time-out on love Paige and he had both agreed they'd taken.

"Can I keep something out?" Riley's fingers smoothed over the red ribbon on a bell door hanger. "Daddy puts all our stuff in the attic, but I don't get to go in there because it's not safe."

"One thing." Evan held up one finger. "But only one Christmas thing."

Riley chewed on her lip. "What do you keep out, Ms. Paige?"

"When I was your age, I kept out a snow globe my grandmother gave me." Paige shook one of the smaller snow globes, setting the snow swirling around a jolly snowman framed in purple-and-pale-green candy canes. She handed it to Riley. "There was a Christmas tree with the prettiest, brightest star on top guiding all the friends of the forest together. Bears, owls, racoons, deer gathered around the tree to decorate and celebrate."

Riley lightly shook the snow globe. "Was there snow inside?"

"So much." Paige smiled. Her voice was unguarded. "I used to think the animals wished on that star every time I shook it."

He imagined a young Paige had wished on that same star. He wanted to know what she'd wished for. Had her wishes come true? Evan's gaze locked on Paige. "What do you keep out now?"

"Nothing." The cheerful memory faded from her gaze. Melancholy tinted her eyes, making them a faded brown color like a fallen autumn leaf. "It seems I've forgotten my dad's own tradition."

"You should keep something out." Riley handed the snow globe back to Paige. "Then you'll be happy again too."

Riley always wished for those she loved to be happy. And Paige had apparently become one of those people. Evan massaged the back of his neck. Riley was simply too young not to allow her heart to get tangled up with Paige. But Evan could establish a hard stop for himself.

"That's a really good idea." Paige set the snow globe on the shelf and shifted her attention back to Riley. "What are you thinking about keeping out?"

Evan wanted to raise his hand. Admit he was

keeping out all of his suddenly tangled feelings for Paige. Leaving them alone and unexamined.

"The tree in my room." Riley lifted her arms. The bells on the door hanger chimed even louder.

He had to give his daughter credit for her tenacity. She wasn't one to give up easily. A skill that would serve her well in life. Except sometimes it was better to let go. Like he would let go of Paige and anything he might feel for her. "I'm not sure that's a good idea. The tree might like to be outside in the ground, spreading its roots and growing bigger. It can't do that in your bedroom."

"I could water it." Riley shifted from one boot to the other. "Sing to it like Grandma sings to her garden."

Evan searched for something to distract Riley. To turn his daughter's attention away from having her own tree. His gaze landed on Paige again like it always seemed to do. As if Paige was the answer. And the one they were meant to have in their lives.

"What if you got an artificial tree like this one." Paige touched the branch of a tabletop, flocked, prelit tree. "Then you could decorate it all year. Eggs for Easter. Flags for the Fourth of July."

"What about that one?" Riley pointed to a purple tree on a higher shelf and grinned. "It's my favorite color in the whole world. Just like my daddy is my favorite."

Evan wanted to hug Paige. Thank her for the sensible solution. And hold her even longer because he wanted to. Because he wanted to know if he could make her happy. Evan stilled and backed away from Paige and his thoughts.

Paige looked to Evan and whispered, "She's good."

"Too good, I'm afraid." Evan looked for an available salesperson and a quick escape.

A few minutes later, Riley set the boxed purple tree on the back seat of the truck, shut the truck door and clapped her hands. "Time for the hayride."

Riley joined the other kids gathered near the front of the wagon, closer to Santa, who drove the tractor pulling the wagon. Santa gave a hearty welcome and launched into a story about Rudolph's adventure in the North Pole yesterday.

Evan dropped a fleece blanket over Paige's lap and settled on the hay bale beside her. He gave in to his curiosity rather than his urge to wrap his arm around her waist and tuck her into his side. "Whatever happened to your snow globe?"

"My ex accidentally broke it." Paige slipped her hands under the blanket.

Better for Evan. Now he wouldn't want to hold

her hand too. "You don't sound like you believe it was an accident."

"Kyle had a certain way he preferred things. An image he liked to present." Paige's brow creased. Her tone was brittle around the edges. "Handmade blankets and sentimental trinkets didn't go well with his aesthetic."

"But he must have known what the snow globe meant to you." Evan had his father's beechwood-handle pocketknife, cowboy hat collection and old guitar displayed in his home office. Every time he looked at the framed family photographs or touched the strings on his dad's guitar, he was reminded of all the things his dad was. All the things his dad had instilled in him.

"I'm not sure that mattered to him." Paige adjusted the blanket, tugging it farther up her lap. "I should reword that. What mattered to me didn't matter to Kyle."

"That's…" Evan started to say and stopped.

"Not how relationships are supposed to work," Paige finished for him.

"I was left at the altar." Evan shifted on the hay bale, seeking a more comfortable position. "I'm hardly an authority on how relationships are supposed to work."

Paige shifted toward him, and her knee knocked against his. "But you know what you don't want in your next one, right?"

"I do." Evan nodded. He knew he wanted someone who would be there through the ups and downs and every stage in between. He wanted someone willing and ready to stand beside him. To fight for the life they shared and wanted to build. That's what he'd want if he was looking for someone. He kept his gaze fixed on the passing rows of Virginia pine trees and not on Paige. "How about you?"

"I have a very clear idea of what I'm not looking for." Her voice was steady against the rocking of the wagon.

"What's that?" he asked.

"The usual." She shrugged. "A little less jealousy. Less negativity. Fewer criticisms."

There was nothing usual about her list. Usual would've been a less party-focused partner. Or a less selfish boyfriend. Or a less messy apartment. Evan rolled a piece of hay between his palms. "I take it your ex was all those things."

"And more." She glanced at him. "Not at the beginning, though. Or maybe I just didn't want to see it."

"I get that." There were things he hadn't wanted to see with Marla. Evan smashed the hay between his palms and watched another row of Virginia pines roll by. "Love makes you blind."

"At the very least, love lets you overlook the warning signs and step around the caution flags." Paige shook her head as if clearing her thoughts. "I kept thinking if I was more. If I loved harder, stronger, better even, then the criticisms, the negativity would stop eventually."

"If you loved enough for both of you, then you'd both be happier." There was that word again. *Happy*. He was beginning to wonder if it was even attainable. Content, definitely. But truly, definitively happy. Could that ever be reached? The wagon rocked and swayed. His knee brushed against Paige's. There had been moments this past week with Paige when he'd been...

"But you can't love someone happy." Paige's voice was monotone. Yet her candid, turbulent gaze was far from neutral. "If they're miserable at their core, you can't ever fix that. And your love will never be enough."

If he wrapped Paige in his embrace and told her she was enough, would she believe him? If he wrapped Paige in his arms, he'd want her to stick. He'd forget their time together was only ever supposed to be brief. Evan tossed the piece of straw on the wagon bed. "I couldn't change Marla either."

His ex might not ever be the parent Evan wanted her to be. He had to accept that and help his daughter understand. He was determined that his love would be enough for two parents. What was left of his heart belonged to Riley. There just wasn't room for more.

"Rather than fix someone else, I'm concentrating on myself." Resolve pushed through Paige's words. "It's why I'm so focused on my career. It's what matters the most to me. My trial period at the clinic is ending and I'm under consideration to become a partner."

The wagon hit a bump and bounced Paige into his side. She straightened away from him. One more pothole. One more wobble. Evan gave in and wrapped his arm around her waist and anchored her against his side. The restlessness inside his chest subsided. "Why haven't you opened your own practice?"

"That was something Kyle promised we'd do together after we married." She draped part of the blanket over Evan's lap. "He knew it was my dream. But the timing was never right. I had student debt to pay off. Then we had a wedding to plan."

"He used the practice like bait." Evan frowned.

Her hand stilled on the blanket. "How did you know?"

He tipped his head toward his daughter. "I always wanted children. A large family. Maybe because I'm an only child. Marla knew that."

"Did she get pregnant on purpose?" Paige leaned back to look at him.

"She would deny it." Evan gently held Paige in place. "But I think Marla thought she could use our child to get me to do what she wanted."

"That's cold." Paige shivered.

"Ironic really." He ran his hand up and down Paige's arm. "I thought our child would get Marla to change for the better. Turn her into someone she isn't. Instead, we doubled down, and any chance of a compromise evaporated."

"There was never any compromise with Kyle," Paige said. "When I broke off our engagement and walked out, he had me removed from our joint bank account and cut me off. If I apologized and came back, all would be forgiven and return to normal."

"That's not right." Anger arced through him. "You would have what rightfully belonged to you and a relationship you didn't want."

"What's important to Kyle is control," she said. "I refused to give mine to him. I moved into a small town house and began rebuilding my life."

"What happens when you become an equal partner?" he asked.

"I'll have a voice in the management of the clinic," she said. "I'll be able to have more of an impact on how we treat our patients and employees."

"You don't have that now?" He was confused and couldn't stop it from slipping into his words.

"It's a little bit complicated." She stiffened beside him.

The strain in her voice confirmed that it was more than a little complicated. Evan kept his gaze fixed on the trees and waited.

"I left Kyle, but I didn't get far. Kyle is also a well-respected veterinarian in the city. We work at the same clinic."

The wagon swayed again. Evan braced his cowboy boots on the floor, steadying himself and Paige. "I'm guessing he's a partner already."

"Yes." Paige brushed the blanket against her cheek as if warming her face. "Two weeks ago, we argued about the treatment of a patient. He wanted invasive, immediate surgery. I proposed a different approach, questioned him in front of staff and the patient's owners. It got ugly quickly."

She'd stood up to him. From what she'd described of her ex, he doubted Kyle appreciated that very much. The words sounded grim even to himself. "What happened?"

"We were put on administrative leave for a two-week cooling-off period." She brushed a stray lock of hair off her face. "On my way out the door, I gave them an ultimatum. I wanted to be made an equal partner or I was taking my patients and most of the staff with me to my own practice."

Her courage impressed him. "Can you do that?"

"In a few years, maybe. I need to save up more money. Take out a business loan," she explained. "It's not that simple to start a practice. Kyle had the funding we would've needed. I have the reputation. And I just wanted the other partners to finally see me and the value I bring."

"So, the cooling period ends, and you go back to work," he said. Back to the city. Back to her life. And out of his. Evan anchored his arm around her.

"I have a meeting with the other partners three days before Christmas." She sat up. "I'll see if they took my threat seriously. If they take me seriously. It's all I've wanted. All I have been working for the past two years."

There was power in being treated like an equal. She hadn't had that in her relationship. Heck, he hadn't had that with Marla either. But he had the ranch to pour himself into and his family. Paige was alone in the city. "What about Kyle? What will he do?"

"You're thinking he might have me fired." She never hesitated. Never flinched. "Kyle has been asking me to come back. Give our relationship another chance. About a month ago, he told me it'd been long enough. He'd given me plenty of space to get over myself and his patience was wearing thin."

"Did he threaten you?" Evan was ready to defend her at any cost. Although, Paige wasn't his to protect, even if he wanted to.

"Kyle is more subtle than that."

"If he gets you fired, you'll have no job and no place to go," he said.

"Don't forget my reputation will be stained. Then suddenly Kyle becomes the one place I can go. He'll offer to rebuild my reputation and promise we'll open our own practice." She exhaled, long and deep, then looked at Evan. Her gaze guarded. "Yes, I've already considered that might be Kyle's plan."

"But you don't think he'll do that?" Evan guessed.

"Kyle will do anything to protect Kyle, right or wrong." Paige rubbed her hands together as if she were still cold.

"Firing you could potentially look bad on him." Evan stubbed the toe of his boot in the hay on the floor of the wagon. It didn't nudge his curiosity aside. "Why haven't you left? Gone to work at another clinic?"

"Because I helped build this clinic into what it is. One of the premier animal hospitals in the city." Pride strengthened her words. "I've invested my time and my heart into that place. It's home to me. It matters to me. That probably doesn't make a lot of sense."

She was mistaken. He'd done the very same. "It makes a lot of sense to me. My heart is invested in the ranch. I couldn't just walk away from that." Not for Marla. Not for anyone. He had to respect Paige for her conviction and her loyalty. Qualities he admired. If only they weren't the very reasons tying her to a city more than a thousand miles away from him.

"What can I do?" *How could I convince you to stay?*

"You just did something." Her surprised gaze settled on him.

"What's that?" He hadn't given her one good reason to stay.

"You listened." The sincerity in her words rang clear. "I haven't told anyone the truth."

Surprise filtered through him. "Not even Tess or Abby?"

Paige shook her head. "They think I'm here for a vacation."

"They should know what's happening. They care about you. But you don't have to go back," he said. *You could…* He flatlined that thought. Offering his heart and love, none of that was on the table. And not a part of his dreams or hers.

"Just promise me that you'll be careful when you go home."

"I will be." She nudged her shoulder against his. "You don't have to worry about me."

He didn't have to, but he would. Now, tomorrow and he feared for a long time to come. He could tell himself to stop caring about her, but he feared a part of him—a very large part—wouldn't listen.

CHAPTER SIXTEEN

PAIGE GREETED EVAN as he carried the potted Leyland cypress to a spot in front of the window near the recliner. He grinned at Tess and Abby, then peeked at Ginger and Tyne sleeping in their puppy box. "I'm off to put up our tree and leave you ladies to your sleepover puppy party."

Evan's arm brushed against hers. She would've been content staying on that hayride for the rest of the day and talking to Evan. He listened to her. Never judged. "Thanks for today. I had fun."

Evan linked their fingers together. "Thanks for trusting me."

She did trust him. And suddenly she wanted to hold on longer. Keep him beside her. She may have opened up to him about her life, but she hadn't opened her heart. She knew better than that. "I'll see you in the morning."

He squeezed her hand. "Your secrets are safe with me."

I want my heart to be safe with you too. She loosened her grip and let his hand slip free. "Night, Evan."

She shut the door before she wished him something silly like sweet dreams, or did something foolish like kiss him.

"How was your day?" Tess stirred a pot of hot chocolate on the stove.

Truthful. Honest. Eye-opening. Everything she would've wanted in a first date with Evan. But it was a Christmas-first outing, not a date. The word chased through her. She worked to keep her voice from sounding frazzled. "Busy. There were arts and crafts, hayrides, great food booths to sample. And of course, choosing and cutting down the best Christmas tree."

"You picked out a perfect one for this room." Abby peeked one more time at the puppies and joined them in the kitchen. "I've got lights for the tree and everything to make our own garland. It's going to look really special."

Paige forced herself to smile. A special tree would only remind her of the special day she'd spent with Evan and Riley. And it wasn't supposed to be anything more than an outing. An item to check off their list. Now it was almost a date. Almost something special.

"I brought our favorite sleepover snacks." Tess tapped the spoon against the pot.

"Please tell me you brought your homemade marshmallows." Paige lifted her eyebrows, her voice hopeful. If she splurged on marshmallows, she could blame the sugar for the fluttery sensation in her stomach, not Evan and labels like dates and good-night kisses.

"They're in the container." Tess aimed the spoon at a holiday striped tin.

"Paige, you need to change into your pajamas." Abby pointed to her feet and wiggled her toes in her thick fuzzy socks. "Then we can get the sleepover part of this shindig started."

Paige sneaked a marshmallow from the tin. Any minute those butterflies would still and thoughts about a second date with Evan would cease. "I'll be right back."

Upstairs, the blue, red and green lights twinkled around the bedroom window frame, illuminating the paper snowflakes Riley had insisted Paige hang up there. She looked out at the main house. Wondered what ornaments Riley would hang first.

The exhausted little girl had slept the entire drive back to Three Springs, but woken up in the driveway, refreshed, reenergized and ready to decorate their tree. Riley had wanted Paige to help put the star on the top of the tree. Paige hadn't wanted to intrude on their family tradition. She'd already unloaded too much on Evan.

Yet he'd acted as if he could've handled more of her company. He'd been engaged, at times angry on her behalf and constantly supportive.

He would've been what she wanted in a boyfriend, in a partner, if she'd wanted a relationship.

Paige turned away from the window and grabbed her flannel pajama pants and sweatshirt. Her time left in Three Springs was limited. She needed to spend as much of it with the people who mattered the most: Tess and Abby.

In the hallway, she glanced again at the decorated window, then went downstairs, determined not to let Evan matter more than he already did. But every hour that brought her closer to leaving Three Springs, her goodbye loomed larger. And her dread increased.

Everything she wanted was in Chicago. Everything she'd worked for was there. She couldn't turn her back on all that. Not for her heart. What if her heart was wrong? Like before.

Paige checked the puppies, ensuring they were warm and comfortable. Then she inhaled and pushed her shoulders back. She had to leave. She'd known that all along. And Evan had to stay here, along with any of her wishes for another date. Or something more.

But there were two people waiting for her that she would not turn her back on. Not leave on the fringe. Not anymore. And she could thank Evan for that. Talking to him gave her the courage she needed now.

If she'd learned anything from her time at Crescent Canyon and from Evan, it was the importance of family.

"You're back." Abby set two boxes of lights on the counter. "I wasn't sure if you wanted all white lights or colored ones. I brought both."

Paige wasn't sure how to begin.

Tess poured hot chocolate into three mugs and added large dollops of whipped cream. "White lights are timeless. Elegant."

"I agree, but never mind the lights right now. I have a confession." Paige moved into the kitchen, closer to Abby and Tess. "And I'll go first because I want us to be like we were when we were kids. We didn't keep secrets from each other—we shared them. We didn't lock each other out, but I feel like we have been for a while."

Abby set the garland-making supplies on the island.

Tess put down her spoon, her movements slow and precise.

Paige told herself to be brave. She had a foundation to build and trust to offer. "These are my truths. They aren't pretty, they're complicated and messy, but there are important things you should know."

Abby blurted, "Wait. We need to sit for this. I can feel it."

Tess handed out the mugs of hot chocolate

and the trio headed into the living room. Paige sat on the recliner and tucked her feet up under her. Abby lowered onto one side of the couch and propped her feet on a pillow on the coffee table. Tess curled into the other side of the couch and kept her fingers tightly wrapped around her mug. It was the only clue to her tension.

"I'm not here on vacation." Paige sipped her hot chocolate. The rich, creamy texture and melted-chocolate-bar taste had her checking the kitchen for Grandma Opal. Their grandmother would've been disappointed in them. She would have encouraged Paige to fix things. Paige lifted her mug in a silent toast to her grandmother and continued, "I was put on admin leave earlier this month for two weeks. The partners called it a cooling-off period. Kyle and I got into an argument in front of staff and a patient's owners. It was loud and pretty nasty. And I threw down a challenge when I left."

Abby's hands stilled on her belly. Her cousin's surprised gaze slanted toward Tess. Paige's sister remained statue still. Only the slightest of creases dented her skin between her eyebrows.

Paige exhaled and launched into those truths about her relationship and broken engagement to Kyle Lawson and detailed Kyle's shift from criticizing her in their personal lives to doing the same at work. Explained her most recent refusal to get back together with Kyle. Then finished with her ultimatum to the partners, which was more bluster than anything and could potentially end with her being out of a job. She shared as much as she could. Some scars were her own and those she would keep for herself.

The tick of the mantel clock broadcast the lengthy silence. Seconds turned into minutes as her sister and cousin absorbed and processed. Paige went into the kitchen for more marshmallows and a refill. Confessing had switched on her sweet tooth.

Or perhaps it was that she'd shared with Evan first, worked through her fears beside him on the hay bale. Under a blanket, she'd hid her shaking hands and worry that he'd think less of her. But he'd tucked her into his side and listened. Such a gift. And now, she didn't want to hide anymore, especially not with her own family.

She returned to them, set the marshmallow container on the coffee table and sat in the recliner.

Tess swallowed a mouthful of her hot chocolate and set her empty cup on the table. "Why didn't you ever say anything?"

"I didn't want to be a burden." Paige lifted her legs and wrapped her arms around her raised knees. "Or a bother. I don't want to be that, either."

"You're still doing it." Accusation and awe mixed in Tess's startled expression.

"Doing what?" Paige asked in a strangled voice.

"Going along." Tess settled her earnest gaze on Paige. "Not giving your problems and your emotions a voice as if they aren't as important as someone else's. As if they don't matter as much as someone else's."

Paige pushed herself farther into the recliner, as if the smaller she made herself, the less of a target she was for Tess's accusations.

Tess shifted her focus to Abby. "After our dad died, Paige never made another fuss. It was like she believed she belonged in the background. Paige became the easiest child. The go-along-and-get-along kid. Always respectful, always quiet and never disagreeable."

"Mom had so much to deal with," Paige argued. Their mother had worked two jobs, battled her grief and, Paige suspected, guilt and regret too, while raising two young daughters. "So did Grandma and Grandpa helping us."

No doubt their grandparents had suffered from the same grief, guilt and regret combination—they'd lost their only son after all. Paige had worked hard to be the kind of daughter her mother needed. The kind that wouldn't cause any additional stress or worry at school or at home.

And if it meant she'd tucked away an opinion or her feelings at times, she'd never minded. Her family had been her world and she would have done anything not to see it upended again.

"Your ex took advantage of you." Abby picked a marshmallow out of the container and eyed Paige. "You know that, right?"

Paige dropped her gaze to the puppy box. How many times had she chosen to keep silent to maintain the peace with Kyle? How many times had she gone along to avoid a confrontation? That had been her default. As second nature to her as petting a dog or cuddling a cat.

"And I suspect work takes advantage of you as well." Tess's words were like chunks of ice. "Work was your escape."

Paige shivered. She hadn't hidden as much as she thought from her sister or her sister still knew her better than anyone.

Tess continued, "But they realized you were not only really talented and qualified, you were also always available and always ready to step in. Always willing to lend a hand. So, you became the one everyone at work turns to first. And you've convinced yourself it's part of your job to be indispensable, never say no and never complain."

"That's exhausting." Abby dropped her head back on the couch.

It wasn't wrong to be good at her work. Competent and well respected by her peers. But Paige couldn't deny she was tired. A bone-deep exhaustion had weighed her down the past year. She blamed her constant need to prove her personal life hadn't interfered with her professional one. That she could and would rise above Kyle's petty behavior for the good of a company she'd invested so much of herself in. She set her head on her knees and stared at the sleeping puppies.

All she'd ever wanted to do was care for and treat animals. When had that gotten lost in ownership percentages and partnerships and control?

"You don't have to go back." Tess looked her in the eye. "Stay here. Start over here. With us."

"I have to go back." Paige unfolded from the recliner and stretched her legs out as if preparing to test her footing. "I've spent the past decade building my life in the city and becoming an equal partner." Then eventually, perhaps, when the time was right and everything aligned, she'd step out on her own.

All her hard work couldn't have been for nothing. She had no relationship to hold on to. But she had a career she was proud of. She couldn't lose that. What would she have left then? Who would she be? Her future had always been clear in Chicago. It was where she belonged.

Abby set her hand on her pregnant belly and

offered Paige a supportive smile. "Take it from me—you won't be able to move forward until you've put the past behind you."

But this wasn't about her past. Didn't they understand it was about securing her future?

"If the life you want is in the city, then you should have it. I want you to have everything you ever dreamed." Tess took a long sip of her hot chocolate, then nodded at Paige. "I'm just worried about you. That's my right as your sister."

"And mine too, as your cousin." Abby tapped her mug against Tess's. "We'll worry less if you stay here with us."

"It's not a bad idea." Tess grinned and tipped her head. "It could be possible there's a different path in your future."

"One with a certain rancher." Abby wiggled her eyebrows up and down.

Those butterflies flapped in her stomach. Paige grabbed another marshmallow and took a big bite. "I'm helping Evan with his cattle."

"And staying in his guesthouse," Abby added. "Which is charming and quaint and perfectly lovely."

"I really like it too." Tess nodded. "This place suits you. You're more relaxed here."

Being with Evan suited her too. Paige swished her finger back and forth between her cousin and sister. "I know what you two are doing."

"What's that exactly?" Abby hid her grin behind her mug.

"Trying to matchmake," Paige accused. "But it won't work, so you can give up."

"Why won't it work?" Tess dunked a marshmallow in her mug.

"Well, there's the obvious. We live in different states." Paige pushed out of the recliner, added another log to the fire and hovered over the puppy box. The duo was nestled tightly together. For warmth. Security. Each calming the other. The pair would need to be adopted by the same owner. Separating them would be too traumatic. It was obvious they belonged together. Just as it was obvious Paige and Evan did not. Love was required for a relationship and she wasn't about to let her heart derail her again. "And he has a daughter."

"Who seems to adore you," Abby countered.

And who Paige adored. "You know what I'm saying."

Abby and Tess stared at Paige, quiet and composed as if they were waiting for an explanation.

"Neither one of us is looking for a relationship or love," Paige proclaimed and held her arms wide as if she was an open book. "So, there's nothing more to discuss."

"Except when you aren't looking for love,

that's the exact time it finds you," Abby countered.

Paige set her hands on her hips and studied her cousin. "You sound exactly like Grandma Opal."

"That's the best compliment I've received in a while." Abby's smile notched into radiant. "Thank you for that."

"You're welcome." Paige clasped her hands together and latched on to a distraction. Those butterflies had gone from mild flaps to a flurry of flutters. No more talk about love. Or relationships. Or Evan. "Now, can someone assure me that we aren't too old to have cookie popcorn."

"No sleepover would be complete without our cookie popcorn." Abby held her hand out to Paige for an assist getting off the couch. "We should make some right now."

"Do you think it's as good as we thought it was as kids?" Tess rose.

"I bet it's even better." Paige linked her arm with Abby's. The evening was turning out better than she could have imagined. "Maybe we can skip tinting it blue."

"I remember having blue fingers for days." Abby laughed.

"I'll melt the marshmallows." Tess took out a pot. "You guys get the popcorn going and the cookies chopped."

They debated which cookies to add, then

agreed to add a little bit of every kind. Their popcorn concoction finished and water glasses filled to dilute the sugar rush, they returned to the living room. Puppies checked on, the fire stoked, they settled back in.

"Eric and I had a white-and-gold Christmas tree." Tess tucked her feet under her and set her bowl of cookie popcorn beside her. Her gaze shifted from the fire to Paige. Humor and sadness swirled in the depths of her sister's eyes. Tess added, "He loved it. I hated it."

Paige dropped her handful of popcorn back in the bowl. She whispered, not wanting to push Tess too far, "What did you do?"

"I went out and bought another one." Tess popped a handful of the salty-sweet snack in her mouth and grinned. Her laughter sputtered out slowly. "Set it up right beside his in our family room."

Paige stood, flopped down on the couch between her cousin and sister. Easier to share her bowl of popcorn and she suddenly needed to be closer to her family. "This is absolutely a story I need to hear."

Abby spread a blanket over their laps and smiled. "I need to hear this too."

And just like that, over a shared bowl of cookie popcorn, their connection was restored. One story led to another and another. Fears, wishes and dreams were woven into the evening. They leaned on each other, supported and encouraged.

And for the first time in a long while, Paige felt like herself. She had her family and Evan to thank for it.

CHAPTER SEVENTEEN

THE NEXT MORNING, Paige jacked up the volume on the music app on her phone and set the coffeepot to brew. She was singing about it being a swell time for a jingle bell rock when Abby padded into the kitchen.

Abby's bun was lopsided on her head and her sleep-filled eyes were barely open. "Are you singing a Christmas song?"

"And dancing in my socks too." Paige wiggled her hips.

Paige had woken up smiling. Excited for the day. She couldn't remember the last time she'd rushed out of bed other than for an emergency at the clinic, but today wasn't about that. It was about checking on the last few sick cattle, viewing Riley's Christmas tree and embracing whatever fun she could find. Paige joined in for the last chorus of "Jingle Bell Rock" and they ended the tune in an exaggerated pose, complete with jazz hands.

Abby stared into her empty mug, then filled it with water and set it in the microwave to heat.

She sorted through the herbal teas in the mason jar. "It's too early and I'm too pregnant for this. Oh, how I miss caffeine right now."

"I've been up for an hour, researching those herbs in Grandma's wreath ornaments." Paige had also fed the puppies and visited Luna for a quick check of her healing eyes. She'd then welcomed Luna inside to meet the pups, but that was their secret. Luna's motherly instincts had kicked in. The gentle guard dog would look after the puppies when Paige left. But today wasn't about leaving and goodbyes.

Paige took the creamer from the fridge and set it on the counter beside her laptop. "I think I have the herbs figured out."

"I'd like to figure out how the woman who slept on the couch has the most energy this morning." Tess headed straight for the coffeepot and stared at it as if willing the machine to brew faster.

Paige had given the queen bed to Abby and Tess last night. She'd been sleeping on the older couch beside the puppies for the past few nights anyway. She'd learned the exact positions to avoid unwanted muscle kinks in the morning and springs in the spine during the night. "What's on the agenda today? We've got a tree lighting in the square this evening. What else?"

Tess leaned against the counter. "Was there special air at the tree farm yesterday?"

"Seriously." Abby fluttered her hand toward Paige and opened a ginger lemon tea bag. "You haven't been this...this whatever this new you is since, well, since you were a kid, I think."

"I feel like I woke up in my own skin today." Paige hugged herself. "And it feels really good. I'm not distracted or preoccupied. I'm feeling present. Does that make sense?"

"It will once I have coffee." Tess drummed her fingers on the counter beside the coffee machine.

"It's a really slow drip." Paige laughed at her sister's grouchy expression and shrugged. "Good things take time." Perhaps that was the same for Paige. She'd just needed time to reach her good place.

The coffeepot sputtered and beeped. Tess heaved a long sigh of relief, filled two mugs and handed one to Paige.

"Wait." Abby held up her hand and lifted Paige's coffee mug to her nose. She inhaled deeply. "I'd know that scent anywhere. That's Wes's special blend coffee."

Paige grinned over the rim. "Wes shared a bag with me."

"How did you manage that?" Abby dropped the tea bag into her cup of hot water. "Wes never shares his coffee blend with anyone."

"I told him it was for our challenge. We've turned it into a bet." Paige sipped her coffee and savored the full-bodied flavor of caramelized brown sugar, spicy cloves and nuts. Was it hazelnut? She sipped again. "I haven't given up. I fully intend to keep blending coffee beans at home until I get this exact flavor."

"Let's not talk about you going home." Abby frowned into her tea mug.

Tess nodded. "Let's enjoy today."

And remain present in the moment. Paige clinked her mug against theirs. "I'm so glad I'm here. Now, what's our plan today?"

"I don't have to be at the town square until noon." Abby fixed her bun and positioned it on the top of her head. "It's barely past sunrise. That would give us time to bake."

Paige hadn't baked more than banana muffins for the staff at the clinic recently. Kyle had a distaste for sugar. Which should've been a warning sign to Paige's sweet tooth. And now that she lived alone, baking for one hardly seemed fun. "What do you have in mind?"

"We could use more donations for the cookie swap tonight at the tree lighting." Abby shrugged. "You've both been busy with the store, sick puppies and cattle. I didn't want to add any pressure."

"Never too busy for family." Paige shifted her

gaze between her sister and cousin. The two women smiled and nodded. Tess added, "Family first."

Paige rubbed her hands together. "How many do we need to make?"

"As many as we can." Abby sounded hopeful.

"So we need a kitchen big enough to make several dozen cookies." Tess glanced around the small cottage kitchen and winced.

"This one won't do." Paige pointed outside. "But Ilene has one right next door. Let's get dressed and get baking."

"I bet Ilene has cookie cutters and everything we need to make the stained-glass cookies like Grandma Opal's." Abby walked toward the stairs. "Grandma always let me crush one hard candy and eat one candy at the same time."

"I always liked Grandma's peppermint-cream patties and caramel-nougat-pecan rolls." Tess carried her coffee with her upstairs. "When we made those, she taught me how to use a candy thermometer and temper chocolate. I was hooked after the first batch."

"My favorite were her cutout sugar cookies." Paige headed into the bedroom to her open suitcase. "She had the reindeer cookie cutters and the one small reindeer cookie always ended up with a broken leg. We'd make a cast out of frosting every year."

Her grandmother had always encouraged her. No matter whether it was casting a broken cookie leg, making ornaments, or helping her rescue an injured animal on the side of the road. She missed her every day. Yet somehow the loss was less sharp and remembering her grandparents brought more peace, not pain.

"I bet Grandma's cookie cutters are in the basement of the general store." Abby unzipped her overnight bag. "With her measuring spoon collection and the silver coin."

"We'll find everything when it's time." Tess touched Abby's shoulder, her smile understanding.

"Grandma would tell us not to give up. Palmers never give up." Paige waved her hands in a sweeping motion toward her sister and cousin. "Now, come on. Hurry up. These cookies aren't going to bake themselves."

With their coffee and teacups refilled, the trio walked over to the main house. Their laughter swept out in every direction, dancing on the cool morning air. The back door opened before Paige could knock.

Ilene stood before them, a neon pink apron tied around her waist. She allowed entry only after a morning hug for each of them. "I was just about to come over and invite you to breakfast."

"Are those waffles?" Abby touched her stomach and grinned. "The baby and I both seem to have a weakness for waffles."

"And there's French toast." Ilene motioned to the platters set out on the island. "Fresh whipped cream and fruit. Help yourself."

They were seated at the kitchen table, plates filled in front of them, before Paige could even protest. Not that she'd considered protesting. The breakfast bouquet of aromas smelled too good and tasted even better. Paige swirled a bite of her French toast in the warm maple syrup and readied her question. "Ilene, we have a favor."

"What's that?" Ilene peeled a small clementine orange, quickly and neatly.

"We'd like to borrow your kitchen." Paige motioned to her sister and cousin with her fork. "We want to bake for the cookie swap tonight."

"We've each picked out recipes of Grandma Opal's to make." Abby placed blueberries into the squares of her waffles. She lifted a shoulder at Paige and explained, "This gives me a blueberry burst in every bite and downgrades the guilt factor of eating more than one."

"Isn't there a rule that sleepover calories don't count?" Paige glanced at her sister.

Tess chuckled. "I think it's more like Christmas calories don't count."

"I believe that rule covers the entire month of December." Ilene swiped a strawberry through a spoonful of whipped cream and laughed. "And you're welcome to my kitchen on one condition."

"We promise to clean up and put everything back where it belongs," Paige said.

"And we'll bring our own baking supplies," Tess offered.

"I'm not worried about all that." Ilene waved another strawberry at them. "I'd like to make Opal's chocolate snowflake cookies, if you have the recipe."

"I'm sure it's in Grandma's recipe box with the others," Tess said.

"I haven't found a chocolate snowflake that's tasted quite like hers." Ilene bit into her strawberry. "It'll be nice to have Opal included in this year's cookie swap. Opal used to organize a neighborhood cookie exchange party. It's good to have the tradition back again."

It was even better knowing Paige would be a part of the tradition this year. Paige touched Abby's arm. "You've set the bar high, Abby, with the return of so many Christmas traditions. What's going to happen at the next holiday?"

Abby laughed and finished off her waffles. "That's the thing about Three Springs. They don't seem to lack in traditions. It just seems they've forgotten them, but with even the slightest nudge, someone remembers."

Evan's questions had nudged some of Paige's

memories forward. Riley's questions had done the same. Things she'd forgotten or set aside had come back. She was grateful. Her heart was feeling full that morning. And she liked it.

Tess carried her plate to the sink and washed her hands. "I'll head home, pick up the recipe box and stop at the grocery store."

"Let's make a shopping list, then you can add the specifics for the recipes to it." Paige added her plate to the sink.

Ilene handed Paige a piece of paper and then opened a drawer and frowned. "All I have are crayons."

"Those will work." Paige accepted the box and returned to the table.

Abby moved to the sink and picked up the bottle of dish soap. Ilene protested. Abby never budged.

"Please let me. I need to stand and stretch. We ate too much." Abby bumped her shoulder against Ilene's and smiled. "The baby's first request just might be your waffles, Ilene."

Ilene took a clean towel from a drawer, ready to dry.

"Grandma, you made waffles?" Riley yawned in the doorway. Curls escaped from the braids she'd slept in, sticking out at all angles around her head.

"I did." Ilene draped the towel over her shoulder and opened the waffle iron. "And you're going to get the hottest, bestest one."

Riley grinned and padded in her footed pajamas over to the table. She eased under Paige's arm and leaned into her side. "What are you doing?"

"Making a shopping list for Ms. Tess." Paige shifted, letting Riley climb onto her lap as if the little girl always sat there. She couldn't stop her heart from filling even more. "Want to help me?"

"Sure." Riley picked up a yellow crayon.

"Okay, we're ready." Paige glanced around the kitchen. "What do we need? Besides everything."

"Butter." Ilene poured batter into the steaming waffle iron and snapped the lid closed. "I'm running low on butter. Best add milk too. Riley and I can collect eggs from the coop after she eats."

"Both dark and light brown sugar," Tess suggested, then ran through the staple ingredients for most baking recipes.

"What's going on?" Evan stood in the archway, wearing his usual flannel button-down shirt, jeans and dust-covered boots.

There was nothing typical about Paige's reaction. And that smile she'd woken up with broadened. "Good morning. We are coloring, shopping, then baking."

"I'm making the grocery list pretty like I make for you." Riley swayed her shoulders and picked up the orange crayon. "Now Ms. Tess will be happy when she's shopping."

"I love to shop," Tess said. "I like to explore all the aisles and see what's new."

"Really?" Riley's crayon stilled. "Daddy doesn't like to shop. He says we can only get the food that's on the list."

Tess spread her arms. "But if you don't look around, how can you find the food that you never knew you liked."

Paige liked her hayride yesterday with Evan more than she thought she would and their daily UTV rides around the ranch were always entertaining. But it wasn't about what they were doing. It was more straightforward than that.

She liked being with Evan. And if she hadn't been put on a mandatory cooling off leave, she wouldn't have stopped to look around. Now she couldn't seem to stop looking at him. She concentrated on the shopping list.

Riley finished coloring her flower and handed the completed shopping list to Tess. With the paper folded and stuffed in the pocket of her jeans, Tess opened the back door. "I'm off. I'll be back soon."

"Can we shop like Ms. Tess next time?" Riley relaxed against Paige.

"I'm not even a little bit tempted to say yes." Evan laughed, lifted his cowboy hat off his head and pressed a kiss on Riley's forehead to soften her frown. Then his gaze collided with Paige's. Heat thawed his blue eyes, drawing her closer.

Paige leaned forward, the barest of shifts. Would he kiss her too? *Yes, please.* As if that was their morning routine. Their start to every day. Paige's breath caught in her throat. Her heart raced.

Finally, Evan straightened, but the interest remained in his gaze. "The grocery store isn't for exploring. It's for getting in and out quickly."

She wouldn't want a quick kiss with Evan. Not for their first kiss. Or any in-between one either. Paige swallowed. Her throat had gone dry. Her voice sounded rough to her own ears. "Have you already checked on the cattle?"

"Yes." Evan scooped a handful of blueberries into his palm. "I figured you had a late night, gossiping and having competitions to see who could eat the most chicken wings and waffle fries with Abby and Tess."

Riley giggled. "Girls don't do that at sleepovers, Daddy."

"Really?" Evan's pretend confusion was obvious and charming.

Riley nodded and giggled more.

"Well, they should." Evan grinned and popped

more blueberries into his mouth. "Food competitions are the best. Doesn't everyone want to know who can eat the most hot dogs in under two minutes? Or the most pizza in ten minutes. Or see who can fit the most marshmallow snowmen in their mouth at one time."

Riley's laughter spilled out, shaking her body from her shoulders to her toes. "That's gross."

"I need to call Carter and Wes." Evan pulled out his cell phone. "See what kind of food competition we can come up with. I bet there's a lot of interest in town. Abby, take notes. It can be a new town tradition."

Abby and Ilene offered no encouragement to Evan, not that he needed any. The two women kept their focus on cleaning and drying the breakfast dishes.

Paige smiled, enjoying his teasing. She had to divert her attention before her heart became too entangled. That was a connection she didn't want to make. "I'll visit the cattle, then check in with Conrad."

"I'm going to visit Macybelle and Annabelle after we get the eggs. I need to tell them all about the tree farm and all the stories Santa told us yesterday." Riley slipped off Paige's lap and turned to face her. "Can I make cookies too?"

"We were counting on it." Paige touched the little girl's nose and earned a wide smile.

"I better hurry then." Riley skipped out of the kitchen. "I got a lot to do."

"What about me?" Evan sat in the chair beside Paige. "Are you counting on my help in the kitchen?"

She was counting on him not looking at her like he wanted to kiss her. Not making her think about kissing him. Her cheeks heated. She had to get outside. Inhale the cold, crisp air, and find her balance. Every time she glanced at Evan, those butterflies fluttered. And when had she suddenly become fixated with his mouth? "Don't you have things to do on the ranch?"

"Are you asking if there's something I need to do that's more important than sampling cookies?" He leaned his arm on the table and let his gaze wander over her face. "I can't think of a single thing."

Paige could think of something. Nothing she wanted to share. She forced herself to stop staring at his mouth. "If you're going to be in this kitchen, you need to help and taste testing doesn't count."

"That's one of the most important parts of the cookie-making process," Evan drummed his fingers on the table. "You can't bring subpar cookies to the swap. What will people think?"

What would he think if he knew Paige's silly thoughts? "Those are the rules."

He took her hand, ran his thumb across her palm. That heat curved through his gaze. "We can change the rules."

A sigh wound through her. Her heart raced again, but she couldn't change the facts.

He had a life in Texas. Hers was in Illinois. She was there to cool off. Not fall for a rancher. Not lose her heart. She pulled her hand free. "It's breakfast and baking."

That's all it could ever be.

CHAPTER EIGHTEEN

EVAN SHUT HIS TRUCK DOOR and stuck the key in the ignition. Beside him, Paige buckled her seat belt and set a hefty cellophane-wrapped cookie platter on her legs. Down the street, the towering Three Springs Christmas tree illuminated the entire square. Abby had outdone herself once again. The tree lighting was certain to become another annual event, along with the Three Springs Reunion Rodeo Days that Abby had put together at the end of the summer.

Evan could imagine the Bishop family attending this Christmas outing every year too. Even more, he could imagine Paige beside him next year and the year after that. He started his truck and restarted his train of thought. "Ready for a nightcap with Breezy and Gayle Baker?"

"I'm looking forward to it." Paige smiled at him. The cellophane wrap crinkled.

Evan reached for Paige's hand. "You can't smile and think you're going to distract me enough to sneak a cookie."

"I just want a taste." Paige laughed and wiggled her fingers inside the cellophane wrap. "I've never had divinity before. Freida promised me it would become my favorite. She was once the mayor of Three Springs, so she wouldn't lead me astray."

"You can have anything on that plate but Nora Finch's gumdrop nougats. I call dibs on those." Which was much better than calling dibs on Paige. All day Evan had tried and failed to get the image of Riley sitting on Paige's lap at his kitchen table out of his mind. Talk about distracting. He'd walked into the kitchen that morning and watched the pair chatting naturally and effortlessly as if they'd always been in each other's lives. And his only thought had been, *Everything I want in my life is right there.*

Evan followed Breezy's SUV. "I never knew gumdrop nougat was a thing."

"Do you feel like you've been missing out your whole life?" Paige's voice was playful and upbeat.

Not until I met you. Evan kept his eyes on the road and held his hand out, palm up. "Yes. I do. Can you hand me a nougat?"

"I've changed my mind. No cookies. We don't want to get too full. We have fruitcake to sample at the Baker house." Paige twisted and set the platter on the back seat, where she'd also placed Scooter's special-order blanket.

The elf blanket was the reason they were heading to the Baker sisters' farm tonight. Breezy and Gayle thought it would be lovely to have Scooter's blanket hand delivered by his own doctor. The two sisters had conveniently forgotten that Dr. Conrad Gibson was Scooter's official veterinarian, not Paige. But they'd reminded Paige that she'd promised to come over to meet everyone at the farm.

The invitation had been extended to the group. However, Abby and Wes had been excused from attending, Breezy declaring the couple needed their rest and Gayle assuring them they'd send a fruitcake home for them with Paige to deliver. Ilene had been holding a sleeping Riley and his mother had been granted a rain check. Tess had reminded them she had to be up early to begin searching for Gayle's special request gift and the sisters had wished her a good night. That had left Paige and Evan along with Boone and Sam accepting the sisters' nightcap invite. The cowboy duo was currently seated in the back of Breezy's SUV.

"You make a good point." Evan returned his hand to the steering wheel. "Save the nougat for after. I might need it to wash down the fruit-cake."

"You might like Breezy's fruitcake." Her tone was buoyant, and Evan enjoyed every syllable.

"It has aged for nine weeks in the Bakers' special brandy blend."

"I never knew fruitcake was aged." Evan cringed. "It's cake. Cake should be baked and eaten right out of the oven."

"Not this kind of cake." Paige laughed. "I think we're going to have to taste it. Breezy and Gayle were so excited."

"It's another Christmas first." With Paige. And there was nothing wrong with that.

Ten minutes later, his truck parked behind Breezy's SUV, introductions concluded between Paige and Scooter's six miniature potbellied pals, Evan carried the crock pot of mulled wine to its new location in the dining room.

Breezy and Paige returned from their tour of the century-old farmhouse. Evan overheard Paige assuring the older woman she'd return to meet the alpacas and goats during the daytime.

Evan scooped mulled wine into two glasses and found Paige in the entryway.

Paige touched a large wreath of dried twigs and branches displayed over a hand-carved wood table in the foyer. "Breezy, did you make this?"

"Heavens, no. That's the work of our aunt Francis." Breezy fluffed her short bob of white hair. "I'm named after her. Hope to follow in her footsteps. She's one hundred and one years young. Still has her hair fixed and her makeup applied every morning at the nursing home. She insists a lady cannot be seen without her face on."

Evan had no trouble picturing Breezy at the same spry age.

Paige called out to Boone and Sam, who stood in the family room. The cowboy duo in their faded plaid shirts and blue jeans looked plain against the backdrop of Breezy and Gayle's Christmas extravaganza. It was quite possible that the Baker sisters would outdo Abby in a decoration competition. Mischievous elves dotted the twelve-foot-tall Christmas tree, their grinning faces peeking out between branches. Handmade ornaments mingled with glass collectibles. Not a surface, not a wall had escaped being trimmed for the holiday. The sisters' joy of the season infused even the air. Every room had a bowl of their signature potpourri in case the visual experience wasn't powerful enough.

Boone and Sam stepped into the foyer. Paige pointed to the wreath. "Doesn't this wreath look exactly like the ones Grandma Opal made?"

"It's quite a bit bigger." Boone sipped his mulled wine. Lifted the glass for a sniff and sipped it again.

Sam squinted at the wreath. "Has more of those herbs and things stuck in it like Opal's."

"What did your grandmother make, dear?"

Gayle had a small pitcher of the wine and offered to top up anyone's glass.

Paige was momentarily transfixed. Evan was transfixed by Paige's tender expression and he suddenly wanted to be let in on her memory. He tightened his grip on the glass of mulled wine and tightened down his heart.

The best Evan could hope for would be to become a meaningful memory like that for Paige. When she thought of him later, he wanted her to smile. And when he thought about her, he wanted not to miss her, except, he wasn't ready for Paige to be a memory.

He swallowed a deep drink of the mulled wine. Not even the spices mellowed his growing feelings for Paige.

"We discovered a box of wreath ornaments in the Silver Penny." Paige handed her glass to Evan, then took out her phone. She swiped across the screen several times and turned the phone toward Gayle. "The ornaments had a note card attached. 'When we remember how it all began, we're reminded that we are always stronger together.' It was dated 1962."

"Year of the drought." Breezy touched her throat as if to stop herself from getting choked up. "Bad time for so many folks here."

"But we pulled through." Boone clinked his glass against the two sisters' glasses. "Together."

"We sure did." Breczy's smile was faint and wistful.

Together. Evan had assumed his together would only include Riley and his mom, possibly Sam and Boone. He'd never considered expanding their team though. Not until Paige.

"I don't recall Opal's ornaments." Gayle adjusted the holly berry branch on the wreath. "But Aunt Francis has been making these wreaths for our family and tucking messages inside each one every year since before we were born."

"Aunt Francis always told us she was given the privilege to carry on the family tradition. She's already taught her own daughter and two granddaughters." Breezy clasped her hands over her heart and sighed. "Always adds red clover—it's rumored to protect against evil—and yarrow, which means everlasting love, to her wreaths as a nod to our parents and grandparents."

"The holly is for strength." Gayle circled her hand in front of the wreath. "And the circle means unity. The wreath itself is a sign of welcome. Aunt Francis always told us we needed to hang our wreaths on the front door or in an entryway, so everyone would know they were always welcome here."

The two sisters had always placed a premium on opening their home and their hearts. Days after Marla had left and Evan's tuxedo had been returned, the Baker sisters had come out to the ranch. They'd collected baby clothes and baby items for Riley from the community. They'd also brought their homemade chicken stew, breakfast casserole and biscuits, stating no one should have to worry about cooking when they were caring for a baby. He wasn't sure he'd ever thanked the sisters properly. But tonight, he'd finish the entire fruitcake if it pleased the pair.

"Do you think your aunt might know when the tradition began?" Paige followed the sisters into the dining room. "Or how it began."

"We can certainly ask her tomorrow," Gayle said. "We have a phone call scheduled every Sunday at precisely 9:45 a.m. It's between breakfast and lunch and doesn't disturb Aunt Francis's afternoon exercise class or her nap."

Boone refilled his glass. "Do you think the McKenzie sisters are tied to the history of the Baker family wreath?"

"Ah, the legend. One of our favorite childhood stories." Breezy uncovered a tray of sliced fruitcake. Her gaze gleamed and landed on Boone. "I hear you and Sam might be heading out on a treasure hunt sometime soon."

"You'll need someone familiar with the land." Gayle passed out red napkins embossed with silver bells. "Breezy and I can help with that. We used to play in the canyon while our father searched for fossils. He taught science at the high school."

Sam nudged Boone's arm. "Was it you or Harlan who started that fire in the science lab when we were in school?"

"Neither." Boone tugged on his beard as if working to keep his smile contained. "It was Al Milton. Harlan and I put it out, but not in the most appropriate way. Mr. Baker gave us a stern lecture on fire prevention and the proper methods to extinguish a fire after that. Al wasn't allowed back in the lab for more than a month."

"You didn't use a fire extinguisher?" Paige said.

Boone shook his head. "We used what turned out to be Mr. Baker's best jacket to smother the flames."

The foursome laughed at the shared memory. Breezy asked if anyone remembered the fiasco at the spring dance that same year. Bits and pieces of the event carried into the conversation. The foursome carried their wine and fruitcake into the family room, collectively strolling down memory lane.

Evan took Paige's hand and led her into the kitchen. "I figured we can let them reminisce and check out Breezy and Gayle's platter from the cookie swap."

"Afraid they got something you didn't?" Paige teased.

"I like to know what I might've missed." Even more, he liked Paige. And if inspecting the cookie platter kept her close to him, he would examine every last crumb on the plate.

"There it is." Paige pointed to the plate on the kitchen table. "And no, you can't steal their gumdrop nougat."

But could he steal a kiss from Paige? Not the time. Or the place. "You seemed to appreciate the wreath in the entryway a lot."

"I remembered my first year at the clinic, when I put up a Christmas wreath and a tree for pets in need. I hung ornaments and wrote the pet items needed on the back. Then we donated everything to several local rescues and shelters."

"That must have been rewarding." Evan kept her hand tucked inside his.

"Very." Her smile faded. "But it got voted down the following year. I don't even know why."

He could make a guess, but he didn't want to ruin a good memory for her. "Maybe you can start it up again when you become an equal partner."

"That's a nice idea." She glanced at their joined hands. "Evan, I..."

Gayle arrived in the kitchen and clapped her

hands. "It's time for the fruitcake handout. Come on. You can't miss this."

But he wanted to. At the very least, he wanted to be late. To press Pause and let Paige finish whatever it was she wanted to tell him.

"We should go." Paige tugged on his hand, pulling him toward the family room. "The fruitcake handout sounds important."

He wasn't sure about important, but it didn't last long.

Twenty minutes later, the fruitcake handout ceremony ended with a flurry of hugs and vows to get together again soon.

Evan started his truck and waited for his three passengers to buckle their seat belts.

"Paige, we'd like to give you our fruitcakes as souvenirs of your trip." Boone's voice was magnanimous. He plunked his fruitcake and Sam's on the center console of Evan's truck as if he was presenting her with bars of gold from the McKenzies' lost loot.

"That's very generous." Paige never reached for the fruitcakes. Instead, she shook her head. "But I can't take those from you. They were gifts from Breezy and Gayle to you both."

"Isn't fruitcake one of the things most often regifted?" Evan kept his words casual.

Paige frowned at him, then eyed the twin

fruitcakes as if she considered launching them at him.

"Well, it is." Evan grinned and backed out of the driveway. "And probably for good reason. I can think of many reasons to pass it on."

That encouraged her smile. Her shoulders shook from her silent laughter.

"It packs up and travels well." Sam continued to state his case for regifting his fruitcake to Paige. "It's perfect for a suitcase. Doesn't require refrigeration."

Boone patted the wrapped loaf on top. "You could hand them out as gifts in Chicago. No one would know you were regifting."

"New rule," Evan declared. "No one can regift a Baker fruitcake."

"What are we supposed to do with them?" Discontent rumbled into Boone's deep voice.

"Keep it and eat it." Evan laughed.

"I still don't understand why you two got fruitcake halves and we got whole loaves." Sam scratched his cheek.

"Because Paige and I are single." Evan glanced in the rearview mirror and caught Sam's gaze. "And those are the rules. Singles only get half of a fruitcake in the annual fruitcake handout."

"We're single too," Boone argued.

"I don't think Breezy and Gayle see it that

way." Evan flattened his lips together to block his laugh.

Boone's head appeared between the front seats. "You really expect us to eat these?"

"I'm afraid not even Carter's limited-edition whiskey could rescue these fruitcakes." Sam's voice sounded forlorn and sorrowful.

"Paige, I'll trade you loaves." Boone leaned between the seats again. His words brisk and energetic again. "It's not regifting. It's a simple trade. One for one."

"I'm good." Paige offered Boone the cookie platter. "But have a cookie. Consider it a taste-bud cleanser."

"I need two of those peppermint-cream patties." Sam accepted the plate from Paige and lifted the cellophane. "Knew those had to be Tess's creations."

Evan chewed on his second nougat. "I need the recipe for the gumdrop nougat. It's my new favorite."

"This divinity is in the top five." Paige took another bite of the white meringue.

That started a debate about the best Christmas desserts ever. One that continued during the dropping off of Sam, then Boone. And that lasted until Paige and Evan returned to Crescent Canyon. The only point of agreement had been that everybody must make a list of their top five favorite desserts. They'd compare lists and arrange for a taste testing of sorts. The voting had yet to be worked out.

"It looks like I'm going to have my food competition after all." Evan walked beside Paige to the guesthouse. Luna was curled on the makeshift bed Paige had made from old towels and blankets for her on the front porch. She offered a tail wag greeting and deep yawn before circling around the blankets and flopping back down as if she had settled in for the night.

Evan was warming to the idea of having a houseguest. Or more precisely having Paige as his houseguest. And in his life. Each day it was becoming harder to recall a time when Paige hadn't been living on the ranch. She'd slipped into their lives naturally and easily. And he couldn't quite imagine letting go.

Paige stood under the porch light and pointed at the ceiling. "Did you hang mistletoe over the door?"

"Wasn't me." Evan took her hand and tugged her closer, bringing her to where he'd wanted her all day. In his arms. "Although, I can't claim it was a bad idea."

Evan reached up, tucked her hair behind her ear. Let his fingers linger on her cheek, drift to her neck. Now he knew the feel of her skin. "I want to..."

"Make an impossible promise." Her words held no more weight than a snowflake.

"Yeah." Evan curved his hand up into her hair and closed the distance between them. "Something like that."

She stared at him deeply, rested her hand over his heart. "We can't. We shouldn't."

"No words, then." He leaned forward. She met him halfway. Her fingers flexed against his chest. His pulse beat faster. He blamed himself for getting caught in the moment. For giving in. "No promises. Only this."

Indecision. Hesitation. Regrets. All of it disappeared within their kiss. Traditions were forgotten. Time. Right and wrong.

And what was caught in the moment, sounded like a heart's whisper. *He'd only ever have this.*

CHAPTER NINETEEN

THE NEXT MORNING, Paige entered the Silver Penny, brandishing two fruitcakes, and called out a greeting to her sister and cousin. She refused to consider it might be the last time she stepped into the store. Or the last afternoon she shared with Abby and Tess.

Okay, she was leaving in two days. It wasn't forever. Just for now. Still, she was sad. She'd missed her sister and cousin before. It was nothing she wouldn't handle. But somehow this time felt different.

Paige walked to the back of the store, straightened her spine, and collected herself. Tears and gloom were for later. "I have information about the wreaths and fruitcakes from Breezy and Gayle. Tess, you only get half a loaf because you're single."

Tess eyed the smaller tightly wrapped loaf. "Paige, if you take mine, you'll have a full loaf."

"That's another rule. No regifting of the fruitcake." Paige laughed at their dismayed expressions. "It's yours to eat and enjoy."

Abby lifted her fruitcake in both hands. "It's quite heavy. It really could be used as a doorstop. I thought that was just a silly rumor."

"Did you try it, Paige?" Tess arched an eyebrow at Paige.

"It's insanely sweet." Paige grinned. She'd realized she'd been honored to receive one. As if by getting a fruitcake she had been somehow accepted into the Three Springs community. And now, she could claim the sisters as part of her family too. "Yes, I realize my sweet tooth knows no limits. But their fruitcake also doesn't have those red and green candied cherries pretending to be real fruit. It's dense and moist and lovingly made by two very bighearted sisters."

"Then we have a mission, ladies." Tess raised her half loaf and shifted it around to consider all sides. "We need to find the most palatable way to eat it. Is it toasted with butter? Crumbled over ice cream?"

"Can you turn it into a candy?" Abby suggested. "Everything is better dipped in your chocolate, Tess."

"We can try all of it." Tess set her fruitcake on the back counter. "Now we know what we will be doing this week. It'll be a fruitcake frenzy feast."

"I hope we have enough for this feast." Abby's grin wobbled.

Paige's laughter erupted and blended with Abby's and Tess's. Only one thought sobered her merriment. She wouldn't be there for the experimenting or the taste testing. Or what were sure to be hilarious and entertaining moments. Creating her own fruitcake dishes at home held very little appeal.

"Fruitcakes aside, I have something for you, Paige." Tess set a large, taped moving box on the counter. "I found it in the basement. It has your name on it, written in Grandma's cursive."

Abby gasped and pressed her knuckles against her mouth. "It's like the one Tess found for me."

Paige's stomach dropped. Their grandparents had left Abby an antique ink set. Grandpa Harlan had included a touching and thoughtful handwritten letter to Abby about writing her own life story. Encouraging Abby to be bold, fearless and take a risk on true love. Abby had read the full letter to Tess and Paige during their sleepover. Now Paige had her own box and most likely her own letter.

Her hands shook. This past week in Three Springs, she'd felt the closest to her grandparents since before they'd passed. Surrounded by people who'd known and loved Harlan and Opal Palmer had brought back her own memories and her own deep love and admiration for the couple. Leaving almost felt as if she'd be saying goodbye to her grandparents again too. Paige rubbed her throat, but the catch lodged there remained. "Do you have scissors or a knife so I can open it?"

"I got it." Tess's voice was subdued and scratchy. She used a box cutter and efficiently sliced through the tape, releasing the flaps.

Paige lifted the bubble wrap. A white envelope rested on top of more bubble wrap. Paige's name was once again written in her grandmother's cursive across the front. Paige set the letter on the counter and removed another layer of bubble wrap. Tears pooled in her eyes. Her vision blurred.

Laid in two neat rows were her grandmother's hand-stitched Christmas ornaments. Quilted stars. Three lace angels, each holding a different silver charm. Red-and-white sequined candy canes. Paige touched the red nose of a cork reindeer with the green-striped yarn hat, garland collar and pipe cleaner antlers. Paige bet that she knew the other ornaments layered underneath. They were partners to the very ones Paige had crafted with her grandmother all those years ago.

"These are Grandma's ornaments. I couldn't find them after Grandpa passed. Not anywhere in the house." Wonder wound around Tess's words. "I wanted to give them to you, Paige. They were always your favorite to put up."

Every year Paige would hang her simple child-created copies next to her grandmother's expertly sewn and hand-crafted ornaments and declare, "Now they aren't alone, Grandma."

Her grandmother would hug her and say, "Together, they're stronger. Everyone should have a partner that makes them better."

Someone like Evan. But ornaments were not like life. And partners weren't picked from a ready-made pattern. Or plucked from a Christmas tree.

A life partner took time to meet, and the relationship required even more time to grow. It wasn't something that sprouted from an unexpected last-minute trip. No matter what her heart claimed.

"Looks like Grandma's ornaments found their way to you after all." Abby peered inside the box. A wistful note accompanied her words and fragile smile. "Don't you want to read the letter?"

"I can't right now. I told myself I wouldn't cry." Paige pressed her fingertips against the corners of her eyes. But the dread of her goodbye and now the gift of her grandmother's keepsake ornaments pressed in on her. "I don't leave for another day. It's too soon for tears. And besides, it's only a goodbye for now, anyway."

Tess tucked the letter in Paige's purse. "Read it when you're ready."

"These ornaments belong here in the store

where they can be seen and enjoyed." Paige belonged in Chicago, where she'd built her life and a solid practice the past decade. It was where she'd always envisioned her future before meeting Evan.

But one unforgettable kiss and an amazing adventure wasn't enough to bet her heart and future on. She had a good life in the city. Why risk that for what could amount to no more than a holiday-induced crush?

Paige inhaled a shaky breath and nudged her grandmother's ornaments across the counter.

"Grandma wanted you to have them." Tess set her hand on the box, stopping its movement, and resisting Paige's effort.

"I don't have a tree." There was a lovely one in Evan's guesthouse, potted and waiting for strands of popcorn garland. Its branches perfect for her grandmother's lightweight ornaments and Riley's paper snowflakes. If only they had more time. But that goodbye would eventually arrive, and Paige feared it would always be too soon. Those tears welled up again.

"The ornaments give you a reason to go out and get a tree when you get back." Abby brushed at her eyes.

"It's less than a week before Christmas." Paige would return to the city and dive into her work like she always had. Work had always fulfilled her. That hadn't changed.

"I've known people who've picked up a Christmas tree on Christmas Day." Abby wrapped her arm around Paige's shoulders and squeezed. "It's never too late to embrace the season."

Paige had embraced Evan last night. Out on the porch. It hadn't been enough and yet it had been too much. As for the season, she'd been getting into the spirit thanks to a Christmas-first list and a very special father and daughter, whose list wasn't quite finished yet. The movie marathon and campout in front of the tree was marked on the calendar for Wednesday night.

Earlier this morning, Paige had remembered two holiday movies Tess and she had watched on repeat every year as kids. She'd taken out her phone to text Evan, then stopped. She wouldn't be there. It was Evan and Riley's movie night only. Their memory to make. It should be what they wanted. She'd dropped her phone in her purse. Sadness spread, shading her world a little bit darker.

Tess lifted a hand-stitched Mrs. Claus from the box. Mrs. Claus's sequined apron and beaded white cap sparkled. "It doesn't feel right to keep these."

"How about this?" Paige braced her palms on the counter. "What if I promise to come back next year for Christmas? And then we can put them on the tree together."

Abby watched her.

Tess looked hopeful. "You mean it?"

"Yes."

"What about work?" Tess asked.

"I'll figure it out." If the partners sided with Paige, she'd arrange for a long-overdue holiday vacation next year. If she opened her own practice, she'd figure that out too. Work would always be a priority, but Tess and Abby deserved better from her. "Family first."

Tess's broad smile swept some of the happy back into Paige, scattering her sadness. Tess repeated, "Family first."

Abby wiped at her tears. "I love you guys."

Paige walked around the counter and hugged both her sister and cousin at the same time. She pulled back. "Just to be clear. We agree the ornaments are staying here, right?"

"If they bring you back here for the holidays, then they stay," Tess said with conviction, rubbing at her eyes.

Abby pointed at Paige. "But know that we aren't above coming to get you for the holidays. A promise is a promise. And next year, I won't be pregnant. I will chase you down if I have to."

"I'll be here." Paige hugged Abby again. She knew another pair who would be here too, but she couldn't make Evan or Riley any promises. Couldn't ask Evan to make any of his own. So much could happen in a year. So much had happened in less than two weeks. Her goodbye with Evan should be final. Two different worlds. Two different states. Impossible situation. The distance on several levels was too much to conquer. But that was for tomorrow. Right now belonged to her family. "Tess, you texted that you needed help in the store this afternoon. I'm ready to set aside the tears and get to it. What are we doing?"

"Well, I have it on good authority that it's never too late to decorate and embrace the full spirit of Christmas." Tess grinned and opened a deep bottom drawer in the shelving unit behind the counter. She pulled out a binder and opened it, revealing black-and-white and color photos. "I want to put up the entire Victorian village that Grandma and Grandpa always told us about. I've been going through their old photo albums for pictures of what it looked like in the front window."

"I always wanted to live in that village after hearing Grandpa describe it." Paige slipped a picture of her grandparents out of the plastic protector. Their hair had not turned gray yet. Laugh lines were still settling into their faces. They stood, arms linked around each other, behind the village, their gazes gleaming, their smiles proud. They had always been stronger together. She'd always wanted what they had shared. Perhaps it was enough that she lived her life to the fullest like they had. "You want to re-create the village to look like this?"

"Yes." Tess hesitated. Her gaze locked on Paige. "And I want to keep the village out all year long like Dad taught us to do."

"Wait." Abby glanced from Paige to Tess and back. "What did I miss?"

"Our dad told us to keep a piece of Christmas out all year long so we could keep the spirit of the season alive the rest of the months." Paige took her sister's hand. "It's a lovely tribute to our grandparents and dad. The trains were always his favorite part. I'll build the tracks."

Tess squeezed Paige's hand.

"Why am I only now learning about this tradition?" Abby steepled her fingers under her chin. "I have no idea what I'll keep out. Can I keep it all out?"

Tess and Paige laughed. Paige shook her head. "Only one thing."

"That's going to take some thought. It'll come to me." Abby reached for the photo album. "But first, we need to build a village."

Paige picked up a photograph of Grandma Opal behind the counter, hands on her hips, a Santa hat on her head. Her face was tipped upward as she laughed. Paige could practically feel her grandma's joy. She moved the photograph closer as if bringing it closer strengthened her connection. Then she sucked in a breath. Waited a beat. And exhaled the words, "It's real."

"I hate to point out the obvious." Abby's voice was bland. She pointed across the store. "But all those boxes marked Village are proof it's real."

"Not the village." Paige thrust the picture at Tess and pointed her finger at it. "The silver coin."

"What?" Tess took the picture.

"It's behind Grandma on the wall." Paige wanted to jump up and down like Riley. "You're standing in almost the exact spot Grandma is in that picture."

Tess spun around and stared at the empty wall behind her.

"Let me see that." Abby swiped the photograph from Tess's fingers and gasped. The picture floated to the counter.

"I believed Boone and Sam." Paige waved her hands around as if she was gathering the right words. "I really did."

"But seeing it, even in an old photograph, makes it truly real." Tess pressed her palm against the wall where the frame would've hung.

"Exactly." Paige liked that her sister understood so quickly what she couldn't quite put into words.

"This makes it…" Abby voice's trailed away. Excitement and wonder brightened her gaze. "Now we know exactly what we're looking for. And when we find it, we might discover the map that will lead us to a centuries old treasure."

"Which will be returned finally to the community of Three Springs like the McKenzie sisters had always intended," Tess said.

"I want to search for it right now." Paige rubbed her hands together and bounced from one foot to the other. "And build the village."

"Maybe the coin is in the village boxes," Tess suggested.

All three women turned to look at the boxes. Dozens and dozens of boxes lined the far wall. All marked Village. Abby sighed. "Wouldn't that be something if it was in there the whole time."

"There's only one way to find out." Paige moved toward the boxes. "Let's get started building a village."

WHAT WAS LEFT of the evening's pizza had been pushed aside. The three women stepped back from the completed display. Paige held her hand over the train's power button. "Ready?"

Abby and Tess nodded. Paige pressed the button and steam puffed from the locomotive as the model train started its run. Lights blinked in the houses and stores. The three women cheered, high-fived and watched the train ease across the bridge and around a mountain. Paige set her head on Tess's shoulder. "It's better than I ever imagined."

Tess squeezed Paige around the waist. "So much."

Abby took a series of pictures with her phone. "These need to be posted on the general store's website."

Paige pulled out her own phone and tapped on the internet app. "We're missing something."

"What could possibly be missing?" Tess studied the display. "We have a pond. A bridge. Mountains and snow. More shops than Three Springs."

"A fourteen-inch prelit Christmas tree for our town square." Paige turned her phone and the photo toward Tess. "In honor of Abby. I'm ordering it now."

"And in honor of Tess, a book exchange box for outside the library." Abby beamed and quickly tapped on her phone screen. "Located and ordered."

Tess wiggled her fingers for Abby's phone and swiped across the screen. "And in honor of Paige, cattle for the pastures. Lots and lots of cattle."

"Perfect." Paige grinned, her heart full.

The trio refilled their wineglasses and toasted a successful day. Paige added a silent thank-you to her grandparents for bringing the women together again. They hadn't located the silver coin. But they'd built something special and lasting. There was something precious and priceless in that. Something worth holding on to.

CHAPTER TWENTY

"PAIGE." EVAN STOOD in the back doorway and took in the suitcase on the step. His stomach dropped. "Come in."

He moved to let her inside, but rammed face-first into the truth. Paige was leaving. Time had run out. There would be no more mistletoe kisses. No more late-night nightcaps. No more Paige to turn to. To laugh with. To share the day with. He shoved his hands in the front pockets of his jeans and paced around the kitchen island.

"I'm..." She lost her voice. Inhaled. Waited a beat. Then another. Exhaled, her words rushing out as if she had only a little strength left. "I'm leaving. I'll stay at Abby's tonight with the puppies. Then I fly out in the morning."

"Abby and Wes are really adopting Ginger and Tyne?" Evan thought of the puppies rather than the elephant in the room. The goodbye he didn't want to give. There was nothing good about it.

"Yeah." Paige dropped the key to the guest-house on the island. "They know it's a lot with the baby coming. But they have great help.

Boone has already volunteered for puppy-sitting duty. And Tess babysitting duty."

"It's all worked out, then." And yet nothing was worked out. Not between them. He could ask her to stay, but then what? Fall for her even more only to have to face a more heart-tugging goodbye later. He had to let her go. He had to let go. "I'm not going to find your fruitcake in the back of the guesthouse's freezer, am I?"

"It's in my carry-on." Her smile flashed. There and gone like a firefly's light. "It's quite good crumbled over vanilla ice cream."

"I'll have to try that." *After I ask you to give up your life and all you've worked for. For me. For us.* He squeezed the back of his neck. He couldn't—wouldn't—ask her to choose. This was where he let go. "Paige…"

"I almost forgot." She lifted two gift bags and cut him off. "These are Riley's. For Project Gumdrop. One for you. One for Riley's mom. They're marked."

Another hard conversation he hadn't yet had. When had he become such a coward? "Thanks."

She nodded and set the bags on the kitchen table. "Have you talked to Riley yet about her mom?"

He shook his head. "I will. Soon."

"I should…"

The back door swung open. Riley rushed inside and pointed out the open doorway. "There's a suitcase out there."

"It's mine." Paige tugged on her ponytail, then her ear as if searching for that magic fairy dust that would make it all better. Or perhaps that was just wishful thinking on his part. Paige added, "I brought your Project Gumdrop over for you. Now it's time for me to leave."

"You can't!" Riley pushed the back door closed with a hard shove and ignored the gift bags on the table.

"Ms. Paige needs to go home." Evan rubbed his hand over his mouth as if pulling his words free. "We all knew that she was only visiting." A temporary guest. The same as his feelings for her were supposed to be: temporary. Although, there was nothing fleeting about the dull ache in his chest.

"But you're happy." Riley's hands fisted at her sides. She stomped one booted foot. "And all my wishes were coming true."

"I've always been happy." Perhaps not always, but enough. That counted. And he would be happy again. Maybe not tomorrow. But soon. And if he wasn't, no one needed to know. That was for him to deal with. "We need to say goodbye."

Riley shook her head, quick, angry jerks of her chin. She crossed her arms tightly over her chest and closed herself off. Defiant. Unreachable.

Where was his sweet little girl? He ached for her. "Riley—"

"No! She can't leave." Tears filled her eyes. Was it her anger that kept them from falling? "You won't be happy then. And my wishes won't come true."

Evan's knees buckled. He knelt on the floor, kept his gaze fixed on his daughter. Searched for hope, reached for that last thread of magic. "Santa won't be here for five days."

"Ms. Paige makes you happy, not Santa," Riley charged. One more frustrated stomp. The thud echoed in Evan's chest. Riley rounded on Paige. "You can't leave."

"I'm so sorry, Riley." Paige swiped at her cheeks, lowered to one knee. Her voice trembled. "I wish I could stay, but this isn't my home."

"Then wish harder so it comes true," Riley begged. A tear escaped. Smeared her freckles, slid down her pale cheek.

That single tear surged inside Evan. The lies swelled. So many that he choked. It shouldn't have come to this. His gaze locked on Paige's. The pain—everything he'd wanted to avoid—came through in her eyes. Paige had warned him. He'd put it off. That hard conversation swelled. It would crash around him, knock Riley's world sideways.

Now. It had to be now. He was out of time. He was out of words. And he couldn't stop it. But he could be there after the fall.

Tears, unrestrained, ran down Paige's cheeks. "Unfortunately, it doesn't work that way."

"Wishes don't come true, do they?" Riley whispered.

His daughter's cheeks were too dry. Her voice too clear. Too steady. Only her chest heaved up and down. One bitter breath after another.

Evan wanted to release the shout curdling in his gut. He was supposed to protect his daughter. Keep her from getting hurt. He wanted to cover Riley's ears, hide her and himself from the truth, make even more impossible promises. He ground his teeth together.

Riley fixed her suddenly too-wise gaze on Evan. "Mom isn't coming home for Christmas, is she?"

That tidal wave crashed over him, stealing his air. He struggled to breathe. To fill his chest. He'd never wanted this. Wanted to blame fate. Curse his ex. But he was the only one at fault. "I can explain."

"I hate Christmas," Riley yelled and launched herself toward the kitchen table. She tore into the gift bags Paige had delivered and threw two glass ornaments onto the floor. The bulbs shattered. Riley fled from the kitchen. "I hate Christmas and everyone."

Evan slammed his hands over his face and wrestled with his emotions. His tears sealed his palms to his cheeks. There was so much he hated. He wasn't sure where to begin, except with himself. He scrubbed his hands into his hair, then wiped his palms on his jeans. He stood and looked at Paige.

Her own cheeks were damp. She looked lost. Alone. So out of reach.

But she'd never been his. Never been within reach. Not really. And he couldn't protect his own daughter's heart. He broke hearts. He refused to do that to Paige too. He'd already caused enough damage in his own home.

She cleared her throat. "You should go check on Riley."

He nodded, yet never moved.

"You belong with Riley." Her voice was deep and scratchy. "I belong in Chicago. We always knew that."

He no longer knew what he knew. Other than he despised inevitable goodbyes and shattered hearts. Words failed him. He held his arms out.

She threw herself into his embrace. Hugged him quick, but so very tight. Then she was gone.

Out the door and out of his life in less than a breath. Less than a heartbeat.

And it officially became the worst Christmas ever.

OUTSIDE IN THE DRIVEWAY, Paige loaded her suitcase into the trunk of the rental car. Then she took the puppy box from Ilene and secured it in the back seat, before falling into Ilene's embrace.

Ilene hugged her and framed Paige's face in both of her hands. "You'll text me when you get to the airport. Then again when you get to your town house."

Paige nodded and held on to the dear woman. "I can't thank you enough."

"We owe you the thanks." Ilene lowered her hands, then took Paige's cold fingers in hers. "You saved our ranch."

"I can't say goodbye." More tears spilled free. Her voice caught on the evening breeze.

"Then we'll say for now." Ilene squeezed Paige's hands. "You'll keep in touch. You might not be here, but you will still be in our hearts."

And they would be in hers. Paige walked to the driver's side and glanced up at Riley's bedroom window. A shadow moved in the windowpane, setting the paper snowflakes swaying against the glass. Paige lifted her hand as if she wanted to catch the pieces. She wanted to rush back inside the house, straight into the little girl's room, and soothe her hurt. But that was for Riley's father to do. His job, not Paige's. Besides, she wasn't quite sure how to fix her own broken heart. How could she possibly help Riley?

Ilene gave Paige's shoulder one last squeeze and walked back inside the farmhouse. Paige lingered and watched the farmhouse door. Waited for it to open. Waited for Evan to appear. Waited for him to... She got in the car and slammed the door. He had a life in Texas. Hers was in Illinois. She could stand there and wait all night. But anything her heart wanted to hear only complicated things further. It was better like this. Unspoken. And deniable.

The tears never slowed on the drive to her cousin's house. And only increased when Abby opened the front door and her arms. Paige clung to her cousin. "It wasn't supposed to be like this."

Abby guided Paige to the couch while Wes carried the puppy box from the car to the kitchen. Abby pressed an already steaming cup of tea into Paige's hand and asked, "What was it supposed to be like?"

"I don't know." Paige sniffed and wiped a tissue against her eyes. "But not like this. I came here to cool off. To regroup and reset." *Not to fall in...* She shut down that thought.

Love wasn't ever part of the conversation. Or

any conversation for that matter. Of course, she was sad. She'd reconnected with her sister and her cousin. She had a niece or nephew arriving in the spring and she'd miss out on the baby's special moments by not living in town. And she'd miss her now friends and Three Springs. The community that had welcomed, accepted and supported her as if she'd always lived there. As if she'd always belonged.

She swirled the tea bag around in her cup. "I have to go home. Back to my life in the city."

"We know." Abby set her hand on Paige's knee. "We support you. And we want the best for you. That's all."

The best thing was to get on the plane in the morning. Then convince the senior partners at the clinic she was the one they wanted in their practice. Once Paige secured her position, everything would settle back into place. Life would return to what she'd always envisioned.

As for her heart, those pieces would settle too. Eventually. And then she'd know she was where she belonged.

CHAPTER TWENTY-ONE

THE NEXT MORNING, Evan was back in the saddle, seated atop Clay, his Appaloosa horse, in the eastern pasture. He and Clay watched the last of the recovered cows return to their herd from a small sloping hill.

Rex greeted Evan and returned to guard the cattle. The dog had taken over for Luna, as if Rex had recognized his littermate needed time to heal.

The Crescent Canyon Ranch was finally back to normal operations. The contracts for the branding program had been finalized, approved, and were waiting for Evan's signature at the lawyer's office. It was a dream realized. And one that helped ensure Evan could provide for Riley now and in the future. That's all he'd ever wanted.

He'd misstepped with his daughter but intended to find his footing later that evening. Riley had been asleep when he'd peeked in on her before sunrise. She hadn't wanted to see him last night; only her grandmother had been granted access to her bedroom. Evan had honored Riley's need for space, but he couldn't allow the distance between them to remain. He had to start that hard conversation. He had to see it through, no cutting corners. Honest and open. And then perhaps, the next hard conversation wouldn't be quite so difficult. And the one after that would be even less challenging. Because somewhere between midnight's arrival and the early-morning hours, when Evan had been staring at his ceiling and given up on sleeping, he'd realized this was only the first of the tough conversations between himself and his daughter. More arguments, more disagreements were inevitable. It was how they resolved things and moved forward that mattered.

Moving forward. That was Evan's focus now. For the ranch, for his family. And especially for himself. One squeeze of his knee and Clay turned away from the herd. One more shift in the saddle, and Clay responded to the cue and eased effortlessly into a gallop across the pasture. Evan would've liked to spend the entire day on his horse, roaming from one pasture to the next. But the ranch required his attention. And his mind demanded a distraction.

Fortunately, he had many.

EVAN WALKED INTO the kitchen later than he'd expected. A flat tire on one of the older UTVs, unforeseen fence repairs and a last-minute trough valve replacement had him out on the land past dinner. He'd wanted a distraction and the ranch had delivered. He'd had no time to worry over his conversation with Riley or notice Paige's absence.

He might have looked for Paige once or twice. Thought of something he wanted to tell Paige more often than that. But it hadn't interfered with his work. Or his focus.

With luck, he'd fall asleep the second his head hit the pillow and tomorrow, he'd miss Paige just a little less.

Nothing wrong with hoping. He greeted his mom and washed his hands in the kitchen sink. "Is Riley upstairs?"

"She's already finished her bath. And at last check, she was organizing her stuffed animals for their bedtime story." His mom sat at the kitchen table, a glass of wine and a cookbook on the place mat in front of her. "Want me to heat up the chicken casserole?"

Evan dried his hands and shook his head. "I'll eat later. I want to talk to Riley."

"You're a good father, Evan." His mom eyed him. "Remember that. I'm proud of you. Your father would be too."

"Thanks, Mom." He kissed his mom's cheek and headed for the stairs. His father had been

Evan's hero. One of the best men Evan had known. He wanted to live up to that. Wanted Riley to see him the same way. Yesterday she'd looked at him with loathing. And it had brought him to his knees. Time to repair what he could.

Two quick raps on Riley's door and he peeked inside the colorful bedroom. "Mind if I come in?"

Riley sat in the middle of her bed, commanding the attention of a dozen stuffed animals, and shrugged at Evan. She closed the book she'd been reading and set it on one of her pillows. "What if I'm still mad at you?"

"Well, those are your feelings." Evan crossed the room. Paper snowflakes brushed against the top of his head. So many emotions brushed against his heart. But there was one gift he could give his daughter: unconditional love. If his daughter could trust in anything, it was that he would always love her. "And you get to feel anything you want."

She pursed her lips as if she didn't quite believe him.

He rearranged three bears, two rabbits and a dog to make room for himself, then sat on the bed, propping his back against the headboard. "You can feel anything you want as long as we agree to talk about it."

Riley set her book on the nightstand and moved to sit next to him. "You're not mad I'm mad?"

"No. I'm sorry I upset you." Evan held her small hand in his. "I should have told you the truth about your mom. I haven't talked to your mom in a very long time."

Riley pushed up and studied him. "Is she mad at you?"

"I was very mad at your mom." For longer than he cared to admit. Even now the last threads of his anger hooked into him at unexpected times. It had been Paige who'd allowed him to bypass the old resentment and bitterness where Marla was concerned. He hadn't lost himself hurtling down memory lane. Thanks to Paige and her understanding and support. "But I'm not so mad anymore."

"'Cause Ms. Paige made you happy." Riley grinned at him.

"I like Ms. Paige." A lot more than he should. Evan stretched his legs out on the bed and concentrated on the conversation. He had to focus on his daughter. "But I stopped being mad at your mom because all that anger made me really sad."

"It makes my tummy hurt." Riley's mouth dipped down, and she patted her stomach.

"Mine too." Evan squeezed Riley's hand. "So,

I let it go and decided to think only about the good things in my life."

"Like me," Riley cheered.

"Especially you." Evan pressed a kiss on the top of Riley's head.

Riley sobered and set her head on Evan's chest, resting her ear over his heart. "Why did Mommy go away?"

Evan pinched his eyes closed. Took a breath. Gathered himself. How much to reveal? How much to hold back? He didn't know. There were no rules. No guidebooks. He knew only he couldn't tiptoe around the truth. Not anymore. "Your mom isn't ready to be a parent right now."

"When will she be ready?" Riley reached for her unicorn stuffed animal —the same one she'd loaned to Paige to keep Paige company in the guesthouse. She cuddled the plush animal against her.

"I'm not sure when your mom will be ready to be a parent." That was the full truth. No matter how much Evan wished Marla to change or willed things to be different, he couldn't make it happen. He could only be present for his daughter and hope he could be enough.

"Does she love me?" Riley's voice was grave. Out of tune with her usual animated tone.

"She does." Evan nodded and reached for an explanation. "Your mom doesn't love the same way you and I do. Her love looks different. Just because you can't see her, it doesn't mean she doesn't love you."

"Will she ever love like us?" Curiosity curved around her words. Her fingers curled around the unicorn's horn.

"I don't know." Evan wanted better answers for his daughter. Perhaps one day he'd have them. "But it doesn't mean we can't love her in our own way too."

"I don't want to love her," Riley stated.

"Just keep your heart open." *Don't become like me.* He wanted his words to sound hopeful. "You might change your mind one day."

Riley lifted her head and peered at him through her long lashes. "You're not mad at me?"

"No." Evan kept his gaze on hers. "But if you're mad, it's okay. You know that, right?"

Riley curled into his side again and brushed her fingers through the unicorn's neon-tinted tail. "Do you think Santa is mad at me?"

Evan's shoulders relaxed. The tension finally eased from his body. His feet were back under him. Santa was a topic he could handle. "No, Santa is not mad either."

"Are you sure?" Riley pressed.

"Positive." Evan tapped her nose and drew out a small smile.

Satisfied, Riley propped her unicorn on Evan's stomach and yawned. "I miss Ms. Paige."

His daughter was an expert at instantaneous topic changes in a conversation. But he'd had a lot of practice over the years. He struggled to restrain his own feelings rather than give in. Perhaps if he put it out there, tomorrow he'd hurt less. "I miss her too."

"You should go get her," Riley urged. "Tell her to come home."

Except Paige was already home. And it wasn't in his guesthouse. "I wish it was that easy."

"Luna misses her too." Riley scratched her cheek. "And the cows miss her too. But me mostly."

And Evan mostly too. He picked up the unicorn and smelled the stuffed animal. The faint floral scent reminded him of Paige. She wasn't going to be easy to forget. Or easy to move on from. For a little while, Paige had been one of those good things in his life. "What do you like about Paige?"

"She made my hair pretty and my nails sparkle." Riley wiggled her fingernails. "And she let me help her all the time. And sit on her lap whenever I wanted."

Paige had made his days better. It was as simple and as complicated as that.

"You know what else?" The musical notes

in Riley's voice returned. A hint that her usual spunky energy wouldn't be far behind. She wrapped her arm across Evan and hugged him. "Ms. Paige gave me unicorn kisses and wished me rainbow dreams every night."

Evan returned his daughter's hug. "What are rainbow dreams?"

"You know." Riley giggled and tapped his forehead. "You dream in all the colors of the rainbow."

Evan set his hand under his chin and pretended to consider her explanation. "You even dream in the color red?" It was the one color Riley had declared last year that she did not like.

Riley nodded against his chest. "We wouldn't have cardinals and robins without the color red. Or watermelon, strawberries and ladybugs. It's a very important color."

"It really is." And Paige had left an important, positive imprint on his daughter. One he would be forever grateful for. Perhaps next year Riley wouldn't be asking to change her red hair to brown. "What about our Christmas-first list? Still want to finish it?"

"Yes." Riley yawned with her entire body. "Can you finish the story tonight? Mr. Bear says he's falling asleep."

"Sure." Evan picked up the book from the

nightstand and relaxed into his best storytelling voice.

Minutes later, he read the last page about a mouse's adventure at school and closed the book. Carefully, he eased Riley under the covers. He set the unicorn near her pillow and rose. He'd made it to the door when she lifted her head and called out to him.

He turned to see her holding out the unicorn. "Daddy, you should sleep with Buttercup tonight. She'll keep you company like she did Ms. Paige."

Evan walked back, accepted the unicorn and kissed his daughter good night. "I hope you have a night of rainbow dreams."

"You too, Daddy." She curled into the blankets and closed her eyes.

Evan wandered into his bedroom, dropped the unicorn on his bed and walked downstairs. He was both restless and exhausted. Eating held little appeal. And sleeping he already suspected was going to be hard to come by. He slipped on his jacket and stepped outside into the night air.

A movement on the front porch of the guesthouse caught his attention. He walked over to the small porch. Luna's tail thumped back and forth. The gentle dog stood and stretched, then walked to the guesthouse door as if expecting Paige to open it for them.

How Evan wanted that to happen. He wanted to talk to Paige about his conversation with Riley. He wanted to sit beside her on the couch and hear about her day. He wanted so much just to be with her. One more night. One more week. Forever.

He pressed the heel of his hand into his chest. As if that would slow the ache spreading inside him. How was it possible he could miss her so much? He barely knew Paige and yet he felt as if he'd always known her.

Luna glanced from him to the closed door. She whined, lifted her paw, and scratched at the door.

Evan would cry too if he thought it would help.

"She's gone." Evan walked across the porch and sank into the rocking chair. *Gone*. That ache throbbed.

Luna set her head on the arm of the rocking chair and whined again.

Evan sank his fingers into the dog's thick coat. His sadness anchored inside him. "I know. I miss her too."

CHAPTER TWENTY-TWO

PAIGE HAD CRIED UNTIL she had run out of tears on the flight home yesterday. Then she'd assured Abby and Tess over text and an evening video chat that she was good. And she fully intended to be good. Soon.

She'd fallen asleep, still trying to convince herself there was nothing wrong with being fine. It wasn't good. And okay was even appropriate too. A lot of people were just okay and that was enough for them.

Yet she'd woken up that morning, two minutes before sunrise, her eyes clear and a new resolve filling her. She'd returned to the city, left her family behind for the life she'd always wanted. She couldn't keep crying for something—or someone—she didn't have. Or for a life she hadn't chosen. But that life she wanted was within reach. She just had to take it.

Maybe there had been something in the Texas air after all. Maybe it was reconnecting with her family. Realizing she had people in her corner. That she wasn't completely alone. Maybe it was watching Evan fight for his cattle and his ranch and never giving up on his dreams. Whatever it was, Paige woke up feeling stronger than she had in years. And more than ready to get the life she wanted.

The getting started now.

Paige stepped up to a familiar town house on a quiet upscale street and rang the doorbell. Lights inside clicked on, then the porch light and finally the locks on the front door released. The door swung open, and Paige smiled at her ex-boyfriend. He was the official first stop on her getting-what-she-wanted list. "Hey, Kyle."

"This is unexpected." Kyle's blond hair was sleep tossed, his T-shirt and pj bottoms wrinkled, his feet bare. A mild irritation stiffened the edges of his mouth.

"This is long overdue." Paige pushed by her ex-boyfriend and strode into the town house they had once shared for more than two years. She paused and took in the modern space. Had it always been so sterile and pretentious? There wasn't a single Christmas decoration anywhere. Not even a forgotten Christmas greeting card on the sleek coffee table. Or the typical poinsettia. "And no, we aren't getting back together."

"Then why are you here?" Kyle glanced at his watch and brushed by her. "It's really early."

"I've been awake for hours. I'm still on ranch

time." She waved away his confusion. "Never mind, you wouldn't understand. I came to take back what belongs to me."

He stopped in the center of the formal front room, surrounded by his stuffy, uncomfortable furniture and collector's artwork. His smug expression coordinated flawlessly with the decor. "What would that be exactly?"

Paige cast her gaze around the first floor from the stiff leather couch to the glass-and-metal table in the kitchen. Not a picture frame or knickknack spoiled the aesthetic. Finally, she lunged toward the side table. "This lamp. I picked it out and bought it." She yanked the power cord from the wall and wrapped her arms around the ombré textured-glass base.

"Anything else?" He crossed his arms over his chest, his voice and stance bored.

"Yes, I need a check in this amount." She pulled a piece of paper from her jacket pocket and thrust it at him.

Only his gaze, cool and impatient, lifted from the paper to settle on her. "What's this?"

"My money that was in our joint bank account when you emptied it and transferred all the funds to your personal bank account." Thankfully, she'd kept her own savings account during their time together. He hadn't bankrupted her or anything like that. But he'd been wrong. And she was standing up for the principle now.

"You're serious?" He flicked his fingers against the piece of paper. "This is less than..."

"I know the exact amount." It was less than five hundred dollars. They'd paid their living expenses out of their joint account. She could've let it go. But she'd let so much go over the past several years. She was tired. And wanted to make it stop. And besides, the money belonged to her. She wanted what was hers and she intended to have it. She lifted her chin. "I'll take a check, please."

Kyle crumpled the paper in his fist and padded into the kitchen. He opened a drawer, took out his checkbook and a pen. He studied her as if didn't recognize her. "Is this really necessary?"

More than he could ever know. "So very."

The pen scratched across the check. He tore it out and handed it to her. "Anything else? Would you like to go upstairs, take a pillow from the bed? Bath towels? The teak clothes hamper?"

"I don't think so." She'd never liked the clothes hamper or the generic white towels that had always been abrasive and rough. She folded the check, stuck it in her pocket and adjusted the lamp in her arms as if it was a newborn. "I think I'm good." *Really good, in fact.*

"What now?" He set his hands on the kitchen

counter and leaned forward. "You got a lamp and some money. Have you gotten what you came for?"

Her pride. She'd proved she could stand up for herself. Proved that her inner fighter was still there. And put her past behind her. Officially and with a resounding bravado. And it wasn't even eight in the morning. She had an entire day left to conquer. She strolled to the door. "I'm going to work, where I will convince the partners to allow me to join them as such. My recommendations weren't wrong for your patient. You were being reckless and greedy. You know it and I do too."

"You think you have it all figured out, then?" His derision didn't bother her anymore, she realized.

She faced him, her shoulders straight, her gaze unflinching. *See me. See my strength for once.* "For the first time in a long while, I do have things figured out. I would tell you to have a good day, but you seem incapable of that."

He winced as if her words upset him. "Excuse me?"

"It's not the world that's miserable, Kyle—it's you. And for no reason, other than you choose to be." Paige gathered the lamp and held tight to the check. She didn't care if he took her advice or not. She didn't care if he even listened.

She only cared that she said it. That she put it out there. "And you'll probably remain miserable until you take a real, honest look at yourself and make some hard changes."

"What's happened to you?" he asked.

"I cooled off." *On a ranch. With my family.* And found herself in the process. "Bye, Kyle."

Paige stepped outside and drew the front door closed with a soft click. It was more rewarding than slamming it instead. Satisfaction resonated in the silence on Kyle's front porch louder than any show she could've put on.

Paige hummed one of her favorite Christmas carols, hugged her lamp and headed to work.

Twenty minutes and a cab ride later, Paige stood outside the animal clinic she'd helped establish, grinning from ear to ear. She dared anyone to try to defeat her today. She walked into the business she'd helped to grow and headed upstairs. The vets' offices and a conference room filled the second floor. She greeted Mai O'Neill, their administrative assistant.

"Cool lamp, Paige." Mai stopped typing, adjusted her wireless headset and smiled at Paige.

Paige handed the lamp to the recent college graduate. "Consider it a gift."

"Are you serious?" Mai accepted the lamp. Her expression was slightly stunned.

"It's a pretty cool lamp as far as lamps go.

You can dim or brighten it with just a tap on the base." Paige pointed to the nickel base. "I hope you enjoy it."

"It's exactly what I've been looking for." Mai set the lamp on the filing cabinet behind her carefully. "I moved into my new apartment last weekend. It's official, I'm living on my own. No more roommates," she said excitedly. "I need a lamp in my bedroom for those late-night reading marathons."

"Sounds like a perfect match. Like it was meant to be." Kyle and Paige had not been a perfect match. Or meant to be. Paige understood that now.

And her and Evan, they could've been a match. Perhaps. She stiffened her spine and pushed thoughts of Evan aside. The day was about Paige standing up for herself. Getting what she had always wanted. What she'd worked so hard for, for so many years. Later, she'd let herself miss Evan. Later, she'd give in to the hurt.

She force-stretched her smile a notch brighter. "Is everyone in the conference room?"

"Yes." Mai pointed down the hallway, then straightened the linen lampshade before returning to her chair. "Go right on in. They're waiting for you."

Paige opened the door to the conference room

and greeted her colleagues on the decision committee.

Exactly sixty-eight minutes had passed when Paige stepped out of the conference room as an equal partner in the clinic. And could finally claim she'd gotten the life she always wanted.

CHAPTER TWENTY-THREE

EVAN PULLED INTO his driveway and noted Dr. Conrad Gibson's truck was still parked in the same spot beside the main house. Evan had spent the entire morning with the veterinarian. Dr. Gibson had wanted to personally check on the herds and Luna. But that had been hours ago.

Evan had left with Riley at lunch for Belle-ridge and their ice slide adventure. Riley's best friend, Claire, and her family had joined them. The slides had been twenty feet tall, carved out of ice, fast and fun. The North Pole–themed ice maze and ice sculptures entertaining. Another Christmas first could be checked off the list and declared a success.

With their movie night marathon scheduled to start promptly after dinner, Evan's plate was full again, just like he always preferred it. Yet he was keenly aware of an empty space beside him where Paige should've been. Multiple times today he'd wanted to turn and take her hand. Or tell her about the polar bear stuffed animal he'd bought for Riley. Or listen to her laugh over his mishap on the slide. His life had returned to normal, and here Evan had never felt more lost. But that wasn't possible. This was the life he'd built, methodically and intentionally, over the past six years.

Evan climbed out of his truck and grabbed the grocery bags from the back seat. Riley had stayed to visit the Christmas art walk in Belleridge with Claire and her family. Evan had a little over an hour before dinner and Riley's return. Enough time to reorder feed supplies, pay invoices and shower. Then the night would be about his daughter, her happiness and not his heartache.

Having set the grocery bags on the kitchen island, Evan greeted his mom and Dr. Gibson. The pair sat at the table with an open box of full-sized candy canes and his mom's special hot chocolate pot on a place mat between them. Dr. Gibson had his foot, the one encased in a heavy-duty walking boot, propped up on a chair.

"Your mother was kind enough to let me rest my foot and turn your kitchen into my temporary office." A half-eaten candy cane poked straight out of Dr. Gibson's mouth. The confection's curved end wobbled as he spoke. "I've gotten rather skilled at this video-calling thing. Got to see my patients and exercise my ankle."

"You shouldn't have come out to the ranch, Conrad," his mother scolded.

Dr. Gibson lifted his hot chocolate mug and his thick salt-and-pepper eyebrows. "Can't get this on a video call."

"I'll give you that to-go thermos." Ilene rose and opened a cabinet under the island. "As long as you agree to take it easy tomorrow."

"It's more video calls for me." Dr. Gibson finished his hot chocolate, stuck the candy cane back in his mouth and rose. He set his hand on the table for balance. "Have to say I'm certainly missing Paige. I fear she might be irreplaceable."

Evan harbored a similar fear. And he couldn't quite shake the idea that he'd let the perfect woman slip away. But getting her back wasn't an option. Forcing Paige to choose between Evan and her life in Chicago was far from fair.

Evan unpacked the groceries and opted for a conversation detour. He held up a bag of marshmallows. "Tonight's menu for our holiday movie marathon has been set. It's pizza bites, cheese sticks and caramel-marshmallow popcorn balls."

Ilene laughed and glanced at Dr. Gibson. "You're more than welcome to join us."

"We've got a collection of movies to see." Evan smiled. "Everything from black-and-white classics to the cutesy animated ones."

"I appreciate the offer." Dr. Gibson hobbled

and straightened. "But I don't want to overextend my welcome."

Paige had barely settled in at the ranch. She could've extended her stay. One week. One month and Evan wouldn't have considered it long enough.

"Have you spoken to Paige?" Conrad bit off a chunk of his candy cane and crunched down on the hard peppermint. His inquisitive gaze never strayed from Evan.

"I have not." Evan folded the paper shopping bags and smoothed his expression. "I'm sure Paige is back at work and glad to be home."

Dr. Gibson nodded, an up-and-down slow-motion move as if Evan's words had failed to convince him. He broke off another piece of candy cane with his teeth and shifted his gaze to Ilene. The corner of his mouth quirked. "The young sure do like to complicate love, don't they?"

"They sure do." Ilene chuckled and filled the thermos full of hot chocolate.

Love. When had it become about love? It was about talking to Paige, not about giving her his heart. Love would require an entirely different conversation. Evan crumpled the paper shopping bags in his grip and opened his mouth to say something.

His mother stopped him, one eyebrow arched,

before Evan could launch into his argument. She said, "Evan, you're teaching your daughter to honor her feelings. And yet you're burying your own."

He tossed the smashed shopping bags into the recycling bin. And tossed his denial out into the room. Weak and unconvincing as it was. "I'm not burying anything."

"An excavation crew would be hard-pressed to uncover all that you've buried." Conrad set his hand on Evan's shoulder and made his way to the back door. "My eyesight isn't what it used to be, but even I can see that much."

"I'll walk you out, Conrad." His mom tightened the lid on the thermos of hot chocolate and followed Dr. Gibson outside. The back door shut, blocking out his mom's laughter and the veterinarian's dynamic voice.

Evan tossed a bag of shredded cheese into the refrigerator and grimaced. What would it matter if he was burying his so-called feelings? This way his hurt was manageable and tolerable. No one wanted to pull off a bandage and poke at an open wound. It was best to keep it covered. Best to keep his feelings in check.

His mother returned with a soft smile on her face, her cheeks a shade brighter than usual. He said, "Dr. Gibson was here longer than I expected. Did you two have a nice visit?"

His mother ignored the speculation in his tone and set the air popcorn popper on the island. "We had a wonderful afternoon. Conrad is a very good listener."

Evan had someone who'd listened to him. He hadn't realized what a gift that was until Paige had left. He touched his mom's arm. "I'm happy for you."

Her smile stretched slightly, then faded. She set her hand over his. "But you're not happy."

"Now you sound like Riley." He'd also told his daughter it was okay to be sad and upset because it would eventually pass. He just needed to wait out his own hurt. Evan pulled away from his mom and opened a bag of white popcorn kernels.

"My granddaughter is a very smart child." Ilene placed a stainless-steel bowl beside the popcorn machine. "And she is not wrong to want you to be happy. We all want that for you."

"Can we not get into a debate about happiness." Evan poured the kernels into the top of the machine. "It's three days before Christmas. There's still a lot to do." And even more for everyone to focus on than Evan and his apparent lack of happy.

"Fine." His mom held the cord to the popcorn machine, keeping Evan from plugging it in and ending their conversation. From the resolve in her gaze to the firm set of her chin, his mother clearly intended to have the last word. She added, "Maybe we could get into a debate about the fact that you are in love with Paige."

In love. With Paige. Evan clenched his jaw together. Unclenched it only to press his teeth together. For a moment, the silence between them was telling. Finally, he worked his jaw and voice loose. "I'm not sure that's up for debate."

"Then you do love her." His mom eyed him from across the island.

"I never said…" What if he did? What if he loved Paige Palmer? What if he was head over heels in love with her? Admitting it left him right in the same place he already was: alone and missing Paige. "What would it matter if I was in love with her?"

"It would mean you've finally stopped hiding." His mother's understanding struck a chord. "It would mean you have finally forgiven yourself. You were young. You fell for the wrong woman. And you've been blaming yourself ever since."

"I got it so wrong with Marla." Evan ran his hand through his hair.

"The only thing you got wrong was not seeing Marla for who she really was." Ilene walked around the island, closer to him. "There was nothing wrong about loving Marla."

"Except love made me blind." And he refused to repeat that mistake. But he worried he'd already erred and fallen for Paige.

"Or maybe love made you a better man." His mom's gaze searched his. "You wouldn't be the father you are today without going through everything you did. You wouldn't be the man you are today."

He had no choice back then. His love hadn't been enough for Marla, and she'd walked away and had never looked back. Left him and Riley. What else was he supposed to have done?

"You always loved the ranch," his mom continued. "But it wasn't until after Marla had gone that you started to make it your own. That you started to really invest yourself in the land. In the cattle. In the business."

"I did it all for my family." Family had always been at the center of everything he did.

"And you guarded your heart in the process." His mom reached up and touched his cheek. "But it's okay to open your heart now. It's okay to love someone outside this family again. It's okay to take that risk."

Something shifted inside him. Still, he resisted. "What if it's like last time?"

"How could it be?" Ilene countered. "You're not the same person you were. And Paige certainly isn't anything like Marla."

Paige was everything Marla wouldn't ever be. Paige was selfless, generous with her time, patient. Kind. He could go on and on about Paige and everything that made her the woman he loved. He said, "Paige lives in another state."

"What matters is that you love her." His mom set her hand over her heart. "It's the core. It's the goal. Your father would tell you that the rest are just challenges you can work together to get past. You can let those obstacles stop you or you can figure out a way around them."

"It's a pretty big obstacle," Evan argued. And yet a long-distance relationship could work. Might work. It'd take planning and it wasn't ideal, but it meant he could have Paige in his life. "What if it doesn't work out?"

"This isn't working out for you right now, is it?" Ilene frowned at him, then shrugged one shoulder. "Maybe it's time to try something different."

"This isn't how love is supposed to go." Then again, what did he know about how love worked?

"Who says love ever plays by the rules? And who says you can't make up your own rules?" His mom picked up the plug to the popcorn machine and smiled at him. "Now, go shower. We have a movie marathon to get ready for."

She plugged in the popcorn machine. The

buzz of the air popper fan filled the air. She waved her hand, shooing him out of the kitchen.

But Evan's mind didn't slow. Could it be that simple? Paige and Evan set the rules. The only condition was love.

And he loved Paige. But did she love him? That was the detail that mattered. The deal breaker.

He had let Riley's mother go, had never fought for Marla or their relationship after his ex-fiancée had left and not come back. He had no regrets.

But not fighting for Paige—that he would regret for the rest of his life.

CHAPTER TWENTY-FOUR

IT WAS DECEMBER 23. Paige had gotten the week off from work to enjoy the holiday and celebrate her success. She sat on her couch and stared at the blank TV screen. She had a bottle of white wine chilled and no one to toast with. She had a plush blanket and popcorn popped and no one to share them with.

Her gaze drifted to the coffee table and the handmade ornaments spread across the top. They were the ones that matched the ornaments from the box back at the general store. Paige had ornaments and no place to hang them.

She dropped her head back on the sofa and stared at the ceiling. She should be delighted. She should be ecstatic. She had exactly what she wanted. Exactly what she had returned to the city for.

Why wasn't she dancing around the living room, then? Singing at the top of her lungs and celebrating. And why did the thought of celebrating sound hollow? She should've gotten a tree. She could still do that tomorrow. A potted one, but she'd have no place to plant it. No place to watch it take root and grow.

She pressed the heels of her hands against her eyes and groaned. She'd never given in and refused to do it now. She reached for the TV remote on the side table and an envelope caught her attention. Her grandmother's letter. She'd found it yesterday in her purse and set it aside.

She picked up the envelope and turned it over in her hand. Hesitating, she broke the seal with her finger, inhaled and took out the letter.

Dearest Paige,

It seems only right that my Christmas ornaments go to you. After all, we created so many together. You may not remember, but you wanted every ornament to have a friend on the tree and in the attic during the long wait until Christmas's arrival the following year.

Check your fingertips. I wouldn't be surprised if you still carried the marks from the needle pricks. You were so determined to sew like I had. Because, Grandma, everyone needs someone, no one should be alone.

Paige stopped reading, pulled several tissues from her pocket, and dabbed at her eyes. Paige had created her ornaments the year after her father had died. For an entire year, she'd witnessed her mom's continuous grief. Paige had been desperate to believe if she'd doubled the ornaments, she'd double the Christmas magic. And if her mom saw all those happy duos on their tree, she might see Paige and Tess, her own daughter duo, and be happy again too. Paige wasn't certain her mother had ever stopped mourning the loss of her husband, but Paige had tried to help. Just as she'd tried to do with animals. Paige picked up her grandmother's letter.

True partnerships are a gift, Paige. They can't be forced. Willed to happen. Or dare I say sewn together with a deft hand and needle. If they are meant to be, they are built from love.

Love is the core. The foundation. The reason.

When you find it, and you will, my dear, precious granddaughter, you must let love in your heart and into your life. Be brave.

No half measures now. They don't work. Love with your whole heart, Paige.

Put our ornaments on your tree same as we used to. Find the joy in the past and let it add richness to the present. Celebrate the season with family and friends. And if love hasn't found you, look around you and watch for those signs. Your heart will know which ones to follow. Trust in it.

As for the rest, life is never as we expect. Embrace it and dare it to surprise you anyway. You won't regret it. I certainly haven't. Keep making memories. You want those memories, not regrets, to look back on. Now go live life to its very fullest and you just might find everything you need.

With love past the stars and back,
Grandma Opal

Paige lowered the letter to her lap. She'd rediscovered the joy in the past with her family in Three Springs. She had what she wanted now.

Was it what she needed?

Trust in your heart.

She closed her eyes and listened to the silence. Listened to her heart. And found part of her truth. The city was her past and she'd closed the door on it yesterday when she'd left her ex's town house. But her future… She was scared to look in another direction.

Be brave.

The doorbell rang. Paige opened the door to a deliveryman. Package signed for, she returned to the couch and quickly opened the box. It had to be her grandmother's ornaments. She knew

Abby and Tess wouldn't listen to her. She'd been expecting them to mail her the ornaments with a note telling her to get a tree.

She opened the box and lifted out a sparkling, ornate star tree topper. The crystal glass beads caught the light. The metallic rose-colored iron added a vintage flavor. It was stunning. And exactly what she would've wanted for her tree. A note card dropped onto her lap. Her heart skipped a beat.

Evan's handwriting was scrawled across the note card.

If you ever become lost, use the star to guide you. I'll be here.

She looked from the note to the star. Her gaze caught on her grandmother's letter. She wiped at her damp cheeks. "Yes, Grandma, I'm paying attention to the signs."

With the star carefully wrapped and set back into the box, Paige picked up her grandmother's letter and reread it. She had the sign. Now she had to be brave and take risks. Live her life to the fullest. That meant more than her professional one.

She opened her contact list on her phone, clicked on Dr. Conrad Gibson and pressed the video-chat call button, taking her first risk.

Dr. Gibson answered and his face filled the screen. His silver goatee had been trimmed, his reading glasses were propped on his head and his unruly white hair stood out in every direction. He wore a half grin, held a coffee mug and a partially eaten candy cane. "Merry almost Christmas Eve, Paige."

"Same to you." Paige realized her first genuine smile of the day.

"The secret to getting through December is candy canes and Ilene's hot chocolate." He swirled his candy cane in his mug. "If you ever need a pick-me-up, ask Ilene for her spiked hot chocolate. Although there's no spike in mine. Doctor's orders."

She could've used that pick-me-up right now. "I'll be sure to do that."

Conrad tapped his candy cane against the rim of his mug and leaned into the screen. "Are you coming back, then?"

Paige inhaled and took that risk. "It's what I wanted to talk to you about."

"Heard you're about to have a more equitable stake in the practice up there." Conrad stuck the candy cane in his mouth and gave her a one-sided grin.

"How did you hear that?" Paige frowned. She'd only told Abby and Tess late last night about her success. And she'd asked them not to tell anyone until she'd signed the official paperwork. Abby had never mentioned an issue with the puppies. When had they spoken to Conrad?

"I might live in a small town, speak with a slow drawl, but I have an extensive network. I pride myself on that." Conrad pointed the stem of his candy cane at the screen. "It's something I'll have to insist you cultivate too as my partner."

Partner. Paige fumbled with her phone. "What?"

"Can you hear me?" Conrad tapped the screen with his finger. His voice boomed across the speaker. "Do I need to speak louder? Is that the problem?"

"No, I can hear you." Perfectly fine. His words were the problem. Paige gave in to her confusion. "Did you just say *partner*?"

"You were calling to ask about working for me, weren't you?" Conrad dunked his candy cane back into his coffee mug and smiled at her. His gaze twinkled as if he enjoyed being one—or several—steps ahead of her.

Yes, she wanted to take a risk. Yes, she wanted to believe in love. But she also wanted to be prepared. She wanted to be able to rely on herself financially. She wanted it all and she wanted it all in Texas.

"It'll never work." Conrad waved his candy cane in front of the screen.

Paige's heart sank.

"Gotta be partners," Conrad continued. He swished the candy cane across the screen like an orchestra conductor gripping a baton. "Fifty-fifty. It's better than what you got up there in the city."

Paige gaped at the phone screen. "You're serious."

"I don't joke about snake bites or my practice." Conrad's face filled the entire screen again. His voice lifted an octave as if he was concerned she couldn't hear him again. "Of course, I'm serious. We say it like we mean it here in Texas. Best get used to that."

Paige laughed. She planned to get used to a lot of things in Texas. Mainly, seeing Evan every single day.

"Here's the particular. There's really only one." Conrad grinned. "Fifty-fifty partners. You have full control of the small-animal side."

Paige blinked. Was this really happening? Was a request to work for him truly turning into a partnership? Over video chat? Talk about Christmas wishes coming true. She glanced at her grandmother's letter and sent a silent wish of gratitude out to her insightful grandma.

"In case you haven't noticed, the doctor fixed

my ankle, but not my age." Conrad's laugh exploded across the speaker. "I don't plan to retire soon, but I do plan to retire. You'll need to know those large animals for when that time comes."

Large animals. Small animals. She'd have her career and a practice with a veterinarian she respected. Conrad Gibson would be a great mentor. She couldn't have asked for more. "I can learn."

"Yes, you can." Conrad popped the candy cane back in his mouth and tilted his head. "Now, do we have a deal? Or do you need time to think things over?"

Paige was done thinking. She needed to act. To take one more risk. "I only have one favor to ask."

CHAPTER TWENTY-FIVE

NOT AGAIN. THIS bypass had become her personal nemesis. Paige stared at the orange cones and flashing lights on the road-closed sign blocking all lanes in both directions.

Until this moment, everything had been going as planned. There'd been no weather delays at the airport in Chicago. No mechanical plane delays for her connecting flight in Dallas. The flight had even arrived early to the gate at the Amarillo airport. She'd eaten breakfast *and* lunch.

She was almost in Three Springs. Almost home for Christmas.

One of the construction crew team tapped on her window. "Sorry, ma'am. You'll have to turn around. It's going to be some time before the road opens."

But it'd already taken her too long to listen to her heart. "What happened?"

"Environmental spill." He tugged on his reflective vest. "Going to be a long night. Merry Christmas."

"Same to you." Paige rolled up her window and checked the time. She was running out of time. The drive back to the interstate would ruin her plan to ambush Evan.

She'd promised Wes that she'd be at Abby's house before dinner to surprise her sister and cousin. That was in less than an hour. But she'd wanted to see Evan first. If she stalled any longer, she wouldn't be surprising anyone until Christmas morning.

Paige grabbed her phone. It wasn't the face-to-face reunion she'd envisioned, but she could still surprise Evan.

The ringing stopped. The connection clicked on, although only static came across the speaker. "Evan. Can you hear me?"

"Paige?" His voice sounded like paper being crumpled.

Part of her signal strength faded. Paige clutched her phone and shouted as if talking louder improved her cell signal. "My phone is dying! I'm stuck on the bypass! It was supposed to be a surprise. I wanted to surprise you and Riley. I'm here! But I'm stuck!" One bar disappeared. Paige rattled on, "And everything is ruined. I might miss Christmas. This wasn't how it was supposed to go. I love you!" Another bar blinked out. "And now I can't even tell you."

"Paige." Evan's voice cut in, still garbled.

"I'm sorry I left. But I'm back. I'm here!" Paige shouted again and wanted to yell for better cell service. "I know what I want. I know who I want." She dropped her head on the steering wheel and groaned. "And I can't even tell you in person. I love you, Evan."

"Paige." Evan's voice surrounded her. Clear and close.

Paige shot straight up and clutched her phone. "Evan? Can you hear me?"

"I heard you say that you love me." It wasn't static slowing his words now. It was surprise.

That part of her plan had worked. Tears ran down her cheeks. "That's the most important part."

"Where are you?" he asked.

"The bypass!" Paige wiped her hand under her nose. "I know you know it."

"That I do." Evan chuckled, then sobered. "Wait. You're here? Right now?"

"Yes." Joy and relief lifted her voice several octaves. "That's what I've been trying to tell you."

"I'll be right there." There was a shuffling sound over the speaker as if Evan was on the move.

"I turned around." Paige stuck her phone in the console. "I have to backtrack for a bit now."

"I'm coming to meet you." Evan's determined

declaration had her taking her foot off the gas pedal.

She pulled over to the side of the road.

The only place she wanted to be was with Evan. The call disconnected.

Paige checked the time and her location. Pastures and empty fields stretched in every direction. Evan in his truck, or UTV, shouldn't take long and could handle the terrain.

Exactly twenty-two minutes later, a horse and rider galloped toward her.

Paige got out of her car and watched the sight.

The construction worker called out, "You okay, ma'am?"

She was more than fine. She was perfect. Paige's smile came from every part of her and burst free. The joy and love she could no longer restrain. This was loving with her whole heart. And she had no intention of stopping. It was life changing.

She pointed toward Evan. "Just waiting for my ride."

The worker nudged his partner and the crew paused to watch the arrival of Evan and his horse.

Evan slowed his massive brown-spotted white horse and slid from the saddle before the horse had stopped completely. His boots barely ouched the dirt and he was already in motion toward her.

Paige moved in his direction. It would always be in his direction. "You brought your horse."

"Clay really is the best way to travel around here." Evan came closer.

"There's so much to say." She slowed as she reached him. "To tell you."

"Nothing is more important than this." He lifted her up in his arms and completely off her feet. "Paige Palmer, I love you too."

Such simple words and yet they sent her heart past the stars. She loved this man to the stars and back. Now she understood her grandparents' sentiment. "That's not fair. You arrive on a horse to rescue me. Then literally sweep me off my feet. I was supposed to be the one doing all that for you."

"Do you want me to put you down?" He laughed and hugged her waist.

"No." Paige grinned at him. "I kind of like this feeling of walking on the clouds. A lot."

"I kind of really like you." Affection roughened his voice. Love intensified his gaze. "A lot."

Paige framed his face in her hands and leaned down to capture his mouth with hers. It was everything a kiss was ever meant to be. Honest. Open. An imprint on her heart. A memory to cherish.

Cheers from the construction crew filled t
night sky. Love filled Paige. Slowly, she pulle
away and whispered, "It's finally starting to feel
like the best Christmas ever."

"Yes, it is." He lowered her to her feet but
didn't release his hold. "We should probably
head back. There are a few people at the ranch
who are anxious to see you."

"And then we're supposed to be at Abby's
house for dinner." Paige slid her hand into his.

"We will make it to everything." Evan guided
her to Clay's side, then helped her up into the
saddle. Soon, he was sitting behind her, guiding Clay toward the pastures with no more than
a gentle knee command. His arms wrapped
around Paige. "Ready?"

Paige leaned into his chest and nodded. With
Evan, she was ready for anything.

It had taken two airplanes, one rental car and
a magnificent horse, but she finally made it back
to the ranch. There was just enough time for
quick welcome-home hugs with Riley and Ilene.
Then everyone climbed into Evan's truck and
they were off to Abby's house for Christmas
Eve dinner. Paige sat in the back seat beside
Riley. The little girl slipped her hand in Paige's
and held tight as if she'd never left. That suited
Paige just fine.

Paige stepped into her cousin's house and

...ally had her face-to-face surprise. Abby ...rieked at her arrival and promptly started cry-...ng. Tess wrapped Paige in a warm hug. The sisters held on to each other longer than necessary, giving them time to collect themselves.

"Everyone is here. Everyone is home." Abby brushed the tears from her cheeks and smiled. "Let's eat and celebrate."

Only Wes paced in front of the Christmas tree. Then he paused to pat his pockets. His weight shifted from one boot to the other. It was odd since Wes never fidgeted. The former SEAL was always composed and collected. Wes cleared his throat once, then a second time.

Paige tucked her hand inside Evan's. Suddenly, she was certain her return wasn't the only surprise for the evening. Wes's insistence that she be there before dinner started to make even more sense.

Finally, Wes cleared his throat a third time, then released an ear-covering whistle.

The room quieted instantly.

"Sorry about that." Wes rubbed the back of his neck and shrugged. "It was the fastest way I could think of to get everyone's attention."

Abby glanced around the room. Her eyebrows were pulled together with worry. "Is someone missing?"

"Everyone we love is here." Wes took Abby's

hands in his. He calmed instantly, as if all he required was Abby's touch.

Paige understood the feeling. She eased into Evan's side.

"I had a speech planned. I even practiced. It was good too." Wes reached in his pocket and dropped to one knee in a fluid motion.

Abby gasped and pressed her hands against her cheeks. "Wes."

Evan's arm wrapped around Paige's waist, anchoring her to him. She rested her head on his chest. Riley held her hand and leaned against them both.

"Abby." Wes opened a tiny box, revealing a sparkling diamond ring. "I promise I'll remember all those words later. But right now, I really need to know. Will you marry me?"

"Yes!" Abby cried out and hugged Wes. "A thousand times yes."

The room erupted in cheers and more tears. So much joy. So much love. Here she was, surrounded by family and friends as her grandma always wanted. And the memories—they were certainly going to make those.

Evan squeezed Paige's hand, his grip strong and steady as if he had no intention of ever letting go. Or perhaps that was Paige. She was holding on to love for the rest of her life.

"Do you think we get a full-size fruitcake now from Breezy and Gayle?" Paige strolled beside Evan toward the guesthouse. Riley and Ilene had already disappeared inside the main house. Riley wanted to get to sleep quickly, so that Santa would know he could arrive now. All of Paige's wishes had already come true. Paige added, "Or did Abby and Wes get one tonight because they are now engaged?"

"I'm not sure what the rules are for fruit-cakes." Evan laughed. "I suppose we'll find out next week when we head to the Baker farm for our dessert challenge night."

Breezy and Gayle had offered to host the dessert competition. The final judges were still being discussed, but Riley had made the final cut, to her absolute delight.

"We are a couple, aren't we?" Paige stopped and wrapped her arms around Evan.

His arms guided her closer. His voice was light and teasing. "I'm not much into labels."

"I hear you have quite the charming guest-house." Her fingers brushed against his hair. "Would you be interested in a long-term tenant?"

He pulled her tightly against him. His warm gaze centered on her. "Do you have someone in mind?"

"I do." She leaned up and pressed her lips against his. "If you'll have me…"

"Welcome home, Paige Palmer." He smiled softly and captured even more of her heart.

And she was home. Finally, in the place she belonged. With a man she loved beside her. This was the start of her own happily-ever-after. The beginning of that love story. And she vowed right then to make it the best one she could. "Merry Christmas, cowboy."

"Merry Christmas, Paige." Their lips met. It was the kind of kiss they'd talk about fifty years from now. It was the kind of love that stuck.

EPILOGUE

GINGER AND TYNE were curled up against Luna's side, reveling in her warmth. The big dog was lying in front of the fireplace and watching over the two puppies as if they were her own. The Christmas presents had been opened hours earlier. The bicycle had been taken for its first ride. And everyone Evan cared about was within touching distance.

"Dad! Dad!" Riley called out. "Ms. Paige says it's dry. You can see your present now."

Evan left the Christmas tree and watched his daughter make her way carefully over to him. Her footsteps slow and measured. Her hands were cupped together in front of her. Cradled in her palms was something blue. Pride radiated from her ear-to-ear grin and into her wide gaze. "It's an ornament. It's our family ornament. We're snowmen."

Evan bent to one knee in front of his daughter. He lifted the bulb up by the ribbon. Riley's handprint, in white paint, had been pressed against the round bulb. Each one of her fingers had been turned into a snowman complete with a painted-on hat, scarf and extrawide smile.

Riley leaned against him and slipped her arm around his shoulder. She pointed at each snowman. "That's me. You. Grandma. Ms. Paige. Our whole family."

Our whole family. Her words filled him. Evan touched her thumbprint snowman. "Who's this one?"

"That's Macybelle," Riley whispered. "But Ms. Paige says it could be Dr. Conrad too."

How lucky they would be to include Conrad Gibson in their family. He'd given Paige a direction for her career and Evan a chance with the woman he loved. Evan wanted his mom and Conrad to find their own way, but he would make sure his mom knew he approved.

Riley tenderly touched the ribbon. "Do you like it?"

"It's perfect." Evan kissed his daughter's forehead.

Riley beamed. "You know the best part?"

There were too many best parts to his holiday to even begin listing them. He smiled at his daughter. "What's that?"

"This bulb can't break." Riley tapped her fingers against it. "Ms. Paige says it's unbreakable like our family's love for each other."

"That is the best part." Evan glanced up and

caught Paige's gaze. She was definitely one of the very best parts of his life. Evan rose. "Should we put it on the tree?"

Riley clapped and pointed toward the top. "Put it up high, Dad. That's where the special ornaments go."

The ornament having been hung according to her specifications, Riley sprinted off to the kitchen, where Tess was finishing her white-chocolate-peppermint truffles. And Evan's mom was preparing to serve her cranberry-eggnog pie.

Paige joined Evan at the tree and wrapped her arm around his waist. "Best Christmas ever?"

Evan grinned and held her close. "I don't think I'm ready to say."

"Really?" Paige paused to consider him. "Why not?"

"Well, there's next Christmas. The one after that. And the one after that." Evan kissed her sweetly. "We have so many to look forward to together. I'm thinking the best is yet to come."

Paige laughed and held on to him. "Whatever comes, I'm glad it'll be with you."

They'd barely begun their kiss when Abby interrupted. "There's no time for that, you two. I'm the engaged one and Wes and I aren't standing around kissing."

Evan smiled at Abby. "Maybe you should be."

"We'll get to that later." Abby shooed them into the kitchen. "Now, we need to make wreaths. It's all set up. We just need your hands to start crafting."

As it turned out, Breezy and Gayle's aunt Francis had shed more light on the wreath tradition than any of them had expected. Wreaths of this type had been hanging on the homes and businesses in Three Springs ever since the original community made them as a sign of welcome for Victoria McKenzie and anyone related to her. Every herb, berry and branch had stood for strength, courage, good luck. Everything the community had wanted Victoria to feel if she ever decided to return, with or without the missing loot.

Paige's grandmother had replicated the wreaths for the community during the drought. And now Abby wanted to do the same for the town again. This time for a prosperous New Year.

Evan suspected it was for a measure of good luck in their continued search for the missing silver coin and elusive treasure map. No one was ready to give up looking. As it was, the search squad had expanded to include the Baker sisters and even Dr. Gibson.

Evan pulled out a chair at the kitchen table for Paige.

The table was covered in white pine sticks and other bendable branches, herbs Evan couldn't name but he was certain had a meaning, and ribbons of all colors. Wes and Abby had already started forming their wreath. Boone and Riley were selecting their materials.

Evan rubbed his chin. "How many wreaths are we making?"

"Enough for the whole town," Riley cheered.

"The shops in downtown," Abby clarified.

"Don't worry." Wes checked his watch. "We have reinforcements coming. Sam and his grandsons should be here soon."

"And Conrad is on his way." Ilene blushed and busied herself with her pie.

"Breezy and Gayle should be pulling in any minute." Tess bit into a truffle and chuckled. "They're bringing more fruitcake and even more supplies."

Laughter rolled through the room. Evan was certain everyone was already plotting how to avoid getting another fruitcake.

"These are going to look so special hanging on all the storefronts for the New Year." Abby sat and set her hands on her stomach. She smiled at the group. "I can't thank you all enough for doing this."

"The wreaths remind us we're stronger together." Riley sat on Boone's lap and grinned. "Right, Ms. Paige?"

"That's it exactly." Paige squeezed Evan's hand. "Just what my grandmother always said."

Now Evan understood. Love built on grace, kindness and patience only bolstered him. Made him stronger and made him want to be even better. For his community. For the people he loved and who loved him. For his family.

Because family was everything.

* * * * *

For more Three Springs, Texas, romances from

Cari Lynn Webb and Harlequin Heartwarming,

visit www.Harlequin.com today!

Get 4 FREE REWARDS!

We'll send you 2 FREE Books
plus 2 FREE Mystery Gifts.

Love Inspired Suspense books showcase how courage and optimism unite in stories of faith and love in the face of danger.

FREE Value Over **$20**

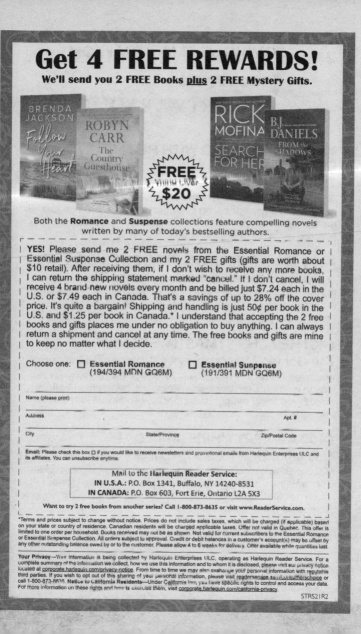

#399 SNOWBOUND WITH HER MOUNTAIN COWBOY

The Second Chance Club • by Patricia Johns

Angelina Cunningham gets the surprise of the season when her ex-husband appears on her doorstep. But Ben has lost his memory—and forgotten how he broke her heart! Can braving a blizzard together give them a second chance?

#400 HIS HOMETOWN YULETIDE VOW

A Pacific Cove Romance • by Carol Ross

Former baseball player Derrick Bright needs a PR expert—too bad the best in the business is his ex Anne. He'll do whatever it takes to get her help...and reclaim her heart by Christmas!

#401 HER CHRISTMASTIME FAMILY

The Golden Matchmakers Club • by Tara Randel

Widowed officer Roan Donovan needs to make merry for his kids in time for Christmas. But he's more grinch than holiday glee. Good thing the girl next door, single mom Faith, has enough Christmas spirit to spare!

#402 A MERRY CHRISTMAS DATE

Matchmaker at Work • by Syndi Powell

Melanie Beach won't spend another holiday alone. But when she confesses her love to longtime friend Jack, he doesn't return her feelings. Can the magic of the season mend broken hearts and point the way to love?

HWCNM1121